The CAVALIER CASE

A Jemima Shore Mystery

Antonia FRASER

BANTAM BOOKS
New York · Toronto · London · Sydney · Auckland

THE CAVALIER CASE

A BANTAM BOOK / FEBRUARY 1991

Library of Congress Cataloging-in-Publication Data

Fraser, Antonia, 1932–
The cavalier case : a Jemima Shore mystery / Antonia Fraser.
p.   cm.
ISBN 0-553-07126-2
I.   Title.
PR6056.R2863C38   1991
823'.914—dc20   90-41943
CIP

PUBLISHED SIMULTANEOUSLY IN THE UNITED STATES AND CANADA

Bantam Books are published by Bantam Books, a division of Bantam Doubleday Dell
Publishing Group, Inc. Its trademark, consisting of the words "Bantam Books"
and the portrayal of a rooster, is Registered in U.S. Patent and Trademark
Office and in other countries. Marca Registrada. Bantam Books,
666 Fifth Avenue, New York, New York 10103.

PRINTED IN THE UNITED STATES OF AMERICA

RRH   0 9 8 7 6 5 4 3 2

Contents

The Meredith Family

Now

DECIMUS ANTONY NORTON MEREDITH (HANDSOME DAN)
18th Viscount Lackland

CHARLOTTE LACKLAND, *his wife*

ZENA MEREDITH, *his sister*

MARCUS MEREDITH, M.P., *his cousin*

BABS MEREDITH, *his first wife*

NELL MEREDITH, *Babs' daughter*

LOUISA, EMILY AND DECIMUS (DESSIE) MEREDITH,
Charlotte's children

also

THOMAS ANTONY DECIMUS MEREDITH (COUSIN TOMMY)
17th Viscount Lackland, recently dead

Then

DECIMUS MEREDITH, *1st Viscount Lackland, Cavalier poet*

OLIVIA LACKLAND, *an heiress, his wife*

ANTONY DECIMUS MEREDITH,
2nd Viscount Lackland, his only child

REV. THOMAS MEREDITH,
chaplain at Lackland Court, his cousin

The CAVALIER CASE

I

The Portrait

Two things happened on the night of the twelfth of July, both of them important to the Cavalier Case (as it was later known). An old man fell down some stairs in a large house in Taynfordshire and broke his neck. And in London, sitting at her desk at Megalith Television, Jemima Shore Investigator fell in love.

Since the object of Jemima's passion was a person in a portrait who had been dead for well over three hundred years and the old man who stumbled down the stairs to his death was seventy-seven years old, half-blind and fond of his late-night whisky, it could scarcely have been expected that this conjunction of events would lead in time to that thrilling mixture of sex, violence and the supernatural, snobbery, historical romance and even sport which went under the general name of the Cavalier Case. It is true that there was one obvious connection between the two events. The person in the portrait, Decimus Meredith, 1st Viscount Lackland, poet and Cavalier, mortally wounded in the Battle of Taynford in 1645, was the direct ancestor of the old man who died thus accidentally if not unexpectedly.

But Thomas Antony Decimus Meredith, 17th Viscount Lackland, had led a career in direct contrast to that of his famous forebear. Decent obscurity might be a way of summing it up, beyond the fact he still lived in Lackland Court, the poet's house. There had been a respectable war record which far from ending in a hero's death had merely formed the prelude to the long quiet life of a country landowner; no poetry in sight (except the works of his famous ancestor reverently enshrined in the library) and certainly none composed. No, surely no-one could have foreseen the chain of events which would link the passion of Jemima Shore to the death of old Tommy Lackland, bringing a chain of destruction in its wake.

Of course there was another way of looking at it. Since the career of the new Lord Lackland—previously known as Handsome Dan Meredith—had been marked by a certain romantic turbulence, it was hardly to be expected that his inheritance of his cousin's title would prove to be utterly peaceful. What with Handsome Dan's two wives, Babs and Charlotte . . . his numerous girlfriends, last but not least Alix . . . Then there was the Meredith family, Zena, the three little ones, poor Nell, and in quite a different sense, poor Marcus. But as Jemima Shore sat moodily in her Megalith office gazing yet again at the portrait of Decimus Lackland, Handsome Dan himself was quite unknown to her, beyond a name cursorily encountered in the newspapers in the past. There was after all no reason why their paths should have crossed. And without the fortuitous appearance of the Lackland portrait (combined with one of Cy Fredericks' notorious "seminals") they would presumably never have done so. Once again the world would have been the poorer—or at least less colourful—for the lack of the Cavalier Case.

The portrait of Decimus Lackland was propped up opposite Jemima's desk. It was in fact a large oil painting: over five feet high. The background was mainly dark, although some kind of pillar could be discerned and a heavy swag of rich reddish material—taffeta perhaps—encompassing it, with a snatch of obscure country landscape beyond. The light fell mainly upon the face and the high pointed white lace collar, falling over the further darkness of the armour. In the poet's face, as in the picture, darkness was set against light: the pale oval contrasted with almond-shaped black eyes, the dark fringe and the flowing lovelocks of the Cavalier. To Jemima, the face itself seemed to rise above the armour and transcend it as though at once disdaining the arts of war, and ennobling them by its participation.

There was a further patch of light on the splayed white hand with its long—perhaps disproportionately long—fingers; it rested on the head of an enormous dog—a hound? a mastiff? Jemima was not good on dogs. A few words were sketched in spidery gold in the corner of the picture: although Jemima could hardly make them out herself, she had learned from the back of the portrait (which confidently proclaimed it on a faded typed label to be "by Sir Anthony Van Dyck") that the legend read: AMOR ET HONOR.

Love and honour: a good if enigmatic motto, perhaps all the more good because it was so enigmatic. Jemima sighed. Love . . . It had to be said that her private life at the present time was fairly lovely without being exactly what you would call honourable (having been exactly the reverse for nearly a year); it was also just slightly claustrophobic, hence perhaps this sudden passion for the romantically unattainable Decimus Lackland. For only recently Cass Brinsley had come back into her life, his marriage on-the-rebound-from-Jemima having broken up with the same startling suddenness as it had begun. Jemima herself still did not fully understand the reasons. All she knew was that Cass was back, and since she was too much of a lady—well, most of the time anyway—to express sentiments like "I told you so," the situation between them seemed outwardly remarkably unchanged.

That is to say, she still found Cass fantastically attractive and probably always would, fascinated by the formality of the lawyer's demeanour in public combined with something much less controlled in private. It was also true that their first sweet reconciliation when he actually spoke the words she had longed to hear: "I was mad . . . how could I ever forget you . . . never for one minute *did* I forget you . . . ," had lasted sexually speaking all one evening, then all one night, then most of two days of a lost weekend. There was no doubt that reconciliation (its own silent revenge on the younger rival who had dared to marry her Cass when she, Jemima, had persistently declined to do so) was a sweet process when it involved sex.

All the same . . . The trouble was that after that, a long time after that, but a moment that would still inexorably arrive, Jemima was still Jemima, she who did not want to marry Cass or anyone else come to think of it, someone who pleased herself and in doing so liked to please others. As and when she chose. Freely and in freedom. In short, once again not settling-down material. Whereas Cass, she had an awful feeling, was so keen to settle down that he would run through several marriages in an attempt to do so. "I thought it was *women* who were supposed to long to get married," he had exclaimed with mock bitterness only last night.

Jemima gazed into the slanting dark eyes of Decimus Lackland and sighed. Love and Honour. Had he found love within marriage immediately? She knew that he had been married off to the famous Olivia of the "Swan" poems when he was a mere sixteen and she fourteen. Presumably love itself, the love celebrated in his poetry, had come later, and the marriage itself had been founded on the seventeenth-century concept of honour: worldly honour in the shape of money, since Olivia Lackland had been an orphan and the heiress to Lackland Court in her own right. Do I perhaps need an arranged marriage? pondered Jemima gloomily. After all, who ever really married for love in any century? Cass, had he really married for sudden overwhelming love of the young and charming Flora Hereford (as Flora Hereford herself presumably believed)? Or had he married because Jemima Shore would not say yes to him—nor no, for that matter—and to marry Flora was the most hurtfully decisive thing he could do under the circumstances?

Another sigh. In her present mood, how much easier to fall in love with a portrait who demanded no commitment, than with a real live man, determined, in that dreadful phrase, to "settle down"! (Why *down*, for God's sake? The mere word gave the game away.) In her present mood, it was particularly easy to fall in love with the man who had written to a woman that poem every schoolchild learned, but was in fact far more explicitly sensual than one realised at the time: "I fain would be thy swan . . ."

The portrait had arrived two days before as a result of a cri-de-coeur from Jemima's friend from Cambridge days, the brilliant, engaging—and disorganised—Dr. Rupert Durham. Since Jemima, like all Rupert's friends, was accustomed since Cambridge to do far more onerous things for him than merely housing a portrait, she was delighted to be able to assist him so easily. It turned out that Rupert Durham had been bequeathed the portrait by the nonagenarian widow of a former President of his old college. (She had fallen a victim to his famous charm at a college dinner intended in theory to raise funds for the college, not a portrait for Rupert.)

As ever with Rupert Durham, questions of scholarship—art scholarship in this case—came first. In fact he had spent some time digressing on the National Portrait Gallery's own fine recently acquired Van Dyck portrait of the poet and what he called "the whole ridiculous early Lely red herring" before Jemima had actually realised what she had been asked to do. Which was to give Decimus Lackland house room, as it were, until Rupert managed to uncover just one portion of a wall either in his large book-filled rooms at Cambridge, or, even less likely, in his room off Ladbroke Grove. Here he had moved "temporarily," without unpacking anything except books, about five years ago after being thrown out for the third and final time by Jemima's friend Becky Robertson. ("The trouble with Rupert," Becky had told Jemima rather wearily on the telephone, "is that he may have a first-class mind, but his famous intellectual powers apparently do not extend to concentrating on one woman at a time. I mean, since when was absent-mindedness a plausible excuse for large-scale infidelity?")

As a cat-lover, Jemima did occasionally cat-sit for friends (one of these episodes—in a flat in Bloomsbury—had resulted in one of her more harrowing investigations a few years back*). She also occasion-

---

*Related in A Splash of Red.

ally allowed visiting cats who belonged to really good friends, although the air of injured betrayal with which her own cat, the proud and independent-minded Midnight, greeted these intrusions was hard to bear; Jemima also suspected that in cat-terms he might be right—it *was* the ultimate betrayal to allow another cat on his territory. Altogether, housing a portrait would be much less trouble, reflected Jemima innocently, having no hint of the upheavals, beyond anything within the compass of the most devilish cat, which this elegant ikon would bring into her life.

Jemima's reverie was interrupted by an inordinately long blast on her buzzer. Even before she picked up the instrument, she knew that the caller must be Megalith's Chairman. She also knew that she had only a brief moment to answer before Cy Fredericks' busy fingers passed on in an increasing frenzy to other buttons . . .

"Jem, my gem," Cy was indeed saying in great agitation into her ear. "Where *are* you?" But before Jemima could answer, reasonably enough, "Right here in my office, just where do you expect?" she was cut off, and a noise of infuriated buzzing began to spread audibly through the other offices. With a last sigh—Decimus Lackland with his romantic looks must be temporarily put aside—Jemima performed the necessary ritual for acknowledging Cy's call by buzzing in her turn his secretary, the estimable Miss Lewis.

"What's it all about?" Jemima asked casually when she had established that she was sitting quietly in her office, and expected a second call from Cy in about ten minutes' time when he had explored all the other possibilities (including the messenger's room and the gentlemen's cloakroom). Miss Lewis and Jemima were old allies; both believed ardently, where Cy was concerned, in the principle that forewarned was forearmed.

"A ghost, I think. Cy wants you to interview a ghost," replied Miss Lewis with equal casualness. Being a loyal ally did not preclude her from occasional throwaway lines like this.

"Of course, what else?" murmured Jemima easily, wondering whether she would after all warn Miss Lewis that she had heard Cy inviting both Jane Manfred and Baby Diamondson to visit India with him in the autumn at a party the night before. The problem being not so much that both had accepted, but that Jane Manfred was married to Baby Diamondson's first husband, a fact Cy might have overlooked at the time but the ladies concerned would certainly not, throughout a three-week trip.

All the same, she was grateful that she had had at least some warning, when she found herself sitting in Cy's baroque office and listening to his excited disquisition on the general nature of ghosts.

"So you see, Jemima," he was saying, "it really would make a seminal programme." Experience had taught Jemima not only to beware the word "seminal" on Cy's lips, but also that Cy's notion of a "seminal programme" differed widely from the meaning generally attached to the word.

All the same: "Tell me more, Cy." That seemed the most circumspect thing to reply under the circumstances. Especially since Cy was certainly going to tell her more in any case. Why this sudden interest in ghosts, she wondered? There had to be a lady—probably two ladies, knowing Cy—at the bottom of it all; as in a murder mystery, once she knew who, she might know why. And what to do about it. If some passing fancy was responsible, then she might by delaying—and if Miss Lewis was in a cooperative mood—sit the whole thing out, and avoid altogether the big series Cy was now busily outlining. But if someone serious was involved—Jane Manfred for example—then quite different tactics had to be employed, an altogether longer and subtler battle might have to be fought—a battle which would not necessarily be won by Jemima.

"Lady Manfred has seen a ghost." Under the circumstances these words, announced by Cy with much gravity as though Lady Manfred had left her husband—hardly likely owing to the totally delightful relationship both complaisant and complacent which existed between them—were to Jemima's ears doom-laden. Before Jemima had decided quite how to deal with this extremely threatening situation, Cy proceeded as though she had actually contradicted him. "No, you must understand, Jemima, this was a . . ." He looked round and ended triumphantly as though using the word for the first time: "A seminal experience."

There was nothing for it but to bide her time in patience. And as a matter of fact what Cy had to relate was not without a certain touching quality. For the ghost Lady Manfred had so surprisingly seen was, it transpired, her *own* ghost; no, not her own ghost in that sense, how could she see her own ghost, queried Cy in slight irritation.

"Her *doppelgänger*, maybe?" References to Cy's own culture—he undoubtedly knew or had once known about the romantic theory of the *doppelgänger*—could sometimes waylay him for hours. On this occasion it was not to be.

"Her *own* ghost! The ghost she had bought, acquired, acquired with the house, the ghost of Taynford Grange," explained Cy. "You see, my dear Jem, up till a short while ago, Jane Manfred, the most charming woman, I must really bring her into your life"—Jemima thought it tactless to mention the innumerable times Cy had already brought Lady Manfred into her life—"Up till now poor Jane has not *seen* the Taynford ghost, despite the absolutely enormous price Max paid for that house, and a house in the country too." Cy shuddered metaphorically. He was not fond of the country, to put it mildly, considering even Saturday dinner and Sunday breakfast in a stone-built Cotswold palace like Taynford Grange an exaggerated demonstration of his friendship.

"At first there was some thought that perhaps change of ownership," Cy continued, "the original family, the—what were they called? The family had certainly been there since Charlemagne . . ." He paused, wondering momentarily if he had the right country, right history, then proceeded, "Yet Jane felt, indeed had complete confidence, that the ghost would soon *settle down*."

"And it didn't?" prompted Jemima. (That word again: she felt some sympathy for the ghost.)

"It did not. Then there was some thought that perhaps the builders, or more to the point the decorators, or more to the point still, the decorator, might have upset him. As Jane said—she's so amusing, Jem, you two share a sense of humour, as I hope you will soon discover—as Jane said, 'I know that Gawain is a brilliant decorator, there is John Steff, I suppose, if he wasn't so tied up at Oare, still Gawain is brilliant, incredibly creative, but I'm not sure I'd come back from the next world to see him.'" Jane Manfred, as quoted by Cy, was referring to a famous decorator, known fondly to his friends as the Green Knight, and by those not privileged to enjoy his friendship as the Green Nightmare.

"It seems that Gawain plans to build a conservatory on the north side of the house, which needs excavation. And that might have unsettled our ghost. Very daring, said Jane, but he's currently interested in the northern challenge. Gawain of course, not the ghost. What challenge would that be, Jem?" enquired Cy, without clearly having any interest in the answer. He was back to the ghost and Lady Manfred.

"And now at last she's seen it!" Cy concluded happily. "And she feels accepted at last. And that, my dear Jemima, is how our series has been born. A series of ghosts and their owners, Jem, beginning with Lady Manfred. Taynford, such a beautiful house, she's promised, she'll see to it that Max agrees. Ghosts—and what they tell us about our time and ourselves; ghosts, who sees them, who doesn't, a new form of who's in, who's out, if you like, don't let *Taffeta* get hold of that one, don't breathe a word; ghosts, how they have influenced history, ghosts, how does history influence them . . . ," Cy rattled away.

"It could be seminal," he concluded. And this time Jemima knew she was finally lost. She had one last weapon on her side, or thought she had: that programme about social attitudes to birth control among the women of Afghanistan as influenced by the Russian occupation—which meant three months' research and filming away from everything, including Cy, Jane Manfred and sundry ghosts; but it also meant three months away from Cass. It was easy, in certain moods, to underplay the sweetness of their reconciliation; and hadn't it been that selfsame kind of programme about child-brides in Sri Lanka, her prolonged incommunicado absence, which had caused him to engage in his precipitate marriage in the first place?

So: "What kind of ghost, Cy?" asked Jemima.

"A romantic ghost," Cy pronounced with great benevolence. For Cy, too, knew that Jemima was lost; vague as he might be about many things such as the challenge of north-facing conservatories, Cy had not built up Megalith Television to its present eminence without being at once feline and ruthless when necessary. What Jemima did not know, for example, was that he had only this morning lured her arch-rival Serenity Saville away from Titan TV, with the offer of just that programme about Afghanistan. And Serenity, a girl with the face of a Madonna, known for some reason as "the S.S. trooper" to her colleagues, had accepted.

"You'll enjoy it all, my Jem," Cy, secure in this knowledge, was promising. "A romantic ghost: a Cavalier, a handsome soldier from the Civil War, long hair, soulful expression, Jane Manfred said. A bit like a violinist, except of course he was in armour. But she will tell you the full history of it all."

For a moment Jemima's heart had given an uncomfortable lurch. Armour, long hair, soulful expression . . . could it be, no, impossible. Besides, if Decimus Lackland's ghost walked anywhere, it walked presumably at Lackland Court . . . Wait a moment, *wasn't* there a ghost? Wasn't there something rather odd in one of Rupert Durham's books about the ghost of Decimus Lackland? A historical reference? That must be it.

The ghost of Decimus Lackland . . . her mind pursued this train of thought while she continued to smile at Cy with an angelic expression worthy of the S.S. trooper herself. Now *that* was a ghost worth investigating. Wait a moment . . .

"I'm sure I shall enjoy it all, Cy," Jemima said in her sweetest voice; in fact so sweet was it that Cy shot a sudden look of suspicion. Docility in Jemima was rare, and in Cy's opinion, generally the prelude to some devious act. Even when their relationship had been a great deal more intimate than it was now—years back an episode

never referred to but in fact the foundation of a warm relationship—
docile was never a word which Cy would have applied to Jemima.
Then the telephone rang on Cy's private line, and Miss Lewis buzzed
him on the intercom at one and the same moment. They were both
saved.

At almost exactly the same time as Jemima was vowing herself
enchanted at the prospect of a whole series on the subject of "Ghosts
and Ourselves"—the working title—the new Lord Lackland, a.k.a.
Handsome Dan Meredith, was professing himself rather less enchanted with a conversation he was having, perforce, at Lackland
Court.

The conversation was being held with his late cousin's elderly butler
and Dan Lackland was sufficiently put out by it to be gazing out of the
stone windows of the house, rudely turning his back on the old man.
Yet even his worst enemies would concede that Handsome Dan's
manners were normally immaculate to one and all, including women
of course and servants, naturally.

"What on earth do you mean, Haygarth, his late Lordship was
frightened?" There was silence, silence with a quality of obstinacy
about it, Dan felt.

"Come on man, out with it. Frightened of what?" The old butler
was shortly to be retired under the will of the 17th Lord Lackland, and
the 18th Lord had time to reflect that his retirement was perhaps not
an unmitigated disaster.

"He was frightened, m'lord," repeated Haygarth stolidly.

"Frightened of death, d'you mean? Well, we're all frightened of that
if we've any sense, death is a frightening business, and his late
Lordship, being nearly eighty, had more time to be frightened of it
than most."

"His late Lordship was not frightened of death, m'lord," said
Haygarth; there was a distinct note of indignation in his voice, and
Dan Meredith thought he detected extra flush in the butler's cheek.
"Ask any of us who were at Dunkirk with him."

"Quite so, Haygarth, quite so," answered the new Lord Lackland hurriedly. Give Haygarth his head about the war and they'd be here all day; what with Charlotte, children and nanny arriving at Taynford station any minute, Babs threatening to drop Nell herself at exactly the same moment with all the possibilities for trouble *that* implied, especially if he had to offer her a drink. As for Zena—when had his sister Zena's presence ever made for peace? "Now, there's a good fellow, tell me exactly what the trouble was. Keep it brisk, if you don't mind. Her Ladyship doesn't like to be kept waiting, and if she did, that nanny doesn't." He laughed companionably before remembering that even in a short space of time, Haygarth and the nanny had managed to get at daggers drawn.

"His Lordship was frightened of the ghost," said Haygarth carefully. "The ghost that steps out of the portrait. He thought that the ghost had decided to kill him."

2

Toast To Decimus

"He—Handsome Dan as he used to be called—Lord Lackland in other words, suggested meeting you at the Plantaganet," said Cherry importantly. From Cherry's tone Jemima could tell that her faithful P.A., one who was not easily impressed, was impressed upon this occasion. Since Jemima herself continued to look blank, Cherry added, "The Plantaganet. The tennis club. In Fulham, down by the river. You know, the one they always write about in the Press." She sounded just slightly reproachful, as though Jemima, her heroine, had on this occasion let her down.

"Of course I've heard of the Planty! Actually I've played there." Jemima hoped that her slightly base use of the Yuppie nickname for the celebrated club would regain Cherry's esteem. "That disastrous Megalith versus Titan tournament, wasn't that played at the Plantaganet?"

"Disastrous! But we won."

"We may have won but that was the fell occasion on which Cy first met Serenity Saville," replied Jemima grimly; she had just heard the news about the S.S. trooper and her Afghanistan programme. It was true that Jemima had recently had her own triumph: all the same these reverses must be remembered and if possible revenged, otherwise Cy would get quite out of hand.

Her own triumph was quite considerable, for all that. For her devious and somewhat prolonged campaign had finally succeeded: the "Ghosts and Ourselves" series would now lead off with a programme about Decimus Lackland and *his* ghost, instead of one about Jane Manfred and *her* ghost, in other words the resident ghost of Taynford Grange. Various people had been of assistance in this campaign. Rupert Durham for example had proved a staunch ally when she had promised that the programme would put an end to the "ridiculous Lely red herring" once and for all. The habitual chaos of his private life by no means incapacitated him from a nice line in academic in-fighting, Jemima noticed, and his mild eyes beneath their large spectacles glinted at the thought of extinguishing once and for all the ludicrous theories of "that woman." What woman? Presumably some rival academic, not one of his rather numerous female acquaintances. (Rupert had addressed Jemima as Becky for most of lunch, with occasional excursions in the direction of Sylvia, Sue and Vicky.) For all his amatory vagueness, however, Rupert Durham was full of good practical advice as to how to lobby who on the whole subject.

What was more, he showed a marked disinclination to repossess his own portrait, when Jemima politely suggested it.

"Where London is concerned, I'm not exactly living in Ladbroke Grove at the moment. At least I don't think I am, am I?" Rupert ran his hand rather desperately through his curly hair, so that the springy brown halo divided itself into two horns. "And Cambridge is impossible." He did not say why. "So Becky darling—"

"Jemima," said Jemima politely but firmly. She had extremely fond memories of a hectic summer romance with Rupert during her second year at Cambridge; at least he concentrated his mind wonderfully when making love, which no doubt explained his continuing success with the opposite sex (punting on the Cam was another matter). But that was another place, another time; she had no wish to revive the memories. And she had observed that Rupert Durham's technique, conscious or unconscious, was to accompany the wrong (but more intimate) Christian name with the kind of intimate approach one name justified but the other didn't.

"Jemima! Then there's another thing. My own television series—did I tell you about it? No? Nothing in your class, just a modest little thing. But one way or another—look, you wouldn't mind holding onto it just a little longer? Till I sort everything out."

"I shall be delighted," answered Jemima with perfect sincerity. If Rupert's chaotic personal life combined with a "modest" television series—which of course he had not previously mentioned—meant that she kept the portrait, she welcomed both.

"I know what we'll do to celebrate," said Rupert, with evident relief—even a picture had the potential power to tie him down— "We'll go to the N.P.G. after lunch" (they were at Orso's) "and compare my version with theirs. You'll find the differences interesting. No, wait, I have to meet someone. You go, Sylvia. Now, back to this old buzzard we need for the programme and how we nail him."

It was in this manner that Jemima found herself ten minutes later on an upper floor of the gallery, threading her way past portraits of voluptuous reclining beauties with visible swelling bosoms and lambent pearls at the neck and ear. Jemima thought of Pope on Lely. How did it go? She would have to ask Rupert. Something about "the sleepy eye that spoke the soul." Here were sleepy eyes in abundance. Indolence must have helped to pass the time wonderfully for these apparently passive, certainly privileged women. Olivia Lackland on the other hand even if passive had not been indolent: for she had had a devotion to learning which according to Clarendon had marked her out from the rest of her sex.

But wait! Jemima had gone too far, gone as far in fact as the Restoration. And there was the Merry Monarch himself, gazing at her, bold, black-eyed and cynical, in frank sexual appraisal from the end of the room (Jemima was sure that he bent the same gaze on every female who entered). Jemima retraced her steps and in a kind of antechamber dedicated to the "Arts and Sciences," found at last the real thing. All the same, Lackland in his armour seemed oddly placed among men in the voluminous dark robes of peace, a man in an open white shirt holding an admonitory skull . . . the ambivalence of his career as artist and war hero struck her anew. There was no dog in this picture, although the pose was otherwise very similar. With his right hand—with its disproportionately long fingers—the poet held a baton. His other hand was hidden. Even the legend beneath the portrait seemed to emphasise the dichotomy. "Decimus Meredith lst Viscount Lackland 1612–1645. Poet and Cavalier," she read. Then Jemima stepped back to study the portrait at leisure, hoping to hold her own version in her mind's eye—and found herself for one moment ensconced in the arms of the only other adult visitor in the room, who had in fact been standing directly behind her.

Hasty apologies on both sides followed. In her embarrassment Jemima hardly took in the appearance of the fair-haired man at whom she had thus apparently flung herself. She had the impression certainly of someone tall and thin, as well as fair, that he was wearing some kind of dark suit, and illogically, she knew, or thought she knew, that he was English—that was because, like Cass, who was also English, the stranger smelt of Eau Sauvage shaving lotion (which was actually French).

The tall fair-haired stranger on the other hand recognised Jemima Shore immediately and followed his own apologies with a quick discreet smile which acknowledged that fact without presuming upon it. It was moreover the smile of a man used, for well over twenty years, to please by his smile; a man used furthermore to pleasing generally, not only women but crowds. Lastly, it was the smile of a man not unused to recognition himself. As a matter of fact, if Handsome Dan Meredith had been wearing a white T-shirt, immaculate white shorts, white socks, white shoes and had been carrying a couple of tennis rackets, Jemima might indeed have recognised him in her turn. But the well-fitting and well-fitted dark blue suit gave her no clues. Besides, Jemima herself was soon utterly absorbed by the portrait before her, as she tried to figure out the differences between the real Van Dyck and "her" copy.

Jemima was oblivious therefore to the intense, level scrutiny which the stranger, confident of his anonymity, now proceeded to focus upon her as she studied the picture. Perhaps that was just as well. There was something just slightly calculating about Dan Lackland's expression. This was not the purely sexual appraisal of the Merry Monarch, forever lustful, forever held back from consummation by the confines of his heavy gold frame. Lust was certainly not absent from the gaze of the new Lord Lackland: yet it did not seem to be his sole emotion as he inspected Jemima Shore.

Lord Lackland silently left the gallery. Outside, in St. Martin's Lane, he turned left and marched rapidly in the direction of Wilton's Restaurant in Jermyn Street. To an outsider, he would have looked not so much calculating as abstracted. At Wilton's, the friendly—but not obsequious—greeting at the restaurant, which was the true sign of its excellence, still did not remove the slight frown from his face.

"Her Ladyship is already at the table, m'lord," murmured the head waiter in what was obviously just one variant of a familiar pattern in which Lordships might already be at the table awaiting Ladyships, graces awaiting other graces (both ducal and physical) and so forth and so on.

It was not until Dan Lackland actually reached his destined table in an alcove that he relaxed. And then the imposing woman sitting there, striking in a red Chanel suit which set off her glowing red-black hair and smooth olive skin, had to command him to do so.

"Darling boy, you smile when you see me," said his *vis-à-vis*—surely a few years older than Dan Lackland himself? "Don't forget." There was something not entirely maternal about the admonition.

"An odd coincidence," he said. "That's all." And he did give the lady opposite the kind of boyish, apologetic smile which she presumably had in mind. "You know I'm working on the Lackland Court problem. And I've had this approach . . ." He leant forward.

Back at the gallery, however, Jemima Shore was not smiling either. She too appeared abstracted. For some reason her thoughts had suddenly turned away from the portrait itself to the ghost of Decimus

Lackland; the bizarre, even horrifying story she had recently been told.

Already her imagination was beginning to play upon the story. In spite of herself, she could not help fleshing it out in television terms, a drama, an investigation. In her mind's eye, Jemima saw Decimus in his lace-decked armour, bidding farewell to his wife. It was a farewell which had of course been anticipated in another celebrated poem: "I could not love thee dear so much"—no, that was Lovelace and Althea. "I could not love thy *kiss*"—And then, long before television, Victorian painters had loved to illustrate the scene: the handsome Cavalier bending from his tall black horse towards his fainting wife with her similarly downcast eyes and her neat little rosebud mouth.

Jemima had an idea that one painter—Frith perhaps? No, someone later, Millais?—had done two pictures of Decimus and Olivia entitled respectively *Their First Kiss* and *Their Last Kiss*. The first picture had shown a similarly modest, highly Victorian-looking maiden seated on a rustic bench under a vast sheltering tree. The handsome Cavalier had his lace matched on this occasion by plum-coloured civilian velvet instead of armour, as he launched himself towards the shrinking Olivia, plumed hat in hand.

But were females really so innocently abashed at a mere kiss in the seventeenth century? Jemima reflected on this with the stirrings of indignation. Surely here subsequent Victorian attitudes were being imposed upon a more robust society. Olivia Lackland herself would survive to bring up that dewy-eyed infant in the second picture; Antony Decimus, her only child. A widow but not altogether helpless. Furthermore she would survive through the rest of the Civil War period as a woman alone: it was she who, following *Their Last Kiss*, would conduct the famous defence of Lackland Court which marked—according to the legend—the first appearance of Decimus' ghost. And she would survive in the harsh times of the Common-wealth—harsh for Royalists that is—and plead successfully for her son's estate from Oliver Cromwell.

The Petitioner, that was another Victorian picture, if not actually depicting Olivia Lackland, some other Royalist widow; more downcast eyes, graceful black garments (but lace-trimmed to reveal Cavalier status) and the grimly patriarchal figure of the Protector himself looming over her, bulbous nose, visible warts and all. According to Jemima's recollection, the gaze which the Protector was bending upon the lovely Petitioner before him, while not the frank appraisal of Charles II, was not quite without its hint of sexual element. As though even Oliver Cromwell was not averse to the spectacle of a beautiful—and vulnerable—female casting herself upon his mercy. A female who might be raised up, pardoned—or flung down at the whim of the dictator.

Was it in this sweetly self-abasing fashion that Olivia, widow of the "Malignant" Royalist Lord Lackland, had pleaded for her son's confiscated property? Everything that Jemima had read about her indicated on the contrary; pride, dignity, and that even included her heroic withdrawal from society following the Restoration. Not for her the louche high jinks of the Merry Monarch's Court. The same, alas, could not be said for her wastrel son, Antony Decimus, who had been the King's boon companion. But then heroes' sons were notoriously prone to dissipation. As the son of both a hero and a poet, what chance in life had the 2nd Viscount Lackland ever really had?

On the other hand, it was possible that Olivia Viscountess Lackland in her petitioning had simply used that secret weapon of apparent frailty always available to the woman in the man's world. Pride and dignity in a woman might be all very well in private but were hardly likely to sway the all-powerful Lord Protector to mercy in public. Nor could Jemima Shore herself, ostensibly living in a far more liberated world from the woman's point of view, really criticise such prudent self-abasement in Olivia Lackland. With her hand on her heart, could Jemima really swear that she had never exercised such "wiles" herself in the course of a highly successful professional career? What about that time she had dropped, well, a tear or two, in Cy's presence over that Sri Lankan child-brides budget? It had of course worked wonders. All in a good cause. The tears moreover had been quite genuine, even if they had been tears of rage, not weakness as Cy had imagined . . . .

Jemima put this uncomfortable moment of self-criticism firmly aside and turned her thoughts back to the death of Decimus and the origins of the ghost story which obsessed her. She saw again the big black horse returning to Lackland Court on the evening of that dreadful day when, in the words of Clarendon, the sun itself setting had not been more red than the blood which stained the King's field. Over the crupper of the horse lay the body of his master. Lifeless—no, not quite.

There was time for Decimus to be laid down, for the frightful wounds to be tended by "clouts" or bandages of linen. There was time for Decimus to embrace his sorrowing and exhausted wife, still weak from the strain of bearing the much desired son and heir. Most of Jemima's knowledge derived from that memoir of the poet "lately dead" by an anonymous author, most probably the Lackland chaplain, entitled "Heaven's True Mourning" or "The Cruel Death of the Most Noble Viscount Lackland." According to this account, Decimus gave Olivia certain last commands concerning his son; he also gave her commands concerning his burial.

Just before ten o'clock Decimus died. The slow booming of the Lackland chapel bell marked the event. That was significant because everyone in the village and around would have known that the Lord was dead.

No doubt Decimus' last commands concerning the boy were carried out by the admirable Olivia. The instructions for his burial, on the other hand, in the family vault in the chapel, had definitely not been carried out.

That was because sometime in the night, under cover of darkness, while the desolated Lackland servants slept and no watch was kept on the corpse—No, Jemima stopped. That was not quite right.

It was Olivia Lackland who had collapsed and been carried away. But there had been a watch kept and she should have remembered that because she found the thought of this particular character so poignant. There had been one person in the room lit only by black candles, Alice, the old nurse, who had in fact been Decimus' own wetnurse. The poet had been the fifteenth child and the tenth son of Sir Marcus Meredith and his City-heiress wife—hence the commemorative Latin name Decimus. He had also been the only boy to survive; Alice must have done well by him. Decimus! You could not imagine such a name being bestowed on a baby today, at any rate not being a tenth child. Admittedly the Merediths had ended up with a mere four children—out of fifteen—since two of their five girls had also died in infancy.

So Dame Alice knelt alone by the great bed draped in its black velvet hangings; plenty of those available in the early seventeenth century when Death was never further away than the threshold of the room. According to "Heaven's True Mourning," Decimus had been laid in the bed in which his own mother had recently died, as his life slowly bled away. That "pious and revered daughter of a City-merchant who brought honour as well as fortune" to the family name, in the words of the memorial, had preceded her single surviving son by only a few weeks. "She led the way, he followed trustingly as when he was a child."

At some time, then, in the night, when the black candles had burnt low, in that "dead of night when men most easily give up their souls to God," robbers had come silently and secretly to Lackland Court. They had found their way without difficulty through the Great Chamber: with the King's cause so heavily defeated that day, and the Lord dying, they had not thought to put guards.

Perhaps Alice slept on her watch, wearied by the long day of horror and its tragic climax. For when she awoke the body was gone. The heavy black coverlet was torn aside, and the corpse was vanished. The old woman had some story of men-at-arms, knights, black knights, visions of the devil, but surely these were merely unhappy visions as she slept. The body of Decimus Lord Lackland had never been found.

It had in fact never been seen again since that night, not his bones, not his skeleton, no trace. The coffin alone had been placed in the family vault: sadly and symbolically empty. The tablet above it had in sonorous and long-winded Latin recorded the capture of the body "and yet his soul they could not take"—*sed animam non raptare posse*. And even that tablet had not been destined to rest very long in place. The chapel, which was much older than the house itself, had been very badly damaged by mortars during the siege of Lackland Court three years later. In a reverse of the usual pious story of miraculous preservation it was the chapel which had burnt and the house which had emerged virtually unscathed. (The Parliamentarian excuse for pounding the house of God was the fact that ammunition and troops were stored there, something hotly denied by the Royalists.) In the eighteenth century the chapel had been allowed to become a suitably ivy-clad folly; the tablet, Jemima believed, had been removed to Taynford Cathedral.

Returning to the abduction of the body, who could have done such a thing? The Roundheads—the Parliamentarian army, as Jemima must learn to call them—were naturally blamed as they were blamed for every desecration. Was it their need to extinguish the legend as well as the life of the Cavalier hero which had led to such a gross deed against the dead? Contemporary sources were either unhelpful or contradictory on the subject, according to Rupert, and Jemima, having checked them for herself, agreed.

Clarendon, for example, in his long eulogy of the character of the poet and his wife, elected not to mention the disappearance of his corpse. "Heaven's True Mourning," while suggesting that the deed was an act of vengeance on the part of the Parliamentarians, on a par with the impiety of those who would five years later kill King Charles the First, had nevertheless not named those personally responsible. Wicked John Aubrey on the other hand, ever one to promote a colourful tale, suggested that Lord Lackland had had a mistress who lived close by—the notorious Lady Isabella Clare—and that she had sent her own men to steal the body and give it secret burial.

As Rupert Durham crushingly said: "Well, he would, wouldn't he? You know Aubrey—" Jemima was just beginning to know Aubrey. "He would have written for the *Daily Exclusive* if he'd been alive today. There's absolutely no proof that Isabella Clare was Decimus' mistress, and as for writing the Swan poem to a woman like that, the mind boggles. We've only got Aubrey's word for the whole thing, and *he* wanted to have a dig at Decimus, I believe. Didn't like the poetic halo round his head. He came up with the same kind of story, if less dramatic, about Decimus' rival, Falkland." And so the matter rested. Until the ghost-who-could-not-rest, the ghost of Decimus, returned to Lackland Court during the 1648 siege and guided the widowed Olivia to victory.

According to tradition Decimus stepped out of the portrait to do so.

"Yes, the portrait," said the present (and 18th) Lord Lackland to Jemima Shore. "As the story goes, he steps out of the big portrait at the head of the stairs. The Van Dyck. The finest version, or so *we* believe. What's more, we all think it's the original, and not the one at the N.P.G., even if Oliver Millar doesn't agree. Something ridiculous about the hands, the hand. I believe you know that picture," added Dan Lackland carelessly. Jemima nodded. She had not however recognised him from their previous odd little encounter, believing him to be familiar to her merely from his famous past as a tennis star.

They were sitting in the coolly elegant surroundings of the Plantaganet Club. Enormous windows opened on the river. Even the factory chimneys on the bank opposite had the air of being composed for the sake of the perfect modernist view. The fact that through another vast plate glass window before their eyes a tennis game was being played made such talk of a seventeenth-century ghost seem for a moment peculiarly bizarre.

Counting the seventeenth century, there were in fact, thought Jemima, three levels of reality. For the surroundings of the Plantaganet bar, a high-ceilinged glass and mirrored area with huge purple bougainvilleas in white tubs (where on earth were they grown?), small tables adorned with pale pink button roses, and a barman in a bright pink jacket, bespoke the leisured luxury of another age; some ocean liner of the thirties, perhaps. The players, on the other hand, whether on the visible "Royal Court" behind the glass, or passing through the bar area on their way to other courts or back to the changing room, indicated both by their dress and their complexion a rougher or at least a sweatier way of life. And the pictures were all enormously blown-up photographs of tennis stars past and present—including, she noticed, Handsome Dan himself instantly recognisable by his thatch of blond hair, in younger days.

The exact nature of Dan Lackland's involvement with the Plantaganet was not quite clear to her. But he introduced Jemima to various members with some style as though he was in fact a form of host. These included various young or youngish women—her uncertainty about their age was due to the fact that tennis gear, with women as well as men, proved a remarkable disguise. The essentially schoolgirlish nature of such clothes could prove delusive: whether very short pale pink pleated skirts revealing brown thighs—did all members of the Planty have to have an all-the-year-round tan by law?—or bright pink track suits concealing unsightly middle-aged spread. One way or another, it was impossible to guess the age of most of the women she met.

Take the energetic girl—or woman—introduced to Jemima as Alix Carstairs, who appeared to run the Club: how old was she? Alix Carstairs sported a thick pigtail of auburn hair beneath her bright pink bandeau and her face, devoid of make-up, was prettily freckled; she might have been any age between twenty-two and forty-two. As she gazed at Jemima, she had the bold bright eyes of some kind of bird; not necessarily a friendly bird, although her demeanour was extremely polite. On learning that Jemima liked to play tennis, Alix Carstairs urged her to come and play a trial game on spec: "To see if you like us."

But the sub-text was, thought Jemima, "And to see if we like you; which I, Alix, may not necessarily do." Charlotte Lackland, on the other hand, Dan Lackland's wife—his second wife, according to the reference books—was extremely friendly and as a result Jemima warmed to her. Charlotte's slight figure—she couldn't have been much more than five foot—coupled with her long straight fair hair tied by a ribbon in a ponytail, and her round blue eyes, made her age once again difficult to guess. Didn't she have—according to the reference books again—three children? But she was gazing at her husband with those round blue eyes as though she was a child herself.

It came as a further surprise to Jemima therefore to discover that sweet little Charlotte, improbably mother of three, also ran a well-known patisserie called eponymously Charlotte's Cakes (whose proverbially charming girl assistants were generally nicknamed, doubtless incorrectly, Charlotte's Tarts). She had been taking part in some form of tournament:

"We were slaughtered," she groaned. "It's true, darling. I'm going to take my serve right back to Costa next week and see if anything can be done about it, otherwise—"

But Dan Lackland hardly seemed to hear her, and soon Charlotte wandered off.

For a moment, Jemima tracked her progress amid the flower-decorated tables; most of the members either kissed or were kissed by her. Then Jemima's attention was caught by a man at the bar. He was gulping down what looked like iced water (but was perhaps a vodka tonic) and dressed, despite his considerable bulk, in a track suit—bright pink like the barman's coat—which was emblazoned with the crossed capital P's of the Plantaganet: to Jemima, with her present bent towards history, they had the look of two crossed swords with large hilts.

She looked again. The wringing wet and curly hair, and a face not much less rubicund than the track suit, the unfamiliar gear, had prevented her from immediately recognising—yes, it was . . . The new Home Secretary. Stuart Gibson. So that was indeed iced water, since he was a self-proclaimed teetotaller as well as health freak. Jemima glanced round and saw the one man conspicuous not so much by his neat dark suit but by the fact that he was ostentatiously doing nothing. That must be the Home Secretary's detective. And who was, or rather who *had* been the Home Secretary's opponent? Medium height, stocky build, distinctly hunched: in his conventional white shorts and zipped-up blue jacket, he looked to be in his forties.

"That's my cousin Marcus." Lord Lackland had evidently read her thoughts. "Gibson's P.P.S. Playing tennis against the boss goes with the job."

"If he's as good as you are—" began Jemima politely to make up for her wandering attention. Then she perceived that in some way the subject of his cousin was inimical to Handsome Dan; his expression had clouded: piqued vanity perhaps because a pretty woman had looked at another man? "He's not likely to be as good as me since he had polio as a boy," Lord Lackland replied quite shortly. "But he's pretty good all the same, gets around the court at the most amazing speed. Stout fellow, Marcus." Jemima felt abashed. She hastened to return to the third—or rather the first—reality of the seventeenth century.

"So Decimus—the ghost—does step out of the portrait! Just as it says in 'Heaven's True Mourning.' The memorial." Jemima hoped that this proof that she had done her homework would start the soothing process. Now for the question, the crucial question which had brought her so eagerly to the Plantaganet Club, the question on which the future of this particular episode in the "Ghosts and Ourselves" series might well depend.

Jemima sipped her Planty Punch (which was actually a non-alcoholic mixture of fruit juices, beloved of the Yuppies who used the Club for its healthful pink froth).

"By the way, have *you* seen the ghost, Lord Lackland?" she asked casually, following the question with a smile, as though the answer to it hardly mattered. But her precise tone, even the sheer sweetness of her slightly cat-like smile, might have been recognised by those she had interviewed on television in that famous hard-hitting programme about women's treatment in the Trade Union movement—"Sisters or Brothers?"

"Call me Dan, for God's sake! I've hardly got used to this Lord Lackland bit. I keep looking round nervously for poor old Cousin Tommy when I hear the name!"

"Dan then! *Much* nicer. And I'm of course Jemima." She smiled again, looking more cat-like than ever. "I just wondered if you'd ever seen the ghost yourself."

Handsome Dan drank from a glass that looked as if it contained whiskey.

"Ah, Jemima—what a pretty name that is, by the way. Do you know, I had an ancestress called Jemima, said to have been the daughter of James II, hence the name. It was originally a form of James. But you knew that." Jemima didn't. "I hope to God she wasn't," he went on. "His daughter, I mean. *Not* one's favourite monarch to put it mildly. Where was I? The ghost. Ah. Jemima, I see you don't yet know everything about the Decimus Ghost. Which is what we generally call him. Or it. But somehow *him* seems right."

"There must be a great deal I don't know. So—enlighten me."

"Children can see the Decimus Ghost quite safely. And many have. Down the centuries. If you believe the stories. He likes children. Because he came back the first time to save his little son. Nell—that's my funny little daughter by my first marriage, not so little now of course, fifteen? I'm hopeless about my children's ages—Nell saw him when she was quite small. And she continues to see him. If she's to be believed."

"Have you yourself seen him often? That's really what I'm getting at."

"Only children can see the Decimus Ghost in safety. If anyone else sees the Decimus Ghost, that's an omen."

"An omen?" Jemima was genuinely startled. This really was news to her.

"An omen of death. His death. Or her death. Or possibly the death of a member of the family. So—" Handsome Dan paused and drank again. "In answer to your question, Jemima, no, I haven't seen the Decimus Ghost and I very much hope I never do." He drained his glass. It seemed like a kind of toast—to Decimus perhaps, *in absentia*.

3

A Ghost Walking

"This is mine," said Dan Lackland to Jemima Shore. There was a peculiar note in his voice which was not exactly family pride, more like personal triumph. Lackland Court at last: as Jemima gazed at the celebrated facade of the Elizabethan house, she felt that compared to other earlier Tudor mansions she had visited, it had the air and confidence of a Renaissance palace. Here were four high storeys serrated by groups of long narrow windows, gables, a parapet and a towering roof; the chimneys were shaped like columns, and decorating the parapet she could see further obelisks and balustrades. Yet it was not architecture which engaged her: she herself was feeling something like the excitement of a lover.

For this at last was the physical, rather than the poetical world of Decimus . . . "Mine." For an instant the word grated on her. Was she in danger of experiencing an absurd jealousy in her obsession over the dead poet? It would never do to start resenting the live owner! That would be ridiculous. Besides, Dan Lackland's remark fitted perfectly into context. He had been giving a courteous disquisition on the Meredith family history, having stopped the Mercedes to let Jemima take her first look at the mellow Cotswold stone of Lackland Court through the arched gatehouse; since that was what the architect had intended.

At first she was surprised that he was so knowledgeable, a mere tennis player to be so expert? Jemima caught herself up. This was definitely elitism, or sportism (if there was such a thing) on her part. The fact that a person was particularly good at some sport hardly meant that he or she had to be an intellectual oaf . . . After a bit she realised that the truth was slightly subtler. Dan Lackland did indeed know a great deal of history—the history of the Meredith family, that is. Presumably he had boned up on it since youth, anticipating his inheritance. On general historical matters outside the world of the Merediths, on the other hand, he was quite as ignorant or indifferent as Jemima had instinctively expected. Perhaps it was just as well that the Meredith family history touched so many points of English history during its three hundred years of progress.

"Built in the 1590's," he remarked. "A good period. Roughly the same as Montacute, if you've ever been there. According to Pevsner, it may even be by the same architect. Montacute is National Trust now, of course." And he added: "This is mine." And Dan Lackland continued with his polite little lecture. The triumphant note had vanished.

"The great thing to remember about the Merediths," he continued, "is that we got the money thing right—aesthetically that is. The Merediths were fairly rich in the eighteenth century when Thomas Decimus the 8th Viscount built up the library and had himself and his wife painted by Gainsborough. But they were fairly poor in the nineteenth century, having got the railway thing all wrong, and very poor indeed by the beginning of the twentieth. So no new nasty Victorian or Edwardian wing to ruin the house."

"You've got two Gainsboroughs!" exclaimed Jemima, Decimus temporarily forgotten, fixing by habit on an obvious point for the television cameras.

"Good God, no. Cousin Tommy's father sold them to the Metropolitan years ago. The money was running out fast. Cousin Tommy would have sold the whole bloody library if it wasn't for the entail. That meant he simply had to pass it on intact. Or pretend to. My clever sister Zena, who knows about such things, thinks there may be one or two valuable books gone missing—" Dan Lackland stopped, as though aware that he had become altogether too intimate in his revelations to one who was after all in effect a total stranger. Jemima however, her curiosity aroused, was not inclined to let the matter rest.

"But how will you manage?" she pursued. "Will you turn to the National Trust? English Heritage, as it's now called."

"I shall manage," said the new Lord Lackland briefly. "No, no National Trust or English Heritage or whatever. As I said, this is mine." He turned to her, smiling and at his most charming. "Not the nation's, I'm afraid. Or not yet."

The car was now drawing up beside the wide stone terrace which fended off the gravel and the grass of the forecourt from the broad stone steps of the house itself. A huge heraldic carving of stone— presumably the Meredith arms—surmounted the doorway with the motto: Amor et Honor, in Gothic lettering. Jemima also saw the date proudly preserved: 1600.

Meanwhile a stout elderly man in a dark suit, bald, with a florid face, was clambering down the steps towards them.

"Haygarth, Cousin Tommy's old butler. He was his soldier servant in the war but he's been here for over forty years, and knows everything about the house: but he's on the point of retiring. He married Cousin Beatrice's lady's maid after the war—a dreadful old bat who terrified me as a child, called Dorothy."

"Then maybe I should talk to them about the Decimus Ghost. That could be useful." Jemima really made the remark out of politeness. She was not particularly interested in interviewing an aged butler and his wife on television when she had other fish to fry such as a former All England tennis player, captain of the Davis Cup team, whose looks alone—unquestionably justifying his nickname—had caused maidens of an earlier generation to swoon. Jemima remembered herself as a schoolgirl fancying him madly.

I suppose he's still quite sexy if you like that fair type, she thought critically, which I don't any longer. He certainly doesn't look much like his famous ancestor. Green eyes instead of brown. Give me a romantic soulful poet over a tennis player however handsome any day.

Jemima was surprised to see Dan frown.

"Not much point in interviewing servants." He sounded uncharacteristically abrupt. "You know how they exaggerate. Dorothy died years ago and Haygarth is getting quite gaga—lives in the past and all that. No, not the seventeenth century, nothing so fascinating. Just Cousin Tommy's wartime adventures. No interviews with Haygarth. I can tell you all you need to know." Dan Lackland jumped out of the car so swiftly and easily that he might have been jumping the net after a victory in a tennis tournament.

But Jemima certainly saw nothing gaga about Haygarth. The man now heaving his master's suitcase out of the Mercedes might be elderly but there was nothing necessarily wrong with his hearing: he could well have heard Lord Lackland's last dismissive remarks.

"Welcome to Lackland Court, Miss Shore," Haygarth was saying; his voice was vigorous and he did not waver as he carried rather than lugged her case up the steps.

But the sight of the Decimus portrait, hanging at the head of the broad double wooden staircase which led directly out of the great hall, put an end to other thoughts—at least for the time being. Perhaps it was the steep perspective of the staircase, the domination exercised by the single portrait at the head of it, perhaps it was her own emotion which gradually accumulated as they approached Lackland Court: for whatever reason Jemima felt a kind of faintness, dizzyness even, on seeing this particular version of the poet's portrait, which she could not remember experiencing before.

With Rupert's portrait she had fallen in love: it was as simple as that. At the N.P.G. she had been mainly occupied trying to train her untrained eye to concentrate and spot the differences between the two versions as Rupert himself had suggested: the big dog—of whatever breed—in Rupert's version, had become for example a page at the N.P.G., a page attending in some wide-eyed way to the sash of his master's armour. Decimus' white hand had passed from the dog's head to a more military-looking baton. Here the dog was back in the place of the page, with the poet's hand spread out upon its head; but his other hand was also visible, one finger raised and pointing, as though in warning . . . At the sight of this third version, she found that by now the intensity of her emotion was different, almost uncomfortably fierce in its quality . . .

A pause for collecting herself, a necessary pause. It occurred to her that this after all was the portrait out of which Decimus himself was supposed to step. No wonder she felt faint. It was at the time a purely ironic thought.

A ghost walking! What an absurd concept, if you considered it properly for one single moment. The further irony of the fact that she, a rationalist, or at any rate one who did not believe in ghosts, was about to make a whole series of programmes on the subject, was also not lost on Jemima. This particular development was however the joint responsibility of Cy's desire to please Lady Manfred and Jemima's own desire to please herself.

It was at this point that Jemima realised, perhaps a little late in the day, that she had never really examined her own truthful thoughts on the subject of ghosts. If Decimus' presence lingered in this world, and for her it unquestionably did, it lingered in his poetry. What need of further corporeal hauntings on the part of a man who had written: "I fain would be thy swan" or "I could not love thy kiss." Decimus Lackland lingered alright, in the reluctant minds of young children, the romantic minds of adolescents, the ardent minds of lovers reciting "No more thy ghost" to each other (as Cass had recited it to her the other night, in an effort undoubtedly to exorcise Decimus on his own terms, if only for one night). And he lingered also in the dry, or to be less stereotyped, the carefully appreciative minds of scholars like Rupert; Decimus also lived there so long as his lines could be analysed, reanalysed, deconstructed and reconstructed again.

Under the circumstances, who needed his ghost to walk? Jemima for one did not. Who needed ghosts anyway? Once again Jemima did not. She rejected all superstition, did she not? The Catholic convent of the

Blessed Eleanor which she had attended as a Protestant day girl had taught her the Catholic catechism as a matter of course. That certainly rejected superstition. Jemima could hear the precise voice of her old headmistress, Reverend Mother Ancilla, on the subject of ghosts now.

"My child, there is the Holy Ghost, and with Him, Our Dear Lord has provided us with *quite* enough to think about in the nature of ghosts."

While remaining a sad sceptic where religion was concerned, Jemima thought that there was nevertheless a good deal to be said for Mother Ancilla's point of view. Let her be clear, if only to herself, that she did not believe in ghosts, and was involved in this programme entirely in order to pursue privately her own literary (and emotional) interest in Decimus the poet. The existence of Decimus the ghost was never going to be her true concern. And what of evil done in dark places, a feeling of brooding terror, savage retribution on the innocent, which still hung over, for example, the pass of Glencoe?

On her single Highland holiday—a disastrous occasion, memories of which she still did not like to confront entirely*—Jemima had visited Culloden moor; had learned of the Highlanders left there to die the night after the battle, left to die of their wounds, their groans for water heard by their womenfolk at the edge of the battlefield, who were yet forbidden to attend them by the orders of the English commander Butcher Cumberland . . . Yes, these "old unhappy far-off things and battles long ago" might leave an atmosphere of tragedy; she could accept that. But *actual* ghosts, that she could not and would not accept, that the ghost of Decimus should walk out of a picture, no.

Jemima gazed at the portrait fixedly, and with the eye of love, not superstition.

"What do you think of him? Our soldier-poet?" It was Dan Lackland at her elbow. He struck a rough semblance of the poet's attitude. "Any likeness? Apart from the colouring?" He was only half joking.

*For these events, see *The Wild Island*.

"I doubt whether he could have beaten Rod Laver in five sets that famous time?" replied Jemima with perfect truth; she had recently been boning up on the details of Handsome Dan Meredith's tennis career; this had undoubtedly been an extraordinary turn-up early in his career.

"You are absurd, Dan! Showing off as usual." It was a pretty, teasing female voice speaking from the gallery above their heads. "You're not half as much like Decimus as I am, face it. I'm the one with the real Meredith looks. One in every generation as the tradition goes." For the first time since she had met him, Jemima saw Dan Lackland look thoroughly boyish, because he looked discomfited. Once again she glimpsed the matinee-idol-cum-tennis-player of Jemima's youth, with his perfect Robert Redford-like features and hair (on which the only visible effect of age was to bleach it still further—and most becomingly—at the wings).

"So you're here, Zeenie. Charlotte didn't tell me you were coming."

"Why should she since she didn't know?" countered Zena Meredith briskly, descending the stairs. "I did ring her up but she was in the middle of some crisis over the shop, as usual. Is it worth her having a shop, I sometimes wonder, with all those crises? Now that you no longer need the money. It's not as if cakes were very interesting—in themselves. Anyway, she'll be here for lunch. It was entirely my own idea that I should come down early and, as the historian in the family, tell Miss Shore all the family history she needs to know. Certainly I shall tell her details about Decimus, Olivia and the portraits. You see, Miss Shore, whatever Dan has been telling you is almost bound to be wrong; you simply cannot trust his version of anything which takes place." She paused and added with a kind of light insolence, "Except, I suppose, on the tennis court."

Jemima suddenly realised who the new arrival was. She had not connected the two names. Zena Meredith. Quite a well-known historical novelist (well-known in the sense that Jemima, who did not read the genre, had herself heard of Zena Meredith). Had they met before? Was it at Cambridge, a few years ago, at a feast at Casey

College where Jemima had been Rupert Durham's guest? She seemed to associate her name with Rupert in some way.

Zena Meredith must now be nearly forty, but with her tall spare elegant figure—she must be nearly as tall as her brother—had preserved a remarkable look of youth. As a matter of fact Zena Meredith had the sort of athletic slimness which would have gone well on a man; one could well have envisaged her in armour. One would for example call her striking rather than pretty; for all her fine features, Zena Meredith lacked a kind of essential femininity, a softness. Indeed, looking at her critically in that connection, Jemima judged that there was indeed a resemblance between Zena and Decimus. She had longish chestnut-brown hair untouched by grey and its stylish layered cut did echo—perhaps intentionally—the flowing Cavalier locks of her ancestor; her eyes were as dark as the poet's own. All this gave her a seventeenth-century air. Whereas her brother's blond American film star good looks were quintessentially twentieth century. The racket not the sword was his weapon.

Furthermore, Jemima could also imagine Zena—quite apart from her resemblance to Decimus—as one of those heroines of the English Civil War who fought alongside their men. Like Olivia Lackland herself perhaps, defending her house and exhorting her troops: "like a man for her courage, like a lion for her heart, but like a woman after the battle for her tender mercy towards the sufferers" in the pious words of "Heaven's True Mourning." She wasn't quite sure about Zena's "tender mercy" but the rest seemed to fit.

"I think you may know a Cambridge friend of mine, Rupert Durham," began Jemima rather diffidently. The absent-minded Dr. Durham, in his reviews, had been known to practice the art of criticism quite robustly but perhaps a historical novelist was immune . . . It turned out to be a gaffe.

"Wasn't that the man who gave your last book such a terrible review, Zeenie?" Dan shot his sister a look of open, impudent malice. From his expression, Jemima had a sense that this was a battle between the handsomer brother and the cleverer sister—reversing the traditional expectations for their respective sexes—begun in early child-hood and continued ever since.

But to Jemima's relief, Zena Meredith ignored both remarks. With a sudden animation which made her look for the first time actually rather pretty, she took Jemima's arm and turned her in another direction. Jemima found that, still looking upwards, she was now facing a door off the hall above her.

"The Long Gallery," said Zena Meredith. "I want to show it to you myself. No, Dan. I want to do it straight away. Why don't you go and return Alix Carstairs' call? She's rung twice since you've been here." In her eagerness, Zena Meredith positively hustled Jemima up the stairs, through the open door—and into a long light room with high arched windows. As its name betokened, it was long. It was also totally empty. There was not even a carpet on the floor, let alone curtains at the enormous windows. Light flooded the gallery, and through the windows, Jemima got for the first time an extraordinary view of the formal garden, realised that the fourth side of the garden was in fact the hills and hedges of Taynfordshire. "So does thy swan in parting soar . . ." This must be the "green world below" to which Decimus had referred! Recalling the lines, Jemima felt her own spirits soar with the swan.

And here too in this Long Gallery Olivia Lackland had once walked, studying her books, she thought. Books written in Latin which some at the time had thought unsuitable to her sex. Rupert Durham, sound about women in the seventeenth, if not the twentieth century, had thrown off some useful guidelines to the habits of the ladies of the day.

"And my brother wants to make this into a tennis club!" The bitterness in Zena Meredith's voice could not be missed. "The Lackland to follow the Plantaganet. Or rather, as no doubt it will be called, the Lacky to follow the Planty. With large photographs of himself in place of the family portraits, which he will probably sell. While Charlotte will run another of her cakeshops in a corner. Later on no doubt the gardens will be turned into a Cavalier Themepark."

"I don't believe it!" Jemima made the exclamation in spite of herself. Was that what Dan Lackland had meant earlier when he declared: "I shall manage—in my own way."

"Now come on, Zeenie, no hysterics please. It's far too soon to be carrying on like that, as though Cousin Tommy's grave was being robbed." Dan Lackland spoke easily from the doorway.

"It's not Cousin Tommy's grave—" began Zena.

"Cool it, Zeenie, will you?" It was a command. Jemima had a feeling that the command was connected more with her own presence than with the subject of the future Lackland Court Tennis Club.

Dan's voice echoed in the long empty room. "We've got Jemima's ghost programme to look forward to, before anything is decided. That's really going to help us get publicity. I've no intention of upsetting the Decimus Ghost with anything as sordid as the sheer economics of running this place until her programme is completed."

Jemima, still reeling from the notion that this stately melancholy beauty, so redolent of Decimus and Olivia, was to be converted someday into a tennis club along the lines of the Plantaganet, said nothing.

"And my biography of Decimus?" persisted Zena. "For which I need the library. The library intact. My first biography, as you know, for which as it happens I have a contract. You promised me. You gave me your word."

As Jemima made a mental note to question Zena at some later date about this, her "first biography," Dan strode rapidly into the room. He stood for a moment without speaking, gazing at his sister. She returned his look levelly, almost insolently. Then both were distracted by the voice of Haygarth from the door.

"I beg your pardon, m'lord, but Miss Carstairs has telephoned again from the Plantaganet Club and asked you to telephone her back as soon as possible. On her private number. And Miss Zena, Mr. Marcus Meredith will be in the office until one o'clock when he goes to the House of Commons. But he hopes to meet you in the Central Lobby at eight o'clock this evening."

"But Marcus *knows* I'm not going back to London," exclaimed Zena. "There's so much to do here." Dismissing the subject, she turned to her brother. "Go on Dan, poor Alix Carstairs is still waiting for your call." All the same, as Dan turned and went down the stairs, Zena Meredith followed him. It was as though she was irresistibly drawn either to his presence or their shared struggle, Jemima was not quite sure which. That left Jemima still in the Long Gallery, and somewhat to her surprise, still in the presence of the butler.

Haygarth stared at her, and then in his formal voice, which made him sound more like a butler in a stage play of the thirties than the kind of Italian manservants Jemima had previously encountered in the homes of the rich, he proceeded to address her: "I wish to communicate to you something concerning the Decimus Ghost, understanding your interest in the same, madam."

Jemima smiled warmly. "I hear you know *all* the family history."

"I did believe so, madam." Haygarth was increasingly lugubrious. "I certainly did believe so. But now I have formed a very different impression about recent events at Lackland Court. I believe there to be danger here and in particular the death of his late Lordship has convinced me—" Haygarth stopped. "The ghost is still walking," he added in a very low hurried voice.

Jemima realised they were no longer alone. Zena Meredith had returned. She scarcely looked at the butler, and therefore it was impossible to tell whether she had overheard his last incomplete remark. Jemima, her curiosity aroused, decided that where the butler was concerned, discretion was probably essential if she was to receive confidential information. So she contented herself with saying rather vaguely: "Thank you so much, Mr. Haygarth, for filling me in on those historical details. I hope we may talk again in the course of researching the programme."

The butler said nothing but merely bowed his head gravely. Nor for the rest of the day, in the course of which he performed a number of services for Jemima, such as serving her food, pouring her drink, and finally helping her back into Dan Lackland's car (he was dashing up to

London and back "for a business meeting"), did he make any allusion to their brief snatched conversation.

Dan did make an allusion to it however.

"Zena told me that old Haygarth did get going on all the family stuff. As I warned you, he can be a fearful old bore, can't he?"

"Oh he didn't bore me for long, just a few dates, and some information about the garden."

The mention of the garden temporarily distracted Dan. "As you can see, there we have real problems," he said gloomily. "Beautiful, isn't it? Cousin Beatrice was a terrific gardener—terrific with the aid of five other gardeners and a boy. Now what do we do? Gawain would love to lay his hands on it, but we can't have that—look what he did to Taynford Grange—and the real gardener is of course Zena, but she wants to restore it to the original seventeenth-century design, which would cost a fortune—" Dan heaved an exasperated sigh. "But you had a good view of it from the Long Gallery. Next time I'll take you up on the battlements, if you've got a head for heights. There's a little spiral staircase just off the Long Gallery; a later addition—one of the few—since the days of Decimus, but convenient."

"Convenient for what?" Jemima was still brooding over Dan Lackland's evident, indeed marked, disinclination to let her interview Haygarth. Jemima Shore was certainly not to be circumvented quite so easily. She had every intention of having a private talk with the butler on her next visit to Lackland Court. Preferably with the agreement of the present Lord Lackland but definitely not in his presence. She felt that she owed it to the shade of the poet, or as Handsome Dan himself would have put it, the Decimus Ghost.

4

Cavalier Masquerade

He was descending the staircase quite slowly; in the dim light the pointed white lace of his broad collar contrasting with the blackness of the armour, and the length of his figure exaggerated by the long boots he wore; there was a cloak on one shoulder and he held his plumed hat in his left hand . . . For a moment the whole image had the quality of a dream for Jemima—one of those recurring dreams she had been having lately about Decimus which both plagued and excited her. One of them had been startlingly erotic: and she had half-awoken in the darkness to find Cass's urgent body seeking hers. In that drowsy instant, she remembered to her shame, she had experienced a strange yearning disappointment that it was familiar Cass, not the unknown poet, before giving herself to him.

But this was not a dream. Nor was a ghost walking: in spite of the fact that the figure of Decimus—as it seemed—might well have been supposed by a more fanciful person than Jemima to have emerged out of the Van Dyck portrait at the head of the stairs. Jemima however did not suppose that, as she stood at the bottom of the stairs at Lackland Court, on her second visit in ten days.

Once she had restored herself to a sense of proper reality, she was busy wondering more practically: who on earth has bothered to dress up for my benefit? It could hardly be Lord Lackland, the obvious candidate in a sense, standing at her elbow as he had done on the occasion of her first visit, but just a little closer, even perhaps just a little too close for the kind of relationship Jemima hoped they were having: that is, strictly professional. On the other hand, she had to admit that the proximity was not quite so unwelcome as it might have been, for example, ten days ago. You had to grant that the man had charm (well, yes, damn it, he was famous for it—nor had the crowd nicknamed him Handsome Dan for nothing) even if it was a charm based mainly on excellent attentive manners and a seductive voice— something to which Jemima was always rather partial. More earthily, maybe it was merely that taste for Eau Sauvage which he shared with Cass . . .

Her thoughts returned to the seventeenth-century masquerader before her. Not Dan Lackland, then, but who? It was Dan himself who gave her the answer in a voice which remained pleasantly low but contained at the same time an audible undercurrent of irritation.

"Zeenie! What the hell are you trying to prove now?"

Zena Meredith had reached the bottom of the staircase and the light fell on her pale face, the dark eyes so like her ancestor's. In spite of that resemblance, in spite of Zena's height, Jemima wondered how on earth she could ever have mistaken her for a man. A trick of the light: it was noon in high summer but the staircase was still encased in its own perpetual dusk (a fact which, it occurred to her, must have helped on the legend of the ghost in the past). The portrait at the head of the stairs, which was dramatically lit by hidden spotlights—a recent innovation presumably—made the gloom of the stairs seem even greater in contrast.

Zena Meredith gave a half-smile, more a whimsical turning of the lips which made the resemblance to Decimus, in face at least, even more remarkable. In her Cavalier boots with their heels, she was able to gaze at her brother directly in the eye.

"Why so sharp, Dan?" she said. "Did you think perhaps I was the Decimus Ghost come to cla-i-m you?" Zena mockingly extended one long white hand—and her hand too had the splayed fingers of the poet.

"Don't be more ridiculous than you can help, Zeenie." Dan was treating his sister as some kind of turbulent little girl, the girl she must have been in their shared childhood. And yet, thought Jemima, this was no little girl, but a woman approaching forty, a woman moreover who had carved out an estimable career as a historical novelist—whatever you thought of the genre, she was a serious exponent of it—even if Zena had not secured the radiant newspaper-headline fame of her brother.

Zena abandoned her predatory pose and turned her attention to Jemima.

"As a matter of fact, I've had it for ages. I had it made for a fancy dress ball—Come as Your Own Ancestor—oh years ago. Don't you remember? You refused to go. Some match or other. So I went as Decimus. But I thought this would be my costume for the Cavalier Celebration," she began. "Since you wouldn't let me enact Olivia—surely Charlotte is not quite right?—and since there are a number of candidates for Lady Isabella Clare, I thought I would enact the ghost of Decimus himself. You be Decimus in Part One, I'll be the ghost in Part Two. Quite an amusing notion, isn't it?"

"No, it bloody well is not," interrupted her brother furiously. "So that's your game. Well, it's not mine. And just to remind you, this is my house, and if there's any doubt about that, the entire Cavalier Celebration, musketeers, schmusketeers and what have you, can go and stuff their pikes up their—" Handsome Dan broke off in what he made clear was deference to Jemima alone.

His sister still looked amused rather than abashed. "Oh, haven't you heard? Then let me be the first to tell you, set your mind at rest, as it were." She paused dramatically and gave a half-bow, half-flourish, that included the plumed hat and cloak on her arm.

"There's a very good chance that the Cavalier Celebration is now going to be held at Taynford Grange," said Zena Meredith. "Nothing to do with Lackland Court at all. Relax," she added. Jemima thought that was all, then suddenly Zena brushed Dan's face lightly with the broad plume in her hat. "Relax," she said again, passing the plume once more very lightly across his face.

It would be fair to say that of the two of them standing there, Dan Lackland and Jemima Shore, to whom this news came as a surprise, Jemima actually looked the most shocked. Either the soft tickle of the feather had soothed him—an unlikely thought—or the deliberate provocation of his sister had left Dan Lackland determined to show no emotion whatsoever. In any case, Jemima had no idea whether Dan felt anything like her own personal dismay.

No Cavalier Celebration, an August pageant re-enacting the various stages in the history of Taynford from the battle to the siege, or rather no Celebration at Lackland Court itself! And yet this recreation, a sort of *son et lumière* with tickets sold to the public, was scheduled to play an important part in the Lackland Court episode of the Megalith ghost series. A good deal of the episode had been positively planned round the Cavalier Celebration. Schedules had been drawn up. Furthermore Spike Thompson had been tentatively engaged as cameraman: Spike Thompson, Megalith's most famed and feared employee, famed for the imaginative brilliance of his camera-work, feared for the imaginative brilliance of his expense sheets. (Already cynical members of the Megalith staff such as Cherry and Guthrie Carlyle were laying bets as to whether Spike would, among other things, claim to have purchased his own seventeenth-century outfit for verisimilitude at the Cavalier Celebration.)

Worse than that, it sounded as if the whole Cavalier Celebration had been hijacked by Lady Manfred and would now take place at Taynford Grange. No, to be fair, Jane Manfred had not necessarily instigated the transference; it might be that Zena Meredith had organised the whole thing as part of her cradle-onwards fight with her sibling. All the same, Jemima did not underestimate the magnitude of the disaster (for her) if this news was true.

For behold, here was Taynford Grange, now with its very own ghost, details of which Jemima had by now quite forgotten, but which had been enough to fascinate Cy. More than that, Taynford Grange now had its own highly picturesque—in any terms including televisual—Cavalier Celebration. And Taynford Grange had Lady Manfred. How was she, Jemima, to hold off Cy Fredericks now from cancelling the Lackland Court episode altogether—poetic images of Decimus, manuscripts of the poems and all? Jemima desperately tried to remember where Cy was supposed to be at this precise moment, never an easy act of recollection at the best of times. Zimbabwe, Salzburg, Buenos Aires? What ill luck if he was in fact in England, now of all times when he was definitely not needed, in England and at Megalithic House!

"Taynford Grange indeed! Do you realise we were raising funds for this house from that Celebration?" Jemima, who had not realised it, suddenly understood that the famous Cavalier Celebration was actually going to support the future Lackland Court Country Club. Dan went on: "Zena, I could kill you," said without emotion however. Then he added: "We'll see what Jane herself says about that. She's coming to lunch. To talk about the Lackland Court Tennis Club. As a potential investor. She understands the need to save Lackland. Perhaps *you* didn't know *that.*" He shot a sardonic look at his sister.

The ensuing lunch was an awkward meal. Jane Manfred—as usual without Lord Manfred—was not the only unexpected addition to the party, unexpected not only by Zena but also, it transpired, by the hostess, Charlotte, although she tried to cover the fact up with a welcome which was almost embarrassingly warm. Then Marcus Meredith arrived just before lunch, that sober-looking man Jemima had last seen at the Plantaganet Club. Marcus, unlike Jane Manfred, was not expected by Dan, but was expected by Charlotte and Zena.

The fact that the sudden arrival of halcyon weather allowed a long table to be set outdoors on the terrace overlooking the stately garden probably saved the whole occasion from being even more awkward than it was. Haygarth simply went on adding chairs and additional little tables, to be buried beneath a heavy white linen cloth laboriously but efficiently. Meanwhile Dan poured out Pimms and Charlotte handed round home-made lemonade with her usual placating air.

Jemima studied the Meredith children. There were four of them altogether: two bubbly flaxen-haired little girls and a rather pugnacious small boy, also white-blond, a miniature version of his father; then there was Nell, quite a lot older, her face half-shrouded in a bush of very curly dark hair, darker altogether, quieter, presumably the daughter of Dan's first marriage. The prattle of the younger Merediths, to say nothing of the prattle of the nanny, an Irish girl called Nuala (with strong views on early-evening television which she was determined to share with Jemima), did bridge some of the awkward silences. All the same, for all the apparent prettiness of the pastoral scene, she felt that the family group was ridden by tensions unknown to her, quite apart from Zena's dispute with Dan.

Was it Jemima's imagination or was there something additionally Cinderella-like about Nell Meredith? It was hardly surprising that the children of Dan's second marriage should have this angelic fairness, given the blond looks of both their parents; but it did have the effect of making Nell the odd one out. Then she seemed much less well dressed in a conventional sense than her siblings; or perhaps it was her own choice to wear a dirty T-shirt and jeans which were clearly too big. The scarf she had tied round her curly hair also had a dingy or at least ragged look. At any rate Nell had, on close inspection, a sad sulky air, which contrasted both with the celebrated debonair charm of her father, and with the other children's ebullience. When Nuala—in full spate on the subject of *Neighbours*—appealed to her to confirm some point, Nell said absolutely nothing, but merely looked resolutely at her own plate. The small boy known as Dessie (for Decimus) blew a kind of raspberry at his stepsister before collapsing in a cloud of giggles.

"Dessie," began Nuala sternly. Jemima left her to it. Besides, behind her she could hear the butler Haygarth giving a heavily impatient sigh. It was ironic that Jemima had actually engineered this second visit to Lackland Court in the first place—although Dan Lackland had cooperated eagerly—partly to have a calmer look at the library and partly to talk privately with Haygarth. Here at lunch she was involved at one end in nursery politics—"I'll get you, you horrid little brat," she heard Nell suddenly hiss at Dessie. Nell's sullen expression was momentarily transformed into one of quite violent dislike, which had at least the effect of bringing an elfin face beneath its fuzzy curtain of hair to life. At the other end of the table there was warfare too, equally malevolent if less overtly insulting.

It was all very well turning romantically back to the past, thought Jemima; she herself was looking forward to a session in the library after lunch with Zena as her ostensible guide (Dan permitting) and Rupert Durham as her unseen companion. They would discuss the interesting contemporary variants on the Swan poem: "I fain would be a swan," for example, was surely a copyist's error for "I fain would be thy swan," since it completely changed the meaning. As for "I fain would be thy swain," that was surely too dull a rendering for Decimus, who was already Olivia's swain in every sense of the word. All the same it would be good to hear Zena's own ideas on the subject, from the family point of view as it were.

But these modern Merediths appeared to be dominated by another more immediate past than their glamorous literary ancestry: their own childhood and youth. Then there was Charlotte's engaging child-wifeliness, treating Dan the male as the ultimate court of appeal in a way which made the middle-class only child Jemima—not used to such built-in deference—uncomfortable. Did Olivia Lackland and the seventeenth-century Meredith sisters, let alone the debatable Lady Isabella Clare, treat Decimus with that kind of female submissiveness?

As for Marcus Meredith, the only other male present, if you did not count Dessie as being a mere child (or Haygarth for being a mere butler), his personality was even less forceful at Lackland Court than it had been at the Plantaganet Club when Jemima had witnessed him obediently playing tennis with his political boss. Jemima put Marcus' age as nearer to that of Dan than that of Zena. She gathered that he too had formed part of the Meredith nursery in his youth, since his father had been killed in action on D-Day. There was even some family banter—slightly more friendly family banter—about Marcus having been his cousin Dan's heir up until the birth of little Dessie, his fourth child.

"Seeing as young Dessie did me out of my position as heir presumptive he might at least stop kicking me under the table. In fact I should really be kicking him"—that sort of thing, ponderous perhaps but not particularly lethal.

So what did Marcus see in Zena? For it was clearly Zena that he had come to see. His eyes hardly ever left her, even when he was supposedly talking to someone else—Charlotte, for example, or Jane Manfred, who attempted to engage him in up-to-the-minute Westminster chit-chat. Marcus Meredith was not unlike an earnest kind of dog, thought Jemima, the sort of dog on which Decimus posed his hand, altogether lacking the glamour which she had to admit his cousin Dan possessed. Then of course there was the matter of his polio, which had given him that hunched lopsided look; although it was much less obvious now that Marcus was wearing a suit than it had been in his tennis clothes.

Was it Zena's slightly stern remoteness which appealed to him? Unmarried at nearly forty, there was something of the military female saint about her, a Joan of Arc too dedicated to history perhaps to marry into the twentieth century.

Hey, thought Jemima, is that how I sometimes strike people? She put the unwelcome idea aside. Zena certainly treated Marcus casually enough. No doubt his devotion was at once convenient and irritating to her, as was often the case with dog-like affection. And there was a moment when—having criticised his Trumper's hair lotion as "impossibly square"—she began to pick on his actual hair-cut.

"You should really go to some unisex hairdresser," Jemima heard Zena say crossly. "As if you ever would."

Only Jane Manfred sailed serenely through the whole of lunch without allowing the surface of her chic calm to be ruffled. The pretty white wool and navy suit she wore (Chanel? Yes, and an original to boot—no copies for Jane Manfred) was neither suited to the weather nor to the country. She had to be on the way to sixty—and yet the smooth beauty of her faintly olive skin made her look quite as cool as Charlotte the English rose. As for her jewellery—was that perhaps what the Duchess of Windsor had looked like at an English country house in July? You could argue that the glistening golden wheat-sheaves Jane Manfred wore dangling from her ears were a seasonal touch, but as for the rows of pearls . . .

And then there was her perfume, strong enough to knock out any kind of delicate competition, the scent of the old-fashioned roses for example, or Charlotte's equally pleasing and pervasive lily-of-the-valley (Diorissimo probably), a taste which she apparently shared with Zena since both women smelt of it—unless one had borrowed from the other. Then there was Dan's own rather heady (to Jemima) Eau Sauvage, and Marcus' distinctly un-heady hair lotion. But Lady Manfred's perfume, unknown and with a strong musk-base, overrode all these smells, pleasant or unpleasant.

Jane Manfred sensed Jemima's appraisal and, leaning forward, whispered theatrically in her direction: "Afterwards we must talk about Cy, that naughty boy . . . I'm in despair. He threatens marriage . . ." Jemima's mind, taken rapidly back to Megalithic House, whirled—marriage? Cy? Who to, for God's sake? Surely Jane Manfred herself was safely married? It must be Baby Diamondson. But wasn't she married too? —Did Cy ever notice awkward things like husbands? At this point Lady Manfred triumphantly changed the conversation.

"Darling!" she cried towards Dan. "Really I shall make no difficulties about the Cavalier Celebration. So long as you are not unkind about my own ghost, that poor much maligned Sir Bartleby Potter, M.P. If it is all to take place here instead of Taynford, then he must have a very good part in your son et lumière. A sympathetic part. So far as is possible."

Lady Manfred turned towards Jemima. "Sir Bartleby was a Puritan," she explained in her kindest voice. It was as though she was explaining to her own butler that a guest at her dinner party was—unexpectedly and with no warning in advance—a vegetarian.

Jemima, to tell the truth, had forgotten all about Lady Manfred's own ghost, that allegedly romantic figure, all long hair and soulful eyes, "looking like a violinist," which had been described to her so vividly by Cy Fredericks. The Puritan M.P. Sir Bartleby Potter did not *sound* as if he looked like a violinist, but that was obviously pure Royalist pro-Decimus prejudice on her part. Frankly, she hoped that Sir Bartleby was not now going to provide a further distraction from the subject of Decimus—thanks, presumably, to Zena's interference— since whatever the quality of his looks, he had certainly not been a poet.

It turned out, however, that what Sir Bartleby had been, if not a poet, was the Parliamentarian commander in the siege of Lackland Court, who had been killed towards the end of it (hence his ghostly status). He had also fought at the battle of Taynford three years earlier. And all that Lady Manfred was asking, most fortunately from every point of view, was for a representation as a character in the Celebration, something to which Sir Bartleby was surely fully entitled. Jemima heaved a sigh of relief.

"I gather you actually saw him at Taynford!" she exclaimed in her relief, rather overdoing her enthusiasm.

"Yes, I saw him once." Lady Manfred adopted an expression in which pride and nostalgia mingled. "Only once. Gawain and I saw him once late in the evening when we were working out the shape of the new north conservatory. It was as though he set the seal on our work. He gave us a sign of acceptance. He looked *exactly* like his portrait, which Gawain had just brought back for us from America—"

"Cy said he looked wonderfully romantic," Jemima went on. "Like a violinist." Her words died away in face of Lady Manfred's amused stare.

"Cy said that? How enchanting! You see, I do not think our beloved Cy has ever noticed the portrait and he has certainly not seen the ghost. Our ghost. No, what I said was that Sir Bartleby Potter looked just like Cy himself, an impressive public figure, do you know, except for the complexion, Sir Bartleby's complexion and for that matter his nose being very red. Cy's nose and complexion are *not* red. They are distinctly pale given his aversion to good country air. But if you imagine our dear Cy in armour, with a broad yellow sash—"

It was an agreeable picture. But the general message received by Jemima was that Lady Manfred's ghost, being "an impressive public figure" of a ghost, looking like a bottlenosed Cy Fredericks rather than a romantic soulful vision, could now be safely down-peddled so long as his earthly role was properly acknowledged.

Only Zena, irritated no doubt by Lady Manfred's defection, tried to drop a little vinegar into it all. "I've never much believed in that Potter ghost," she murmured to Jemima in her turn. "It was probably just Lord Manfred coming home unexpectedly. After all, Sir Bartleby Potter himself only got hold of Taynford a couple of years earlier. Before that it belonged to a heavily Royalist family." So much for Cy's second bold assertion of the family owning Taynford Grange since "Charlemagne" thought Jemima.

But Jane Manfred elected not to hear Zena. She helped herself to an enormous second plateful of summer pudding and double cream as she spoke, which recklessness, given her by no means sparse figure, endeared her to Jemima.

"We will discuss it tomorrow. At the Planty. After our game. Have you forgotten? We're playing a doubles at some unearthly hour tomorrow morning. Dan, you're going to do all my running for me. Before discussing my investment in the country tennis club. You, me and that woman who runs the Planty, Alix, what's her name."

"Oh yes, Charlotte," began Dan hurriedly. "It is true that I'll have to go up later tonight—"

"I wonder if on the subject of the Cavalier Celebration and the characters involved, the cool voice of television could be heard—" Jemima spoke politely but firmly; Megalith Television must not be ignored altogether in favour of plans for the new country club.

"Of course it can!" cried Dan. He beamed at her. "I've had a brilliant idea. Why don't you play tennis with us tomorrow morning? Alix is longing for you to test out the Planty. And then we can all talk about this television thing."

In all this Nell's anguished cry—"But Daddy, you promised *me*"—passed unregarded by Dan, if not unnoticed by Jemima. For the rest of her visit, however, Jemima found Dan to be in an ebullient mood which seemed to be connected to his projected escape from Lackland Court later in the day (or night in fact—"when the traffic dies down"). Even her tentative suggestion of a further quick "chat" to Haygarth about the history of the place was perfectly well received. Jemima, in the general atmosphere of *bonhomie,* seized the moment to mention it.

"Anytime after tomorrow!" responded Dan jovially. "He finally retires tomorrow morning. This lunch was his swansong. Then there'll be all the time in the world for the old boy to take you down memory lane. I fear he's suddenly turned pretty depressed about leaving so it will be a pleasure to him. One warning: *don't* let him get on to Cousin Tommy's war record."

"And the ghost?" Jemima decided to press her luck since the sharpness with which Dan had dismissed Jemima's appeal to talk to Haygarth on her last visit was noticeably absent.

"Ah, the ghost!" There was a pause. Dan drummed his fingers on the table, a habit he had, Jemima noticed, only when in the presence of his family. "Of course. That's your subject. As the tennis club is mine, I doubt if Decimus will come a-haunting the players. Ghosts outlive their usefulness like everyone else." He was interrupted by a cry from the nursery end of the table. It was Nell once more.

"Oh Daddy, can I go up on the battlements after lunch? Please, Daddy, will you take me up? You promised."

This time she did get her father's attention. Dan's face cleared; it was as though he had seen an opening for a classic passing shot on the tennis court. To accompanying cries of "Me too, Daddy" from the younger girls and a shout from Dessie, he turned to Jemima.

"The view from the battlements. I promised you that last time. I must look after—" He gave a vague indicative wave in the direction of Lady Manfred, who did not contradict him. "But Nell will take you, won't you? And she can tell you all about the ghost. She's seen it quite recently, or so she tells me. First the library with Aunt Zena, then the battlements with the Little Nell. A delightful family tour." He smiled at Jemima, that boyish grin which made it so easy to remember the Wimbledon favourite, Handsome Dan Meredith, he had once been.

"Delightful indeed!" said Zena Meredith sardonically to Jemima a little later when they were standing together in the Lackland Court library. "It would be—if I could get out of my mind that this is going to be the club room—including vast bar—for Dan's country club."

It was a remarkably beautiful room, as dark as the spare and empty Long Gallery at the top of the house was light. Leather-bound books in predominantly sombre colours, books of carefully graded sizes, not only lined the shelves on every wall but the deep embrasures which led to the six long windows. There were only two pictures in the room—every other inch of space was covered by books: two full-length portraits of a man and a woman in eighteenth-century dress, he with a long gun under his arm and some kind of sporting dog at his heels, she with high powdered white hair, long dress of celestial blue and a bust to keep her company rather than a dog.

"The Gainsboroughs!" exclaimed Jemima, remembering her conversation with Dan Lackland in the car before her first visit.

"Copies," corrected Zena drily. "Since the originals went to the Met . . . Not too many originals here altogether, I fear, among the pictures. The famous Van Dyck at the head of the stairs is almost certainly a copy, if a historic copy, a few years later, after the Restoration perhaps. Although the Decimus Ghost doesn't seem to have noticed."

A series of busts, similar to that depicted in the fake Gainsborough, stood at the tops of the book shelves. Philosophical worthies? Roman emperors? Under their sardonic gaze, the room, for all its beauty, had a feeling of sadness and neglect about it. Unlike the drawing room, which already showed signs of Charlotte Lackland's fashionably pretty Fulham Road taste (including copies of *Taffeta* cast about and

new-looking lamps), the library betrayed no signs of the new ownership. Did any of the present Meredith family ever visit it, Jemima
wondered. Except Zena, of course. Would this room really become the
club room—plus bar—in Dan Lackland's projected country club? The
ghost of Decimus, the real ghost, which was the memory of the poet
in the room where he had once written his poems and where his
manuscripts were still housed, would vanish. Copies of *Taffeta*, *Vanity
Fair* and *Vogue* would invade; the books would recede and would
perhaps be sold.

Zena was standing in one of the shafts of light in the furthest
window. Jemima could hear the cries of the gambolling younger
Meredith children on the lawn outside. Zena's pale face looked quite
haggard in the brilliance of the light. There were deep lines suddenly
visible not only round her eyes but surrounding her mouth. Then
Jemima realised that for all her light sarcasm she remained deeply
angry.

"Either you feel it or you don't," Zena was saying; she clenched her
fist on the book in her hand—"Heaven's True Mourning" in a red
eighteenth-century leather binding with the arms of the 8th Viscount
(he of the Gainsboroughs) on it in gold.

"The importance of inheritance?" Jemima, both of whose parents
had died in a car crash when she was eighteen, had never inherited
anything much in her life except her father's medals and her mother's
photograph albums of life as an army wife in India (she treasured the
latter more than the former).

"Not so much inheritance as *heritage*. The Lackland family heritage,
beginning with Decimus and of course Olivia the heiress. This is—
was—a perfect gentleman's eighteenth-century library. The Merediths
didn't read—and they didn't sell. Up till very recently." Zena paused
briefly but she did not elaborate. "A perfect combination you might
say. And he's going to dig up the ruins of the chapel to make a
conservatory-type club dining room there. Conservatories are all very
well for people like Jane Manfred." She stopped. "Those perfect

Gothic ruins we used to play in as children, scaring ourselves silly."
The bitterness was unmistakable.

Then Zena started to take out Decimus' precious manuscripts from
locked cases. The inspection seemed to calm her. No more was said
about the Lackland Country Club. And when together they looked
again at the Van Dyck at the head of the stairs, Zena was at her most
rational and historic-minded. There was no mention, frivolous or
otherwise, of ghosts stepping out of pictures.

Instead: "It's the hand which gives it away," Zena explained. "That
perfect white hand with its assertive pointing finger. Daring us to
point out that the whole hand is a fake, and thus the picture a copy,
a much-improved copy. Decimus lost all the fingers of his left hand in
a tilting accident at court as a young man, according to 'Heaven's True
Mourning.' Defending the honour of Lady Isabella in a duel, says
Aubrey, but we needn't believe *that*. He was a mere boy when it
happened. There are various references to it in letters of the time. You
never see the left hand in the contemporary pictures. This was
probably done after his death, either Olivia or his son decided to give
him back his fingers."

"I think I prefer my portrait," exclaimed Jemima. "It's more tranquil
and thus more poetic."

Jemima's second visit to Lackland Court ended, however, as it had
begun with thoughts of Decimus the Ghost not Decimus the poet.
This time it was not the unexpected sight of Zena Meredith descending the stairs in her Cavalier costume but Nell Meredith, a generation
younger, whose words recreated the ghostly presence for her. Nell's
peaked little face became quite pink as she poured out the story.

"I *did* see him, not just when I was little, now, nobody believes
me—"

"Your father does—"

"They didn't believe me then. Besides, my father wasn't here."

"Here?"

"At Lackland. When Cousin Tommy died. Just before Cousin
Tommy died. The night he fell down."

"*You* were here?"

"I was staying here. I do sometimes. I did sometimes. Lots of times. Mummy used to park me here. Actually—" Nell looked rather embarrassed, "I think it was a way of getting at Daddy. To show the world Cousin Tommy hadn't deserted her, even if Daddy had. When she had to go abroad for her shop. She runs this sort of gift shop called Goldentimes for things which are really pretty and sweet. She used to buy lots of them abroad. She even went to China once and India lots of times. So I used to come here. Cousin Tommy was sorry for me. And he loved Mummy. He loved her. Ask Mr. Haygarth.

"I *saw* the ghost," continued Nell earnestly. "I used to go wandering about sometimes at night. I've never slept, all my life, Mummy says, since I was born. And the night Cousin Tommy fell down the stairs I saw him clear as clear. So did Mr. Haygarth. Even though grown-ups aren't supposed to see the ghost. Otherwise something horrid happens. Well, it did happen, didn't it? Poor Cousin Tommy died."

From the battlements it was possible, as Dan had suggested, to overlook the whole broad sweep of Taynfordshire, all the way to the winding slate-blue ribbon which was the River Tayn; Jemima had not realised the river, between its guard of pollarded willows, ran so close to Lackland Court. The soughing of the summer wind among the strange turreted chimney pots which fringed the parapet—they were extremely high up—and the wheeling screams of the rooks above their heads, made a strange accompaniment to Nell's story, like the sound track at the start of an eerie movie.

There was a loud noise behind them. Jemima started nervously and clutched the turret behind her. There was in fact a narrow iron bar between the two turrets before them—"We're not allowed to go beyond here," Nell told her—but she was suddenly glad of the additional security. Then she realised that it was only the small door in the narrow east turret which led up to the roof—or down into the Long Gallery—which had slammed violently shut, presumably in a gust of wind. The sound sent the screaming birds above their heads higher still in an arc of protest.

5

Disaster

It was quite dark that night at Lackland Court, with no moon to illumine the gardens lying below, when the little spiral staircase to the battlements was once more found convenient. A noise awakened one of the sleeping inhabitants of Lackland Court, who by now numbered quite a few: not the new Lord Lackland perhaps, gone up to London after dinner for his "business meeting," but his wife Charlotte, his cousin Marcus, his sister Zena, his daughter Nell and his three children by his second marriage, down to the boy Dessie. Then there were the members of the staff who still slept in the house such as Nuala the nanny.

One of these sleepers awoke; one who was never a heavy sleeper at the best of times. After listening for a while, he thought there must be intruders in the house, and after all, his property—which is how he saw it—must be defended. So he rose and with surprising lightness of tread, made his way from his bedroom to the Long Gallery. The first thing he noticed was that the little door at the end of the gallery which led to the roof was open. He hesitated; an intruder or intruders? Could he tackle more than one by himself? But then he had never lacked courage, had he? No-one had ever accused him of that.

He advanced towards the spiral staircase through the darkness of the empty gallery. His footsteps sounded hollowly on the wooden floor, and preoccupied by finding his way—so little light came from the arched windows on the moonless night—he did not realise for a while that there were further footsteps behind him, footsteps which stopped—almost—when his did, like someone playing grandmother's footsteps in the dark. It was not until he had begun to ascend the winding staircase to the roof that he had some suspicion that he might not be alone. But since he had no choice, he went on. He went, bending, through the little door which led to the roof. Now he was certain he was being followed.

Courage! If only he had a weapon of some sort, any sort. He should have picked up one of those heavy ancient swords from the landing, off the wall.

As he turned, determined to do his damnedest to protect Lackland Court, he had the extraordinary impression of a man in full armour rearing up in front of him, against the background of the turrets and the parapet. It was the last thing he saw, before he hurtled downwards to a certain death.

Early the next morning, about the time that the body of the butler Haygarth was found spread-eagled incongruously among the shrub roses of the big Lackland Court border, Jemima Shore was having an acerbic argument with Cass Brinsley. It was eight o'clock; they were both in bed and furthermore they were both in bed in Jemima Shore's flat in Holland Park Mansions. (Cass' overnight stays, welcome in the dark hours, added to the tension when daylight came, Jemima found.)

The rumpled scene presented by Jemima's enormous low white bed bore a resemblance to the mess of earth and broken branch which surrounded Haygarth's sprawling body, only in the similar chaos produced by both love and death. Jemima's bed displayed a mess of hastily discarded garments, male and female, white jockey shorts entangled with black stockings in a happy parody of their owners' own entanglement. Jemima's favourite very high-heeled black satin evening shoes, the ones she sometimes thought were too much (but Cass never did) were on the other hand separated from each other on the white carpet, one marching to oblivion in the wrong direction, the other lying tipsily on its side; only one of Cass' shoes was visible.

The chaos of death was less aesthetic. But amid the wreck of an enormous Mme Isaac Pereire rose bush, deep pink petals everywhere, Haygarth's clothes also were shed around, his dark red woollen dressing gown ripped half off his body, his striped pyjamas gaping and torn. There was absolutely no doubt from the unnatural angle of his head that he was dead, and there were contusions on his face and chest as well as scratches from the roses. At least this was the conclusion of the young woman gardener who found him: actually a student whose parents lived in the village, filling in as a gardener for a holiday job.

Gingerly, Cathy Smith touched the bruised scratched face with the void staring eyes; Haygarth was cold to her touch although the morning sun was already beginning to beat down on the east-facing wall quite fiercely. Her first thought was: that rose, it'll take years to recover. Then she leant away from the corpse, supporting herself on a great wooden pyramid of white Colbert roses, and began to sob.

She sobbed first with shame at her unworthy thought about the rose, and then with further shame because she had never really liked old Haygarth when he was alive. He had several times made it clear that he disapproved of young women students acting as gardeners, "not what we had under his late Lordship." Now that he was dead, the first dead person she had ever seen, Cathy Smith cried because she could not summon up the appropriate feelings, whatever they were. Besides, who on earth did she summon in this emergency? Since the answer to this question would normally have been old Haygarth himself. The sight of young Nell Meredith—Little Nell as the staff were inclined to call her, not knowing that her father did likewise—approaching down the path, swinging an ancient wooden tennis racket, filled Cathy Smith with additional panic. At least she was alone; no sign of the younger children.

"Don't come any nearer, Nell," she shouted. Rapidly Cathy Smith pulled the red dressing gown over Haygarth's battered face before wondering whether she should really be touching either him or his clothes. And as Nell still advanced she cried more desperately: "You mustn't look. It's Mr. Haygarth. I'm afraid he's—dead." It was in this way that Nell became the first member of the Meredith family and the second person—other than his murderer, of course—to know of Haygarth's death, a fact which was to have some bearing on the subsequent course of the Cavalier Case.

At roughly the same time in Holland Park Mansions, it was, ironically enough, on the subject of Haygarth and Nell that Jemima and Cass were having their acerbic argument.

"If you rule out a real live ghost—" began Jemima.

"Rather an odd concept, that, darling—a real live ghost." Jemima realised that, argument apart, Cass Brinsley was cross. This was because she had just proposed putting on the new white track suit Cass had given her for her birthday "to dazzle Handsome Dan." And she added: "I must go. The Planty is miles away down the Fulham Palace Road and then you have to find it. That maze of streets, near the river."

"The Vanderbilt is so much closer." Cass spoke pointedly.

Jemima had to accept that Cass remained insecure about even such tiny aspects of their relationship as the fact that she had chucked a tennis single with Cass the night before—at the Vanderbilt—on (genuine) grounds of work; yet now she was finding time to play at the Plantaganet and in the sacred working morning too. Useless to explain at this juncture that this too was (genuine) work, whereas playing with Cass was . . . well, pleasure; if pleasure which contained within it a good deal of healthy competition.

Sometimes Jemima thought that all the complexities of their present relationship should be fought out on the tennis court. Rather than in bed for example. Last night—and on other nights recently—Cass seemed determined to prove to Jemima with his physical ardour that something permanent existed between them which, whatever her reservations about "settling down," whatever his brief "infidelity" with Flora Hereford (as his precipitate marriage was now tacitly accepted to be) could not be denied. But Jemima saw no reason to deny it. Why should she? It was true enough. It was just that she had never quite worked out the exact value to be placed upon a deep, and as far as she could see, permanent physical attraction existing between two people.

Jemima put these unresolvable thoughts aside and concentrated on the argument in hand about the case of the Ghost, the Girl and the Butler (as Cass had sarcastically once termed it). "My point is merely that *something* must have happened to have frightened them both. And if not a ghost—which it wasn't because we don't believe in ghosts, you and I, and we are right—if not a ghost, what?"

"Autosuggestion! A trick of the light or of the imagination. A failing old man about to retire and a neurotic teenage girl. Not very convincing witnesses in court, as it were. And by the way, darling, you do look ravishing in that white track suit and do put it on, and do ravish the eyes of the ageing tennis star—God damn him!"

"I wish I could believe you. No, not about the track suit—thank you—I mean about the failing butler and the neurotic girl. My instinct tells me—don't laugh, Cass, the past should remind you about the value of my woman's instinct, and I'm extremely proud of possessing such a thing. The time for apologising for women's instincts is definitely past. To put it another way, I'm in touch with myself. Whereas you, a man—Cass—no, Cass—listen. My instinct tells me that there's something going on here. The old Lord died; nothing wrong with that except that he was beginning to sell things from the library. At least according to Dan, who got it from Zena, the historically minded sister. So that it was convenient he popped off when he did rather than later. More than that you can't say. He was nearly eighty. And he did drink, especially late at night. Got lonely and depressed and then hit the whiskey bottle. Haygarth, in his starchy way, didn't deny that."

"No trouble with the inquest, I take it."

"None whatsoever. That's my point. *If* something was going on, it was very cleverly organised to seem utterly natural." She paused and added rather unhappily, "Here, since I don't believe in ghosts, I suppose I *have* to be talking of someone impersonating a ghost, don't

I?" The image of Zena Meredith, the pale wraith in the dark suit with its white lace collar, which had startled her on the stairs the day before, came uncomfortably into Jemima's mind.

She had not in fact mentioned that episode to Cass—and in any case Zena had hardly benefited from her ancient cousin's death, rather the reverse, in view of the hated country club now projected by her brother. All the same, Jemima decided not to mention Zena's masquerade now. It would only complicate matters. "Someone impersonating a ghost," she repeated. "Or someone making ghost noises. Or whatever else you do—outside a Hallowe'en party—to impersonate a ghost."

"The only other possible explanation, m'lord," said Cass in his most reasonable voice which he reserved for really difficult judges, "being that the events of the night in question were perfectly natural. So that there's no case to answer." He hugged Jemima again, but it was no longer a demanding hug, something kinder, more brotherly and under the present circumstances more welcome. Jemima, realising that Cass had decided to be reasonable about her tennis game (as well as about alleged psychic phenomena), decided that the moment was propitious to take her departure as fast as possible. Especially as she was already in danger of being late, which she somehow did not think would be appreciated by Cy's friend, the somewhat imperious Lady Manfred. To say nothing of Dan Lackland himself. (The only good thing about all this was that Jemima had no time to worry about her actual tennis.)

For all Jemima's expeditious driving of her smart new Mitsubishi Colt (chic navy blue with her initials on the doors) she arrived at the Plantaganet Club at five past nine. It was definitely a maddening journey from Holland Park to this part of the world. The time was recorded on the big, reproachfully big, clock above the reception desk. Jemima, seeing Alix Carstairs standing there in bright pink shorts, white Planty T-shirt, and a white snood bundling her red hair away, rushed forward muttering hasty and breathless apologies. But Alix Carstairs' expression was abstracted and her manner was friendly but absent: the exact reverse to the hostile studied politeness of their previous meeting. She even looked rather white beneath that thick powdering of brown freckles.

It was only when Jemima murmured the words "Ghastly traffic at Hammersmith" that Alix sprang briefly to life.

"Ghastly!" she echoed rather loudly and then stopped. "Oh, the traffic. Yes. Yes, ghastly. Look, don't worry, actually Dan's not around just at the moment. Whereas Lady Manfred is around. So perhaps—" Alix Carstairs waved her hand in the direction of the bar where Jemima saw Jane Manfred sitting at one of the little tables, apparently inspecting the arrangement of pink roses in its centre for signs of dropping petals.

Lady Manfred's thick hair, which on Sunday in the harsh sunlight had given the impression of a busby so vibrantly black—even improbably so—was its colour, was now neatly confined in a white bandeau pulled low on her forehead. An enormous pair of faintly tinted sunglasses covered a great deal of the rest of her face. From a distance she created, as ever, an impression of graceful composure. It was not until Jemima actually approached her that she realised that Jane Manfred too, like Alix Carstairs, was suffering from some kind of agitation.

"Darling!" Jane Manfred had seen Jemima and the moment was gone. "Now where is our naughty Dan? Ten past nine! Impossible. Are we to play a single? No, certainly not, look at your long English legs. What am I to do against legs like that? And at my age." Jane Manfred looked deprecatingly down at her legs, exquisitely brown between the dazzling expanse of white represented on the one hand by her exquisitely pressed skirt, on the other by her immaculate socks and shoes. Everything she wore had the air of being brand new: except the enormous pear-shaped pearl earrings which dangled from her ears. These were the sort of thing you saw being featured in a sale at Christie's.

It was true that Jane Manfred's legs were somewhat shorter than Jemima's own (generally agreed to be exceptionally long). They were still excellent legs, and strangely slender compared to the rest of her rather matronly figure.

"So, let us play!" Jane Manfred, however charming her tone—and it was very charming—made it sound like a command. She tossed her head. The enormous pearl earrings which contrasted so oddly with her tennis gear (could they be real, at that size?) swung in her ears. She was an Empress, Jemima decided: so would Cleopatra in ripe middle age have commanded some slave to a tennis game. "This is not like our darling Dan. Some crisis, I think. And that woman with red hair, what is she called, hardly seemed to take in what I was saying." All signs of agitation or melancholy were gone.

"Alix Carstairs." Jemima did not believe in the putting down of functionaries by the forgetting of their names, nor for that matter for the colour of their hair (was not her own distinctly reddish? Corn-coloured, as Cass sometimes described it, but red to others).

To Jemima's relief, Jane Manfred led the way through the empty "Royal Court" (so embarrassingly visible to spectators in the bar through its vast plate glass window) and through two more courts to the fourth and last in the sequence. The second court was labelled "Agincourt," and the third "Crecy" and their own "Black Prince." Both "Agincourt" and "Crecy" were occupied, the one by a girl coach and a small boy, the other by two men, who looked like Arab princes out of uniform, playing an energetic singles. The courts, draped in green plastic along the walls, were a good deal less elegant than the reception area, for all their great names—and in marked contrast in style to that future country club, mellow and gracious Lackland Court. Inwardly, Jemima shuddered at the thought of an invasion of green plastic into Decimus' world.

There was no other way, it turned out, to reach "Black Prince" other than by processing through the first three courts. As they processed, Jane Manfred continued to chat vivaciously to Jemima. The coach accepted the interruption with a smile and wave to Lady Manfred.

"Hi, Jane! Good game—" she called out cheerfully. The "Arab

princes," on the other hand, one of whom was delivering a bullet-like serve more or less at his opponent's head as Jemima and Lady Manfred passed, were both visibly and audibly disgruntled at the interruption.

There was a shout. "Would you guys mind waiting when the ball's in play?" The accent was heavily American. Jemima could not see that the bullet-like serve would ever have fallen within the service area; nevertheless she felt embarrassed.

But Jane Manfred, with a style that Jemima could not help admiring, paid no attention to either greeting, friendly or unfriendly. She simply continued to discourse—now on the subject of English history—in her low but richly carrying voice, a thrilling mezzo-soprano from one who had been trained—where? Poland? Vienna? There was something about Jane Manfred's elegance, the smoothness of her bone structure, which suggested Poland to Jemima; her feeling for luxury on the other hand was distinctly Viennese. Or was Jemima simply thinking of Cy?

"These historical names, darling, for the courts, my idea, so amusing. I love your history."

A few minutes later, the need to concentrate on scoring even a handful of points against Lady Manfred drove all reflections concerning history out of her head. Jemima had somehow imagined from Jane Manfred's appearance, her broad hips and full bosom, discernible soft shapes more discernible in her tennis dress than beneath the elegance of her Chanel suit, that she would play tennis like a stately galleon in full sail . . . it proved a singularly inappropriate analogy. In fact she played like an athletic well-trained man with a gammy leg.

That is to say she hit every shot, forehand and backhand, with remarkable, one had to say masculine, strength and a more or less unerring eye for the place Jemima (by no means a slow runner) would be unable to reach. And her serve seemed to Jemima quite as bullet-like as that of the "Arab prince," while seeking out strange corners of the service area which Jemima once again found difficult to reach. Should Jemima, however, manage to deliver or return a ball to any spot on the court more than a few feet away from her opponent—

that is to say, out of reach of the formidable swinging punishing racket—Jane Manfred made absolutely no effort to retrieve it.

She simply stood stock still and directed towards Jemima an ironic smile that had more than a hint of a reproach about it, a suggestion that someone with Jemima's "long English legs" and twenty years'—at least—advantage in age, should not indulge in such gratuitously aggressive play.

So Lady Manfred's Cleopatra-like earrings hardly moved in her ears and Jemima Shore, after twenty-five minutes of play, found herself losing 1:5. (The only game she did win was the result of her rushing desperately to net and volleying Lady Manfred's fierce drives; a technique which incurred even more gentle reproach from her opponent: "Now, that sort of shot, darling, I could never get.") All in all, as Jemima told Cass afterwards, the sudden unheralded arrival of Dan Lackland at the doorway to "Black Prince" was by no means unwelcome.

"Or so I thought at the time. That swinging pearly queen was all set to beat me, and then I caught sight of Handsome Dan just standing there. So my serve went out. And still she claimed the point . . . Good news, I thought."

"But it wasn't." Cass was busy cooking an Indonesian dinner in Jemima's kitchen; cooking ethnic, she remembered, was always a gesture of reconciliation with him. There had been a famous Thai dinner which absolutely *proved* to her that he had had a fling with Flora Hereford—ah well. That was the past. Unlike the Meredith family, she must not allow herself to be dominated by it—not the immediate past, that is. Decimus was another matter.

"Good news! No, it absolutely was not. Disastrous news in fact. As he—Handsome Dan—was the first to say."

Without preamble, Dan Lackland spoke directly to Jane Manfred.

"There's been a disaster," he said. "Haygarth's dead. The old butler at Lackland. They just reached me. It was a fall apparently. Unbelievably, he fell off the battlements. What on earth was he doing up there? And at night. I've been talking to the police. They—well, they're asking a lot of questions. Accident? They won't say. I have a ghastly feeling they're hinting at suicide. And it is true that he did suddenly become very depressed. Retirement—well, I suppose it's inevitable after so many years. All the same, to go and fling yourself off the roof! Christ!" He broke off. "Look, you can understand. I have to go back there immediately." Dan Lackland suddenly focused on Jemima, who was still standing, one tennis ball in her hand, for her second serve. "Ah, Jemima Shore. And, yes, the gutter press are there too."

"*The Press?* Already? Why?" Jemima hardly considered herself in the category of the gutter press but she was too busy taking in what Dan Lackland had just told them to make the point.

"You tell me why they're there. Charlotte's trying very hard to hold the fort but the trouble is that Nell, my daughter Nell, she seems to have found him, or at any rate seen him. And she's talking all the time about the ghost. Amusing, isn't it? Your ghost programme and now this. Little Nell is talking all the time to the gutter press about the Decimus Ghost and how the ghost killed Haygarth. Pushed him off the battlements!" But Dan Lackland neither sounded nor looked as if he found it at all amusing.

"But that *is* a disaster!" echoed Jane Manfred. She dropped her racket and running swiftly towards Dan—more swiftly than she had moved through the whole tennis game—she embraced him. "A disaster for everybody! Most of all, of course," she added quickly, "for the poor butler."

The word "disaster" hung heavily between the three of them. Most of all, a disaster for Haygarth: that was true enough. Another old man had died at Lackland Court, and died as a result of a violent fall, conceivably suicide. But a disaster also for Dan Lackland and the Lackland Country Club? It was possible. Anything was possible where the ramifications of a public disaster—in the Press sense—were concerned. Much less importantly as it seemed, the death of Haygarth might turn out to be a disaster for the Decimus Ghost programme— but of the three of them still awkwardly standing within the "Black

Prince" tennis court, Jemima Shore guessed she was the only one thinking of the programme.

What would be seen long afterwards was that with the death of Haygarth and the arrival of what Dan Lackland called the gutter press (but others might term the tabloids) the Cavalier Case had begun in earnest.

6

Mission To Frighten

The Decimus Ghost was frightened: how ironic that a ghost should feel frightened! Such a feeling was surely not in the ghosts' charter. Or was it too close to cockcrow? Then traditionally ghosts had to vanish. In fact it was only three o'clock: the clock in the gatehouse just chimed its familiar note, sonorous and cracked (although it had actually only sounded twice, being too venerable to adapt to summer time).

But it was not entirely dark. It had never been entirely black throughout the sultry summer's night. As the Decimus Ghost looked out of the windows of the Long Gallery, processing through it from the little battlement staircase, the lawns outside were dark and shadowed rather than the ultimate black of winter's night. The ghost had better move fast . . . courage . . .

The face of the sleeping girl was turned towards the window as the ghost entered her room; quite silently, since the door was partly ajar. Her bundle of curly hair, lying across the pillow, was tangled and slightly damp in the heat. She was wearing a white cotton nightie, slightly ragged like most of her clothes. There were no fastenings: the ghost could see her small breasts, with their tiny puckered nipples. Nell Meredith dreaming had a certain beguiling sensuality, a young girl painted by Balthus perhaps, or her slightly older sister. Sleep had ironed out the sadness or petulance from her pointed little face and replaced it with something more innocently open.

But the ghost was not interested in sensual experiences—as ghosts should not be. The Decimus Ghost had a mission, a proper ghost's mission. You could call it a mission to frighten. The Decimus Ghost, in short, wanted to make quite sure that there would be no repetition of Nell Meredith's inconvenient behaviour following the butler's death. Some thought had been addressed to the subject of making quite sure. Perhaps that hysterical babbling to the sympathetic young woman who turned out to be a journalist from the *Daily Exclusive* had been a natural reaction to shock. Certainly it was a maddening coincidence that Nell of all people should arrive in the chapel garden just after the girl gardener had discovered the body. The girl gardener alone—no connection to the family—would have created far less trouble. Natural reaction to shock, maybe—for all that, the ghost suspected that Nell had thoroughly enjoyed the attention following her revelations.

What was that new government policy towards young offenders called, a while back? There had been a lot of fuss about it; then the fuss had died down as fusses of this sort usually did, in favour of the next fuss. A short sharp shock—that was it. The perfect phrase, whatever the demerits of the policy. The Decimus Ghost intended to give Little Nell Meredith a short sharp shock. The ghost extended a hand. The deep lace cuff which fell back from the black glove did not rob the glove itself of its air of menace, as, casting a faint shadow in the greyish light from the window, it hovered over the face of the sleeping girl.

At that moment Nell Meredith opened both her eyes, wide. For one instant she stared up without blinking at the shape looming above her, the outline of the plumed hat just discernible against the window. Then she shut her eyes again.

Throughout this time—which seemed like eternity to the intruder but could not in fact have lasted longer than two or three seconds—the Decimus Ghost remained arrested over the girl, quite motionless, hand still outstretched. For a moment too there was not even the sound of breathing in the bedroom. Then, as the ghost drew back the gloved hand and backed silently away, there was a sound of exhalation. Nell at least was breathing again. After a while, as the ghost stood at the doorway, her breathing became soft and regular. If you had entered the room for the first time at this point, you would have confidently imagined the girl to have been fast asleep.

But the Decimus Ghost was not under any such comforting illusion. Nell was merely pretending to be asleep, that was unpleasantly clear. By faking sleep now, she was trying to establish, ostrich-fashion, that she had never been awake, that the fatal—as it might prove—clear upward glance of her wide apart brown eyes in the direction of the ghost had never taken place.

The question was: what had she seen? Or rather, what would she make of what she had seen? The information could prove rather important for the lifespan of the Decimus Ghost (if a ghost could have a lifespan, maybe timespan was a better word) or even, to put it another grimmer way, for the lifespan of Little Nell. But the ghost did not want to put it like that. In fact, would not dream of putting it like that. That sort of thought was absolutely out of the question. The whole Decimus plan was working out so well, was it not? If only that wretched man Haygarth had kept his mouth shut! Instead of intending to tell Jemima Shore not only what he had seen but what he had worked out for himself, what he had come to understand. But Haygarth had been an old man; like his late master. No point in spilling too many tears over him. One had to be realistic about these things: the death of the old was all part of the cycle—the cycle of history.

Little Nell was a very different matter. She simply had to be punished, firmly but not unkindly punished, for all those newspaper headlines. Warned might even be a better word than punished. And her mouth had to be shut for the future. In a manner of speaking: *only* in a manner of speaking. She must simply be persuaded not to tell

That is, if she knew who the ghost was—beyond being Decimus, that is.

"Who are you? I won't tell." The clear, small voice from the bed was so uncannily accurate in echoing the ghost's own thoughts, that for a moment it was the ghost—the ghost on a mission to frighten—not the girl who was startled. Then a mild kind of bitterness followed.

"I won't tell!" That was all very well, reflected the Decimus Ghost. But did someone who had given a full sensational story to the *Daily Clueless*—quickly copied and embellished by other hounds on the trail—really have a right to say: "I won't tell"?

The *Clueless*—which on this issue had shown itself not really so clueless after all and in any case respected the laws of libel if only because an alternative course in the past had proved expensive—had begun comparatively mildly. Rather unpleasant prominence was given to the fact that the butler had just been retired by the Meredith family after "years of faithful service": even if Haygarth's age might have been thought to make that inevitable, there was at least a whiff of reproach about his treatment. But Nell's "own story" as told to an *Exclusive* reporter, was first run under the headline MY PHANTOM CAVALIER. Here, far more prominence was given to Nell Meredith's alleged frequent sightings of a romantically handsome "phantom Cavalier" up and down and roundabout her stately home (and its equally stately battlements) than to the phantom's alleged threats. Although these threats were mentioned, they were carefully quoted in Nell's own words ("They say the phantom brings death especially to our family but I knew he would never harm me"); the threats were not coupled explicitly with the death of the old Lord Lackland following one fall nor with the recent death of his butler following another.

Other papers, subsequently, were less restrained. THE GHOST AND THE GIRL screamed one headline, followed by LITTLE NELL'S PHANTOM BEAU, and most lurid of all: TEENAGER SEES HEADLESS GHOST "KILLER." (For somewhere along the line in this story the ghost had lost his handsome head or at any rate tucked it under his arm.) Most ominous of all for the future, however, was the treatment of the story in the sober *Jupiter* coming up fast on the rails as the paper of record. It was the *Jupiter*, for example, who first came up with the headline THE CAVALIER CASE. And that after all was the headline which stuck.

The story that followed, although written in that quirkily authoritative style the *Jupiter* was making its own, contained in fact all the elements of a romantic Cavalier ghost appearing to a young girl, presaging death, which had so titilated readers of the *Clueless*. And there was a very fine photograph of Nell Meredith gazing upwards, her face half in the shadow of a battlement: for the *Jupiter*'s quirkily brilliant photographs were also establishing their own authoritative style. Moreover it was the *Jupiter* which introduced the true historical dimension to it all, for to the conventional photographs of Handsome Dan Meredith, tousled and desirable at the height of his tennis career, used by the tabloids, the *Jupiter* added a large reproduction of the Decimus portrait from the National Portrait Gallery with the "Cavalier Ghost" caption and beneath it: "Is this what she saw?" A short description of Decimus' career and achievements followed the work of Dr. Rupert Durham of Casey College, Cambridge.

It was, however, what came next on the page, rather than this sober assessment, which really boosted the Decimus story. This was a separate article by one D. J. Smith, described as "a leading historian of the Civil War in Taynfordshire" (of whom no-one had previously heard including the normally knowledgeable Dr. Rupert Durham). I was D. J. Smith who gave an account of the siege of Lackland including "the local tradition" that the ghost of Decimus Lackland had come to the aid of his beloved wife "Lady Olivia." So far, so good: but D. J. Smith also repeated the story—another "local tradition"—that Decimus' body had earlier been snatched from the chapel by his mistress, the notorious beauty Lady Isabella Clare, and interred secretly somewhere else.

Although this second local tradition directly contradicted the unalloyed devotion Decimus was supposed to have felt for his beloved wife, this fact did not appear to worry that hitherto-unknown local historian D. J. Smith. And it did enable the *Jupiter* to print another fine picture from the National Portrait Gallery: that of Lady Isabella Clare as St. Agnes. Gazing at her slightly foxy little face, that big pair of exophthalmic eyes above the matching pair of equally globular breasts revealed by her shepherdess' dress, a little white lamb posed suggestively in her lap, long be-ribboned crock to one side, readers of the *Jupiter* had no need to feel themselves left out of the delights of Page Three in the papers of lesser record.

It was several days before the bemused (and besieged) Meredith family at Lackland discovered that D. J. Smith was in fact none other than Dave, the enterprising ex-student brother of their girl gardener, Cathy Smith, whose self-created credentials as a local historian were now considerably enhanced.

In all this the police had remained publicly silent. They were, said a representative of the Taynfordshire Constabulary, making investigations, pursuing their enquiries and so forth. Was the Haygarth case being treated as acccidental death or suicide? No straightforward answer to that one; just more talk of pursuing enquiries, making investigations . . . The anodyne predictable official phrases did of course nothing to allay the intense interest which now surrounded the butler's death. Nor for that matter did the coroner's inquest, opened and duly adjourned, at the request of the police. Could it in fact be an accident? If so, what was the butler doing at night up on those dangerous battlements? Had he really killed himself, heartbroken at the idea of retirement? Was it even possible—delicious menacing thought—that he had been frightened to death by a phantom Cavalier?

The ghost thought momentarily that if there was a general mission to frighten, then haunting Dave Smith might be rather fun: getting into that small house in the village street lived in by the Smith parents would be comparatively easy since they had built on a pretentious conservatory, more suited to a stately home than a terraced house, at the back . . . Maybe something a little bit more positive than haunting . . . "D. J. Smith, leading local historian of the Civil War" might live to regret those vivid stories he had spun, especially about Lady Isabella Clare . . .

Then the ghost heard the sleepy cry of a child, also on the upper floor but from the other side of the wide staircase which led up from below to the floor where the various Meredith children slept. The ghost was alarmed. This was a complication. If the cry was from the boy Dessie, the cries were liable to get louder and become continuous. Someone—one hoped—would soon come and attend to the cries. And the cries were starting to get louder. It was time for the ghost to be gone, as silently as it had come. Had the mission to frighten been accomplished or accomplished in part? Only the future—Nell's future behaviour in short—would show. No time to linger now.

The ghost padded away by the route it used on these nocturnal visitations. The problem originally had been the safe storage of the Decimus costume including the boots, the boots with their rubber soles. In the days of the previous Lord Lackland, the house, lacking effective female supervision for many years, had been quite a run-down and ramshackle place with plenty of dark and dusty corners. But although the old Lord, safe in the embrace of the whisky bottle after darkness fell, would hardly have noticed if he had stumbled over a regiment of Cavaliers, Haygarth had been another matter. Loyal to his master and possessive about the house and its furnishings, little escaped his eye in that direction—except dust itself. And even the disturbance of the dust had constituted another danger: for Haygarth might not reckon dust sufficiently to instruct the daily women to remove it, but he would certainly have noticed footmarks.

The discovery of a kind of cubby hole which could be locked, behind one of the odd sixteenth-century chimney pots on the roof, had been providential. One or two brushes stored there looked as if they dated back to the same period—some antique method of chimney cleaning perhaps? No doubt they should by rights be transferred to the Victoria & Albert Museum, and maybe they would be one day, but for the time being, the antique apparently mouldering brushes served admirably to conceal the costume in its black plastic wrappings. All this, however, was in the old days, when the ghost had not been all that active, had not needed to be in fact, except for rehearsals and the ultimate successful daring coup.

Even then, though, the ghost should perhaps have identified another potential troublemaker beyond Haygarth in the shape of Nell, so inconveniently dumped at Lackland by her irresponsible mother— and what a tiresome woman *she* had become! To sort her out would also be a pleasure—but no, the thing must not *grow*. Although it was tempting, the ghost could see that, to act the ghost in all sorts of ways, a wonderful foolproof way of carrying out all sorts of vengeances . . . but the ghost had made a solemn vow at the beginning. The thing must not *grow*.

Nowadays the stowing of the costume was not such a problem since—conveniently enough—there were now a number of costumes, not all identical, but all vaguely seventeenth-century, in various parts of Lackland Court in anticipation of the forthcoming Cavalier Celebration. It must be possible one day simply to integrate the ghost's own costume in to the general store, which would solve a number of problems to do with discovery. Even the rubber soles on the ghost's boots would then pass unremarked, for example, and that other special problem to do with the costume which could make discovery awkward now, would then pass unremarked.

It was while standing at the entrance to the Long Gallery that the ghost was aware of not being alone. It was at first a feeling, an instinct—perhaps human beings did begin to develop a version of the nocturnal instinct when it was necessary. The ghost stood quite still for a moment, listening.

Beyond, the Long Gallery was replete with shadows in the cold shimmering greyish pre-dawn light. But it was silent.

The ghost suddenly realised that, to an observer in the properly dark hall below, its form must be visible against the background of the Decimus portrait at the head of the stairs. More irony! If this was a proper ghost story, the phantom Cavalier—in Nell's famous phrase— would now smoothly disappear back into the Van Dyck picture. How convenient that would be. As it was, the ghost felt in a most unghost-like quandary.

How was it best to escape? The child upstairs had mercifully stopped crying. If the ghost could manage to achieve the roof, dump the costume in its hiding place by the chimney pots, then the ghost knew how to escape after that without returning to the Long Gallery. A private escape route using the roofs, planned for an emergency but never tested. But what if the watcher lurked in the gallery itself?

Courage again. The ghost stepped softly into the Long Gallery and, hardly breathing, began to traverse the gallery by touching the wall opposite the windows, clinging close to it, like some mountaineer on a dangerous rock face. The outline of the huge Jacobean floor-to-ceiling pictures served as a strange kind of guide to the route. The ghost began to name them, so as not to lose count of the moment when a big carved oak chest also against the wall acted as an invisible but dangerous obstacle. Number one, that ugly old Alderman from the City or wherever, founder of the family fortunes but no prettier for that; number two, his equally ugly first wife; number three, his second wife, a great deal younger, a great deal prettier. Number four, Decimus' mother, more in the style of the Alderman's first wife.

In this manner, mouthing the pictorial history of the Meredith family like a litany, the ghost maintained a stealthy progress along the wall, eluding the awkwardly placed chest at the appropriate moment with success. There seemed to be no other movement in the gallery, beyond the slitherings of the ghost. Number twelve, one of Decimus' plain sisters—Decimus had had all the looks in *that* family. On to that reproving old chaplain, the Reverend Thomas, with eyes that followed you in the daylight, then time to cross the narrow far end of the gallery in the direction of the spiral staircase and safety. The ghost was beginning to breathe more easily now.

But the small door to the staircase was shut. A quick turn of the handle revealed that it was also locked. And the key was gone from its usual hiding place.

Don't panic, even though that meant returning through the gallery.

There was no way of reaching the roof now except from the fire escape at the far end of the top floor, which would be even more risky. The ghost had better make for the empty old servants' quarters via the landing outside the gallery. The death of Haygarth—who had lived in the house looking after the old Lord—had removed the only person who would have had cause to investigate those back passages.

Sooner or later all that area of the house would be transformed with the coming of the country club, architect's plans had already been drawn up, but for the time being it was the best route. The side door which lay through the ruins of the old chapel, now a garden centred round a mossy Gothic folly, was barred from inside, shut not locked. Would it be safe to dump the costume, especially that hat with its feather, which the ghost was beginning to hate, in one of the old cupboards there? Those endless dressers beloved of Haygarth! If one could be sure the costume would lie there undetected for a while, at least until it could merge with the general trappings of the Cavalier Celebration . . . Wait, yes, there was a wicker basket full of costumes somewhere, that had arrived the other day, hadn't it? Not yet investigated fully so perhaps its contents wouldn't be listed.

Besides, no one was exactly monitoring the arrangements for the Cavalier Celebration in the confusion following the wretched butler's death. If the ghost could locate that wicker number. Yes, that was the solution. Then out into the chapel garden and somehow resume normal life. Another ironic phrase that. Normal life. But it could be done. It had to be done. There was too much at stake to fail now.

Once the ghost had a plan, some measure of relaxation followed. The ghost was able to cross the landing through the far green baize door and achieve the back stairs without the kind of palpitations which had been so troubling earlier. All a matter of planning. And here was the basket; no need for a light, which could be risky; the ghost could feel it and the metal clasp undid quite easily. Now for the chapel door. Keep nerves steady. Now for the chapel gardens and away.

About twenty minutes later, the silence which prevailed in Lackland Court and its environs, in the widespread gardens with their pyramids of shrub roses and shaped yews, difficult to tell apart in the dark, was rudely shattered. There was a loud shout, a crash of something heavy falling and a male cry of "Christ, Zeenie, what the fuck are you *doing* here?" Then another loud rude shout which sounded like "shit" but in a different male voice. The voice of the woman which followed was far more composed.

"Dan," said Zena Meredith, "one might well ask: what on earth are *you* doing here? Is that horrible light a torch? Do put it out."

"Yes, darling, do put it out," said another softer woman's voice, softer and not so composed. "I mean, I'm terribly sorry Zena, we shouldn't *be* here."

Zena Meredith, whatever she had been wearing when her brother shone his torch on her on the grass of the chapel garden, entangled whether willingly or unwillingly in the arms of her cousin Marcus, was now struggling to right herself. Marcus Meredith, so far as could be seen, was in a thin black silk sweater and dark trousers, possibly the trousers of the dinner jacket he had worn at dinner. Dan Lackland was wearing only a pair of white cotton trousers and white tennis shoes. Charlotte Lackland had on some kind of sprigged cotton short nightdress which made her look as young as her step-daughter Nell. Of the four of them in the garden, Dan Lackland was the only one who seemed outspokenly angry; even if Marcus' attitude was slightly defiant beneath his politeness and Zena had a measure of defiance too beneath her composure; Charlotte Lackland on the other hand was plainly rather upset as well as nervously apologetic.

"Dessie started to cry and woke Charlotte." Dan Lackland broke the awkward silence. "Nuala's away on one of her endless weekends so Charlotte was sleeping upstairs. Then she thought she heard something going on downstairs, an intruder, as they say, so she came and found me."

"Ever since poor Haygarth's death I've been so nervous at night!" exclaimed Charlotte still rather apologetic. "With all the children in the house. I insist on sleeping upstairs even though I do have the youngest Smith girl in from the village to help me."

"Spare us your domestic arrangements, darling," interrupted Dan. His usual seductive timbre of voice was noticeably missing. "You really don't have to apologise for what was a perfectly reasonable concern. For that matter, Zeenie, what were and are you doing out here? And Marcus? In the chapel garden of all places! I don't want to sound rude, but aren't you both a bit old to go romancing out of doors? You've both got bedrooms, so far as I know." But Dan Lackland did in fact sound extremely rude, to the extent that Charlotte made another effort to smooth things over.

"Darling, this is all a silly mistake. Why don't I make some coffee? I'm trying out some super new biscuits for the shop. First I'll check that Dessie went back to sleep, Penny Smith is only fifteen, Nell's age . . ." Her voice trailed away. "And anyway why *shouldn't* Marcus and Zena have a late-night date? I think it's a jolly romantic idea. I wish we could have a romantic late-night rendezvous in the garden . . . ."

"There's been a mistake." Marcus Meredith broke in sharply. "We didn't have a rendezvous. Any kind of rendezvous, romantic or otherwise, Zena and I. We met each other by chance."

"You met each other by *chance?* My dear fellow, do please explain." Dan's tone remained sarcastic, but was perhaps just slightly less angry than it had been.

"There was someone out here," Zena explained. She addressed her brother alone as though Charlotte and Marcus did not exist. "I looked out of my window, which as you know has this view." She pointed upwards. "And I saw someone. The traditional lurking figure, if you like."

"How could you, Zena?" Charlotte objected. "Considering there's no moon or anything. Or if there is, it's gone down or whatever you call it."

"I tell you I saw *something*, something white, or a flash of white at any rate. It showed up in the dark. I decided to come down and look.

I couldn't sleep. It's too hot to sleep. Anyway, I came down, let myself out of the chapel garden door so as not to wake the whole house using the heavy front door. And then I found Marcus. But he's all in black, so it couldn't have been Marcus I saw."

"*You* gave me quite a fright, Zena." Marcus went as if to put his arm round Zena's shoulders but she shrugged him away; not roughly but unmistakably. "I was merely going for an innocent nocturnal walk. A walk not a prowl. And I too couldn't sleep. It is bloody hot, as you pointed out."

"And then? What happened then when you two innocent ramblers got together?" asked Dan.

"What happened then, dear brother, is strictly private," replied Zena in something of her old bantering tone. "Or was until you two blunderers came along."

"Perhaps Zena saw the Decimus Ghost," suggested Charlotte brightly.

"For Christ's sake, Charlotte." Dan Lackland sounded once more both rude and angry. "Let's have none of that nonsense. Haven't we had enough trouble from the Press, thanks to Little Nell? Quite enough trouble, and now the whole family wandering about bumping into each other in the dark. What's more you've got Penny *Smith* upstairs, sister of the unbeloved Dave. Let's not have any silly talk about ghosts."

Dan Lackland turned on his heel and walked back in the direction of the house, leaving the three of them, his sister, cousin and wife, to watch him as he went.

"I did see something," said Zena Meredith, once her brother was out of earshot. "And it wasn't a ghost." Then she followed her brother in the direction of the house.

"Oh dear, I shouldn't have said that about the ghost," Charlotte half-whispered to Marcus. "Deep down, Dan hates any talk about the Decimus Ghost. Even before the Press got going on it—and he's right. As for that ghost programme, I just wish he'd never agreed. But he thought it would help the club publicity. He's so keen on that club—well, Marcus, we do need it, if we're to hang on to the house."

"And you must hang on to the house," said Marcus. "For the sake of the family."

Charlotte rattled on. "I must do something about Penny Smith. We can't have any more stories. Because if it's *true*, seeing the ghost means someone is going to die. Whoever sees it dies—unless it's a child. But of course it's *not* true," she added hastily, "is it?"

"I very much hope not," replied Marcus Meredith in his suavest tone; he might have been politely correcting his Minister in his private office. "Because according to one theory, seeing the Decimus Ghost actually means that the Lord Lackland of the day is going to die. It depends which story you believe. And we can't have that, can we? When Dan has only just succeeded that drunken old reprobate Cousin Tommy—to one's immense relief."

Charlotte gave a little cry. At which the arm which Zena had recently rejected was put comfortingly round her shoulders. "Now, Charlotte, don't be silly," said Marcus, sounding now quite tender, "I was only joking. I don't believe in ghosts. And nor do you. Come on, let's follow them inside."

7

Body-Snatching

"There's something very odd going on at Lackland Court," said Zena Meredith abruptly to Jemima Shore. "To do with poor old Haygarth plunging to his death. The police are officially inclining towards suicide, I hear. At least according to my brother. Because he was retiring the next day, losing his lifetime's work as it were. Dan of course is just hoping that doesn't become public at the inquest: it looks so bad for the family image as he rather crudely puts it."

She went on: "But Haygarth's supposed to have talked about his heartbreak to that wretched Smith boy. Not that you can believe what Dave Smith says in or out of print. And 'heartbreak' doesn't sound much like old Haygarth to me. Even if he had been latterly a bit down—which is true—Haygarth certainly never wanted to stay on after Cousin Tommy died; he was perfectly well provided for in his will, didn't want to work for the new regime, let alone the *club*. So where's the heartbreak, I ask you. D. J. Smith, local historian indeed!" Zena snorted. "But I mustn't get going on *that* subject. On the other hand, if it wasn't suicide, what was he doing up there? He must have gone up on purpose. No wits-a-wandering about old Haygarth. Sleep-walking? That's ridiculous. As for Nell and her ghost frightening him to death. That's equally ridiculous? Isn't it?"

"I do see what you mean," replied Jemima carefully and non-committally.

"Supposing it was neither accidental nor suicide?" went on Zena. "Have you thought of that? There is a third possibility." She hesitated as though searching for a euphemism. Then: "Why beat around the bush? Murder. That is the third possibility. Murder is the third possibility," she repeated. "I can't believe the police have ruled it out altogether, whatever Dan says. What do you think?"

"I did rather wonder . . . ," replied Jemima honestly. "Two deaths." She stopped.

Of all the places to be discussing a violent death and possible murder, thought Jemima, Taynford Cathedral must rank as one of the weirdest. Unlikely you took account of the historical novels of Harrison Ainsworth (her childhood passion) in which most dramatic scenes took place in some such Gothic surroundings. Zena and Jemima were actually walking between two ranks of tombs; high banks of carved stone, effigies of crusaders, dogs and ladies, crowned heads and mitred ones.

Near the entrance, the cathedral contained quite a number of visitors gazing with awe at the vast Norman pillars of the nave. To Jemima on entry these mighty grey cylinders of themselves had a positively post-Industrial look; contradicted by the elaborately fretted, painted and gilded fourteenth-century roof above (which other visitors were inspecting with dangerously tilted heads). A discreet but encouraging buzz from the Cloisters hinted at the existence of a cathedral shop; Jemima suspected that the safer pleasure of buying postcards of the nave and roof was being enjoyed by an even greater number of tourists.

But here in the apse it was quite cool as well as silent. The July sunlight, which made the stained glass of the huge heraldic east window almost too vivid for modern taste, did not penetrate here. In this opposite end of the cathedral they were in fact quite alone. The footsteps of the two women echoed on the flags as they walked between the tombs, or rather perambulated slowly. At first Jemima attempted, out of reverence or superstition, to avoid stepping on those stones which marked some kind of further burial beneath them. But after a while, familiarity dulled her reverence—or her superstition—and she was in fact treading quite blithely on the serried stones beneath which lay further embattled gentry, their wives and children.

Recently the shadow of the Cavalier Case had begun to hang very heavily over the Decimus Ghost programme—haunting it, you might even more appropriately say. Cy Fredericks had not exactly banned a programme being made at Lackland Court, still less had he insisted that the same programme be made at Taynford Grange; such straight-forward decisions, leaving everyone precisely informed, were not the stuff of which her infinitely variable employer was made. No, Cy had merely taken refuge in travels of such a frenetic sort that even Miss Lewis—dare one breathe it—had found herself madly putting through a call to him in New York when he was actually sitting next door in his office. The sound of Cy's voice, and its familiar cry: "Miss Lewis, Miss Lewis, where are you?" while she was in mid-call, had so unnerved her that Miss Lewis had actually begun to reply: "Here in New York with you, Mr. Fredericks," until saner counsels prevailed.

Jemima Shore, walking in on this communicational farce, had only made things worse by observing innocently, "Why not send him a fax?"

"He's right next door, Jemima," observed Miss Lewis, rapidly recovering her famous cool.

"But I thought—never mind. Still, it's an idea. I say, Audrey, if you installed a separate fax machine in his office, *on* his desk, then you would fax him from here, lo and behold the jolly bits of white paper would come popping out, they'd arouse his curiosity, he'd read them and then at last we'd get our answer about the Decimus programme."

"How?" enquired Miss Lewis sweetly.

"*How?* You just order another fax machine . . ."

"*How* would we get our answer? Are you suggesting that Mr. Fredericks would be able as well as willing to make use of a fax machine personally?"

Silence fell as the long history of that great conflict on a global scale, Cy Fredericks versus technology, any technology, passed through Jemima's mind. It was broken by a further anguished cry from Cy himself: "Miss Lewis, Miss Lewis, I'm looking at my diary. How can I lunch with Lady Manfred at Le Cirque if I'm in London? Surely I'm in London?" Since Le Cirque was in New York, yes, Miss Lewis was definitely rattled.

Thanks to Cy's cunning elusiveness, it was extremely doubtful that Megalith would actually get to film the Cavalier Celebration, destined to take place in about a month's time, even though Lackland Court would definitely have the honour of holding the Celebration. That decision, however, arose from the fact that Lady Manfred herself was no longer advancing the claims of Taynford Grange. Moreover Cy—when Jemima did get to see him—was giving vent to some ominous remarks about "poor Jane Manfred's" absolute horror of unpleasant publicity: "as Jane said only the other day: it's not the sort of thing that you expect to happen to a friend's butler."

"Perhaps that was a joke," suggested Jemima politely. Cy shot her the suspicious look that such suggestions were apt to elicit. It was, however, when he revealed that "poor Jane" had recently been appointed Chairman of the prestigious Euro-Opera 92 Appeal—"with the little Princess as Patron—so wonderful in view of what happened at Covent Garden,"* that Jemima had an inkling of why Jane Manfred was now fighting shy of the ghost series. Which meant that the series itself was very likely doomed.

At this point Jemima took a firm decision that her own newfound interest in Decimus—the poet who was the subject of the portrait, not the ghost—would not similarly wane. She would attend the Cavalier Celebration in her own right—why not? Also, she had to admit it, her curiosity was aroused about the whole situation at Lackland Court, that natural inquisitiveness which was really her dominant characteristic . . . It was under these circumstances that she had accepted

*For these events, see *Your Royal Hostage*.

Zena Meredith's slightly bizarre invitation for a tryst in Taynford Cathedral.

It was true that Jemima had yet to inspect the tablet commemorating Decimus—*sed animam non raptare posse*—"and yet his soul they could not take"—which she knew had been moved to Taynford Cathedral after the chapel was burnt and before it was allowed to become an eighteenth-century Gothic folly. Had the programme gone ahead, they might have made some play with the tablet and its allusion to the empty coffin in terms of the Decimus Ghost. That would have depended on the line the programme took on the whole subject of the alleged body-snatching, and for that matter the line taken about Lady Isabella Clare. Since it was to the wife, Olivia Lackland, that the Decimus Ghost had appeared, the whole question of the pneumatically beautiful Lady Isabella might well have been left in abeyance. *Amor et Honor*: the family motto. Where love was concerned, Jemima would probably have kept Decimus' honour as a loving—and faithful—husband publicly intact.

It all seemed rather an abstract issue now. The two women looked at the tablet together: it was set quite insignificantly in a wall at the beginning of the apse. Far more striking was the tablet directly below it, a very recent memorial to a local fox-hunting grandee which included a brightly coloured enamel portrait of the said grandee on horseback in full hunting rig, plus some active-looking hounds. That other essential ingredient of the hunt, the fox, had not however made cathedral status: presumably foxes were considered to be pagans.

It occurred to Jemima that she had never asked Zena—descendant, and future biographer of Decimus—what her own theory was concerning the snatching (or not) of Decimus' corpse. The sight of the tablet—after all it actually *stated* that the body had been removed, albeit in Latin—aroused her curiosity again. Jemima did know the views of Dr. Rupert Durham on the subject just as she did know the views of D. J. Smith, local historian, along with all the other readers of the *Jupiter*. Rupert Durham had once again dismissed the idea of Lady Isabella's participation in the body-snatching as "sensationalist rubbish" just as he had scorned Aubrey's story; it all went along with such other matters generally subject to scorn as "the ridiculous Lely red herring."

"But then what did happen to Decimus' body?" Jemima had asked, reasonably enough.

"I have no doubt that it was buried perfectly decently in a coffin like any other body in those days," Rupert had snorted angrily.

"And the tablet which Olivia erected? And 'Heaven's True Mourning'?"

"You do realise that the tablet is of a much later date?" enquired Rupert in a much kindlier tone; he could be the mildest and sweetest of men once he had scored his point. "Probably the whole story was concocted by that Restoration rogue Antony Decimus, the 2nd Lord Lackland. Used it as a good excuse for *not* rebuilding the chapel post 1660. You might say that he wasn't exactly into chapels. As for 'Heaven's True Mourning,' it's amusing enough in its detail, I grant you that, which is why I put you onto it for the purposes of your programme, but it can't be taken as holy writ. Did I tell you my own television programme is doing rather well, by the way? Rather gratifying. I believe I'm a hit. Or is it a cult?"

"Both perhaps. The two things are not mutually exclusive." Jemima had heard of the success of the programme. Somehow, she had not got around to watching it.

Rupert returned to the subject of "Heaven's True Mourning." "We've only got a later printed copy—the original manuscript, which would have been interesting, has conveniently vanished. In any case 'Heaven's True Mourning' merely says the body was taken away, no mention at all of Lady Isabella. The real reason Antony Decimus, the ungrateful son, spent no money on restoring the chapel was in order to spend more money on cards and all the rest of it. Nothing to do with his father's body being there or not there. The debts they ran up! Even with inflation . . ." Rupert Durham's eyes gleamed behind his spectacles.

Now Jemima asked Zena the same question. "Who do you think did take the body? If indeed it was taken. The infamous Lady I.C. for example?"

But Zena, dismissing Lady Isabella's claims to have done any such thing, was if possible even more scornful about her than Dr. Rupert Durham. "That sort of gesture wasn't at all her style. She was a courtesan, not to give her a ruder name, not a great romantic. She would never have had the guts to carry out something like that the night after a major battle in the neighbourhood. On the other hand, unlike some self-satisfied authorities . . ."—no names were mentioned but an obvious one came to mind— "I do take 'Heaven's True Mourning' very seriously. If only we could find the original manuscript! Everyone has always assumed that the chaplain wrote it. A Meredith cousin incidentally, the Reverend Thomas Meredith, you can see him somewhere in the Long Gallery, white bands, solemn po-faced expression. Looks totally without humour, and no doubt was. And yet I've never been totally convinced. His sermons, such as have survived, mercifully few, are quite deadly. Yet 'Heaven's True Mourning' is written with such verve! I would have been proud of writing that myself." Zena laughed.

She went on: "Anyway, the manuscript always used to be in the Lackland Library. I have a theory Cousin Tommy must have sold it privately, but more of that later. As to the whereabouts of Decimus' body, that's yet another mystery."

Their walk among the monuments continued in silence, with Zena seemingly intending to perambulate the entire apse. So Jemima was taken by surprise when she stopped suddenly again in front of a large marble monument with two kneeling figures, one male, one female, facing each other in prayer, and a multitude of tiny kneeling figures below.

"This is what I really wanted you to see." Zena put her hand out towards the plaque on the nearby pillar. "At least I did want you to see it—before everything happened. So much more interesting than the tablet. The Meredith Monument." Jemima bent down and looked more closely at the tiny figures. "How many of them? *Fifteen.* And the

Jacobean dress—good heavens, am I right?—it's Decimus and his brothers and sisters. Those are his parents above."

"Exactly. Well done. Ten enormous boys, with Decimus—the sole survivor—biggest of all, followed by five tiny little girls. Three of the girls—Decimus' sisters—survived, married and bore dozens of children in their turn but their figures remain tiny. As a matter of fact, Jemima, I bet you don't even know their names." Zena did not pause for comment. "And this was erected by Decimus' mother, don't forget, that black-clad lady above, she erected it to her husband in her own lifetime."

"At least the status of the female has changed for the better since the early seventeenth century!" remarked Jemima with some spirit. "It may not be perfect but it has changed."

"Has it, Jemima?" Zena gave her that same teasing smile which she had bent on her brother, masquerading in her Decimus costume. "Are you saying that if my sweet little sister-in-law, Charlotte Lackland, had to erect a monument to Dan and her children in her own lifetime—which God forbid—that, left to her true inclinations, she wouldn't do exactly the same? Dessie, the boy, the *heir*, would be twice the size of his two older sisters."

Since Jemima could hardly contradict that statement, which sounded to her all too likely to be true, she had an impulse to ask: "And Little Nell, Charlotte's step-daughter Nell, what size would she be on this modern Meredith monument?" Nell's behaviour, in effect blowing the gaff on her family's affairs, was not the least intriguing aspect of what she now mentally, in common with the rest of the world, termed the Cavalier Case.

Jemima curbed the impulse. This was not an appropriate moment to question Nell's aunt about Nell's behaviour. And she had to admit to herself—if not to Zena—that she didn't actually know the names of Decimus' sisters. Louisa and Emily? No, dammit, those were Dan Lackland's daughters by Charlotte. Well, she wasn't going to feel guilty about this particular piece of ignorance. She wasn't a historian—just an amateur lover of Decimus' poetry. And she did appreciate his splendid wife Olivia Lackland: very much so. If her programme ever got made, which seemed more and more doubtful, the world would know about her appreciation of Olivia.

Now Jemima repeated to Zena, but with rather less spirit: "Of course the female status has changed. Look at you for example."

"Don't you mean, look at *you*? Jemima Shore Investigator who won the NIFTA Award for documentaries three times running and also happens to look—I quote yesterday's *Jupiter* review I believe—'good enough to eat.'" But Jemima had already had one screaming row on the telephone with the *Jupiter*'s television critic about his words (such rows were a rare occurrence with her): "Don't bleat to me about compliments," she had shouted—the critic happened to be an old beau from Cambridge: "Even a vulgar sexist like you should have known better than to say that when the programme was actually about starvation in Africa." She had thus no intention of returning to the subject.

"No, look at you, Zena," she replied in her most patient interviewer's voice. "Your books: you've written six of them, I understand, or is it seven? And didn't *you* win some prize recently for *The Young Pilgrim?*" Jemima had, to be honest, derived this information from the blurb of one of Zena's books at Lackland Court. "And now you're going to write Decimus' biography. A new stage. What did Decimus' sisters ever do except have children? To me," said Jemima firmly, "your career is every bit as interesting as your brother's. And without any of his advantages." Jemima was also aware from the same blurb that Zena had had very little proper academic education and had certainly not gone to university; Dan on the other hand, in the intervals between playing tennis, had been at Oxford.

Zena looked at her without answering and for a moment Jemima glimpsed some other more complicated feeling following the mention of her brother's name—be it love, envy, hatred or something of all of these. Then she said in a more relaxed voice: "Originally I wanted you to see the Meredith Monument to explain to you what history means to me. We might have talked about it on the programme perhaps. I gather the programme is unlikely to go ahead." Jemima nodded. "I used to come here by myself as a little girl. We lived the other side of Taynford when Cousin Tommy was alive. I used to bicycle over pretending I was going to see the Bishop's ghastly twin daughters. Instead, I used to come here and gaze at it and make up stories about the fifteen children. That was even before I knew about Decimus' poetry. In fact I made up stories about all the people I found buried in the cathedral and in the stained glass windows."

Zena waved a hand in the direction of the other tombs, the big west window of the Lady Chapel, like the east window, rich in emblazoned figures, was just visible from where they stood.

"I found it almost too exciting at times," she went on, "the thought of all those lives—and deaths. Which I was going to recreate. And I did recreate them in a way. Do you know, a lot of my characters are named from people in these tombs? So you see, I wanted you to understand what history can mean, if it means anything at all. It means everything to me. And oddly enough it means quite a lot to my cousin Marcus and even, in an odd way, Charlotte, because it will one day be her son's. But it means nothing to him, Dan," Zena concluded quite violently. "Not a heritage at all. Just an inheritance—to be turned into a tennis court as fast as possible."

"And now? Because you didn't put me off from this meeting. You said that there was something else to discuss."

"There is, Jemima. Now, I want you to investigate Haygarth's death. And Cousin Tommy's death too, if necessary. I've got this theory that he was selling off the manuscripts and books from the Lackland Library, which may or may not be relevant. I have to say that history didn't mean much to him either—unless you could see it in the bottom of a whisky glass. Except his own history of course: his wartime history. All very tedious, and not my idea of real history at all.

"We never got on," she continued. "You've gathered that. He didn't like independent women. At times, I would have been glad to see him dead myself before he had sold up everything. That is until I knew

about the club. Out of the frying pan into the fire! Dan just broke it
to me after Cousin Tommy's funeral. And I burst out crying. Not for
Cousin Tommy, you understand me, but for the house."

Zena visibly controlled herself. "But above all, I want you to
investigate Haygarth's death and tell me what you find: I know you've
done this sometimes for people in the past. Another mystery you
might solve." She said very solemnly: "There's something odd going
on at Lackland, which I don't understand. I want you to lay the ghost
of Decimus."

"Whatever I find?"

"Whatever you find."

8

The Departed Servant

Just as Zena finished speaking to Jemima, the sound of singing, a sweet perfect unison of voices, broke out from somewhere just above their heads in Taynford Cathedral. The effect was startling, especially as the song was immediately recognisable: it was the *Nunc Dimittis*. Why were these quintessential words of the eventide—life's eventide—soaring out over the cathedral sanctuary, and yet it was barely eleven o'clock?

"Lord, now lettest thou thy servant depart in peace . . ." There was something slightly creepy about hearing the beautiful phrase in this particular setting, since it suddenly seemed to have a sinister relevance to the death of Haygarth, the faithful—and departed—servant. A servant, what was more, who had evidently not been allowed to depart in peace . . . After a moment, Jemima realised that the invisible choir high up above them—she could just glimpse the corner of the huge cathedral organ—was merely rehearsing for evensong. But her discomfort remained.

By now, a body of the visitors were percolating through from the nave to the apse, via the sanctuary and the modern choir stalls, each one commemorating some Taynford worthy of recent vintage. (There were not many series to be made up out of them for an imaginative little girl; the 1920's War Memorial Window in the side chapel on the other hand might provide quite a lot of material since it contained young soldiers with angels' wings sprouting out of their First World War uniforms. But then Zena found war history "tedious.") One or two visitors had even stopped to give the Meredith Monument a cursory glance and strolled on.

But the footsteps which were now approaching sounded already more purposeful than those of the casual tourist. The next moment, the stocky bowed figure of Zena's cousin, Marcus Meredith, appeared, as though by appointment—which after her first surprise, Jemima reflected was no doubt the case. Then there was another surprise in the fact that he was accompanied by a further cousin in the shape of Zena's niece, Nell Meredith.

"I'm sorry if I'm early, Zeenie, I know I am, extremely early, and yes, I have brought her too." Marcus indicated Nell, standing beside him with her shoulders sloping in her characteristic attitude of sulky hopelessness. "She's desperate to talk to someone, she says, other than the police."

Marcus Meredith still did not look at Nell as he spoke; indeed they presented an odd contrast as a pair, the man tidily and conventionally dressed as usual, in a blazer, shirt and tie, all perfectly correct for a Conservative M.P. in a country cathedral mid-morning in the summer; the girl wearing what looked like a sarong top and a mini-skirt which also did not particularly suit her, since it revealed that for all her skinny frame, she had quite strong well-muscled legs and thighs. Nell's bushy hair on this occasion covered at least two thirds of her face.

"So I thought: why not let her talk to you, Jemima Shore?" went on Marcus. Jemima realised that the reason Marcus had not looked at Nell—nor indeed at her, beyond a first polite greeting—was that his eyes were as usual fixed on Zena.

"Yes, I'm desperate to talk to somebody," repeated Nell. Her voice was extremely light and childish, with a very slight whine to it; it might have been one of her little blond step-sisters speaking, except that Nell's accent had a twang somewhere, nothing as strong as Cockney, but not quite the upper-class accents of Dan's children by his second marriage. Jemima realised that she had in fact hardly heard Nell use her voice before—except once to hiss jealously in the direction of Dessie. Nell had the air of one repeating a lesson.

"Well, we can't all have a good talk *here*," murmured Zena crossly. "In the cathedral. Marcus, I don't understand why you brought her here. Wouldn't lunch have done? We were going to meet at The Happy Bishop."

Nell hung her head. Jemima had the impression she was sadly used to having her presence dismissed as unwelcome or at the very least to being treated impatiently. The life of a step-daughter was traditionally hard in fairy stories, generally thanks to the persecution of her step-mother; in the seventeenth century too, the early deaths of numerous women in childbirth must have produced numerous tricky relationships of that sort. Jemima remembered how the admirable Olivia Lackland had—at least according to "Heaven's True Mourning"—declined to marry again after Decimus' death "that my son might not feel the cruel weight of another man's rod, for the weight of a father's blow, be it never so heavy, is given in love which makes it light to receive."

All very admirable, even if Olivia was probably quite optimistic about the light weight of every father's blow . . . However, given that the ghost of Decimus was due to pop up at the siege of Lackland Court, perhaps it was just as well Olivia, unlike Hamlet's mother, Gertrude, had no new husband at her side. Nowadays the endless broken marriages and divorces had the same effect as childbirth mortality: step-parents for a great many children. It was not that Jemima suspected Nell had ever felt "correction" at Charlotte Lackland's hand: on the contrary, Charlotte had been most affectionate towards her at lunch that Sunday. In a funny way, it was more Dan Lackland than Charlotte who treated Nell as a step-daughter.

Jemima wished she knew about Nell's mother—what was her name? Babs? Had there been some talk of her being a secretary? Jemima wished in particular she knew more about the reasons for the break-up of Dan Lackland's first marriage; beyond the strong impression she got that the present Lord Lackland had a roving eye towards every woman he met. About the only female he treated with real respect was Jane Manfred: and that respect probably had money or at least influence somewhere at the root of it. Had poor Babs been in some way inferior—or held to be inferior? A programme on ill-treated first wives of allegedly lower social status—now that was an idea. "First among equals?" How about that for a title? On second thoughts, perhaps not.

"*Nell* wanted to see the Meredith Monument; that's why I brought *Nell* here." Marcus spoke with careful emphasis, his eyes as ever on Zena. "She's never seen it, you know. For that matter, she's never even been in the cathedral."

At this revelation, Nell hung her head with its curtain of curls lower than ever so that her face was totally invisible; it was as though she was deeply ashamed of this lack, which must be her own fault. Zena, on the other hand, had the grace to look ashamed.

"My God, Nell, how awful of me! I'd no idea. And all the times you stayed with Cousin Tommy. I suppose he didn't go in for too much cathedral-visiting, and as for Babs, I can see that—well, anyway, I'm jolly *pleased* you are here. I was just telling Jemima here how I used to make up stories about the people in this cathedral as a little girl."

"I've read all your books, Aunt Zena, well, most of them. I like *The Young Pilgrim* best, the end always makes me cry, it's just brilliant. That's why I wanted to see the cathedral, really, where he sits and prays and doesn't see her, and if he had, he wouldn't have gone on the pilgrimage, it really makes me cry."

Zena Meredith cast quite a new type of look upon her niece, one of dawning benevolence. It was a look Jemima too had reason to give upon occasion when some hitherto thoroughly unlikable person had proved, by genuine if clumsily expressed praise of a programme, to be full of unsuspected good qualities. Zena's previous apology, sincere or insincere, was forgotten. This was A Fan.

Half an hour later, Jemima found herself sitting in The Happy Bishop (which turned out to be a Chinese restaurant, not a pub as she had expected) with Marcus Meredith but without either Zena or Nell.

The aunt was engaged in taking the niece on a full historical tour of the cathedral.

"Isn't Zena wonderful?" exclaimed Marcus. "I've always thought, if only someone would just take an interest in Nell! Cousin Tommy did, oddly enough, or to a certain extent and in so far as he took in anything in his last years—beyond his all too well-known habit. It used to embarrass me so much—all that. The head of the family! And one *is* the local M.P. He once took it into his head to go to the local supermarket. There was the most ghastly scene. I had to rescue him. He was totally plastered of course. But he did, drink or no drink, take an interest in Nell. Since then, no-one."

Jemima forbore to enquire why, if Zena was being so wonderful now—and she was certainly being very sweet—she had not been wonderful or at least sweet earlier. She did not think that Marcus would take kindly to any criticism, albeit implied, of Zena. Instead she asked after Nell's mother.

"Oh, Babs! A pathetic woman these days, I have to say. Just the sort of woman one is glad *not* to have as a constituent. She'd always be in the surgery, or writing to one, you know the sort of person. All the same—one has to say it—it was all Dan's fault in the first place. If you think that getting a young girl pregnant is the man's fault. Which I *do*." Marcus nodded his head vigorously. "I'm a great believer in male responsibility, in fact in a recent speech . . ."

"Wait a minute,"—Nell was fifteen, Jemima did a calculation—"I suppose the pill did exist . . ." From exactly the opposite angle to Marcus Meredith, she suspected (and God save her anyway from politicians quoting their speeches!) Jemima refused to blame the male piecemeal for everything. That could after all be equally insulting to the female.

"Yes, but she was so madly in love with him, how could she resist him? And why not? He was like a god to her; she wasn't even on the tennis circuit, just a secretary. Mischievous, easy routine seduction." Marcus was becoming quite heated at the memory. "She believed every word he said, romantic love, Cinderella and Prince Charming, etcetera etcetera. You can't blame poor little Babs—not then. She was such a pretty little thing! So innocent, yet so attractive."

For a moment Marcus became positively dreamy. "I have to admit I fancied her madly myself. I even once had a little romantic notion that we two might have got together. We had a lot in common: both of us hopelessly in love, she with the brother, me with the sister. Thank God, that came to nothing! Nowadays it's a very different matter, as I indicated." He went on more briskly. "She's terribly bitter. It doesn't help. Dan hates being constantly attacked." Marcus smiled. "I suppose most men do. But he's so used to adulation . . . Then all that making up to Cousin Tommy—just another way of getting to Dan of course. When that didn't work, it became another way of getting *at* him."

"Why did he marry her?" asked Jemima curiously. "If he was such a cad. We're talking about the seventies. Abortions were known in those days."

"Someone intervened and intervened heavily." Marcus Meredith's smile had vanished. He stared at Jemima. They were toying with some Chinese hors d'oeuvres called "Little Cathedral Canapes" (a name which seemed to mix a number of cultures). "Can't you guess who? The only person who has any real influence with Dan—"

"Jane Manfred."

"That was long before her day. No, it was Zena. Zena talked Dan into marrying Babs—I have to say that she probably thought Babs wouldn't be a rival—Zena is a little strong-minded." Marcus smiled. "And then became so jealous about what she'd done that she never spoke to her again."

When Zena finally returned with Nell, the latter was glowing and Zena too displayed an unusual kind of exhilaration. Perhaps it was Nell's newfound confidence which led her to insist—quite determinedly—on talking to Jemima alone. She noticed that Marcus was not particularly happy with the arrangement; but the return of the sulky look to Nell's face, the old droop of the head, led Jemima to say hastily: "I always think one to one is better. In my preliminary interview I always do talk to people alone—"

"You're talking about television, I take it," Marcus interrupted. "But you're not going to be putting Nell on television, I hope, hasn't one had enough—"

"Of course not!" Jemima saw that look of dawning hope on Nell's face which occurred on most faces under twenty—and a good many over it—at the prospect of appearing on television. It was Zena who clinched the matter. With an emphatic look at Jemima—you're my investigator now, it seemed to say—she swept Marcus' objections aside.

"After lunch—what *is* this? 'Bishop's gaiters Chinese chicken,' yes, well I suppose that is roughly what it tastes like—Nell will show Jemima the cloisters. We never got that far. She'll talk to her at the same time. Secluded places, these cloisters. Remember Decimus' sonnet:

In thy dear cloister, secret from the world
So might I dwell and never pine for sun . . .

In my biography, by the way, I shall hope to show that it was the Taynford cloisters he had in mind, not just some imaginary stone arches. That pompous academic at Cambridge simply doesn't understand." Since Jemima had an awful feeling that the pompous academic in question was Dr. Rupert Durham (his public persona being so very different from his private one) she was glad when Nell burst in.

"But in *The Young Pilgrim* he takes her hand in the cloisters, thinking nobody can see them, but the old monk, the one that wants him to be a monk and serve God and all that, not love her, does see them, and he does overhear them . . ."

"Times have changed at least to that extent," observed Zena in her new kindly tone. "Eat up, Little Nell, if you can."

So for the second time that day Jemima, who had frankly not spent much time in an ecclesiastical atmosphere since her departure from her convent school, found herself back within it. The cloisters were indeed secluded, since for all their arched and fluted beauty, the cathedral shop in the far corner drew off all possible visitors. Nell pointed out the monks' work places with some pride: "Zena says they're called carrels. She knows *everything*, doesn't she?" But as they turned the corner so as to be invisible to those in the shop, her mood changed. Nell burst out:

"The Decimus Ghost! I'm frightened. I think it's going to kill me next. I know it doesn't touch children. But I'm growing up. I'll be sixteen next birthday. And that was *ancient* in those days."

"Next?" Jemima took the girl's hand—she couldn't help noticing her fingernails bore the unattractive remnants of bright red polish. Did no-one care about her get-up or her general appearance? Jemima led Nell gently to the stone seats beneath the fan vaulting which closed over their heads like the branches of trees, making an elaborate carved stone tunnel. The brilliant sunshine on the grass sward in the centre of the cloisters contrasted with the slightly dank gloom in which they were now enveloped. The girl shivered.

Nell began her story. At first it was substantially the story that she had related to the *Daily Exclusive,* if presented in a less lurid manner. But all the elements were there: the phantom Cavalier, Nell's sighting of him in the lifetime of her elderly Cousin Tommy, above all her sighting of him on the night of the death of Haygarth. But there were certain new insights for Jemima concerning Nell's mother, Babs— former secretary and now gift-shop owner. (It occurred to Jemima that both Handsome Dan's wives were shop-owners, Charlotte with her upmarket cake shop, Babs with her somewhat more downmarket gift shop; did the man drive his wives to commerce?) The picture of Babs which emerged from Nell's account was an interesting one, given that Marcus had alerted Jemima to the origins of that unfortunate first marriage. If she, Jemima, was to be involved in an investigation of Haygarth's death—and let's face it, she was already involved—then an encounter with Babs Meredith might be instructive.

Nell, she noticed, was prone to repeating: "Cousin Tommy loved

Mum. And he loved having me to stay when Mum had to do her work," to the extent that Jemima thought she definitely protested too much. How had the lonely child spent her time at Lackland Court in those days, other than chatting to Haygarth about his version of the family history? Jemima also treated with a pinch of salt Nell's other repeated remark on the subject of the Merediths:

"Cousin Tommy never liked it half so much when Charlotte came down instead of Mum, and it was worst of all when she brought the children. 'No brats,' he said to her once. I was never a brat to him," she added proudly. "And he didn't like Aunt Zena very much either. She used to come down without asking and race round the library looking for things. And give him lectures about his own history. Well, I see now they were fully interesting lectures," added Nell, with new loyalty. "But Cousin Tommy used to call her the Schoolmistress. He once called her that to her face! 'Here comes the Schoolmistress,' he said."

Nell giggled. "Aunt Zena was awfully cross. He had had a bit too much, you know."

"In front of you?"

"It was quite late. But actually I was sort of listening."

Nell returned to the subject of the phantom Cavalier and her sightings, and Jemima returned to it as well. Babs could wait.

"You've told all this to the police, I take it? About the ghost." She did not add: since you've told it all to the Press.

Nell hung her head again. "They didn't believe me, they thought I was really hysterical, the man was horrible to me."

"What man?"

"The policeman. And the woman too. The policewoman. She was horrible too. And the other one. The nurse or doctor or whatever she was. All those horrible questions. They thought I made it all up, just to be important. But I didn't. I didn't." Nell lifted her head and for a moment her eyes blazed. "I *didn't*. And that's why . . . ," more quietly, "that's why I'm not going to tell them anything ever, ever again."

"Tell me then, Nell."

"You won't laugh or call me hysterical and think I'm silly or call me a typical idiotic teenager or a child of a broken home telling lies . . ."

"None of those things, I promise."

"Okay, so I'll tell you." Nell still spoke reluctantly. Nevertheless Jemima got the impression that talking to anyone she regarded as official (and television *was* official to her) other than the ungrateful police was a relief to her. There was an air of loneliness about her, that Cinderella-look Jemima had noted originally. Nell was a Cinderella on the look-out for Fairy Godmothers to a touching degree: first of all Zena and now Jemima.

So with a flood of detail Nell now described to Jemima how—two nights ago—the Decimus Ghost had appeared to her again, but in her bedroom (which had never happened before). And how the ghost had "vanished" when her little brother began to cry, "as ghosts are supposed to do."

"But supposing it *wasn't* a ghost, supposing all the time it was a person," concluded Nell looking anxiously at Jemima, as though expecting to be mocked yet again. "A person *dressed up* as a ghost. That's what I wanted to talk to you about. And that's why I'm frightened."

In spite of her own suspicions, Jemima was momentarily taken aback. She had been expecting to have to convince an emotional teenager of the non-existence of ghosts; now she was disconcerted to find a situation which was the exact reverse.

"But why, Nell?" she asked finally. And in her gentlest interviewer's voice. "Nell, what made you think that all of a sudden? Considering what you told the police." Jemima did not add: and the Press.

"It was the smell," Nell said at last. "I know it sounds funny but the ghost had a sort of human smell. A smell I recognised. Except I *didn't* recognise it. That's the point. But ghosts don't smell like people. How can they? So it must have been a person." Jemima did not want to argue that point—who on earth could tell what ghosts smelt like since they did not exist? She decided to pursue the exact nature of the smell instead and see if she could get somewhere that way. Familiar—how familiar? Pleasant—unpleasant? Sweet-sour-rank-delightful?

"What sort of person?" she began.

Jemima could have sworn that Nell was about to speak. She even opened her mouth, a rather small rosebud of a mouth, perhaps, but not at all unattractive when she smiled; it was the perpetual sulky droop which ruined Nell's features. When something seemed to stop her. Afterwards, going over the scene in her own mind, Jemima seriously wondered whether Nell could have glimpsed Zena and Marcus advancing on the other side of the cloisters through the arches and that this presence had warned her off the final revelation. Yet even if Marcus and Zena were coming—ultimately—to join them, they could certainly never have overheard what Nell was about to say.

Whatever the truth of it, the girl had looked momentarily quite haunted as though some memory had returned to plague her. Now she merely looked anxious again, her habitual expression.

"I can't say any more. Honestly, there isn't anything else to tell, I'd tell you, Jemima, honestly, I would, but there's nothing to tell. Honestly." The little whining note had returned to her voice. "It was silly really. I just wanted to tell someone about what happened to me and now I have. But I expect it's all imagination just like the police said. I have got a very strong imagination you know, my school reports often talk about my strong imagination."

Nothing more could be got out of her.

From the cathedral itself the distant sound of singing reached them only faintly in the cloisters. It was too early for evensong. Another rehearsal of the *Nunc Dimittis*? Certainly the case of the departed servant—as that part of the Cavalier Case which concerned Haygarth's death might be termed—grew more complicated hourly. And more surely than ever Jemima knew that the servant Haygarth had not been allowed to depart in peace.

9

Sport For Spectators

The huge wash of smart women's clothes in the Plantaganet changing room alerted Jemima Shore to the fact that some kind of multiple female event was in progress. Which was not quite what she had expected.

Without any warning the weather had turned much cooler overnight. It was now what might be described as a traditional English July day, overcast with a threat of rain and a temperature that made you shiver in a summer dress. The Planty members were evidently not prepared to shiver. Rows of immaculate silk blouses and linen jackets, both heavily shoulder-padded, and pale perfectly creaseless skirts faced Jemima hanging languidly on the Plantaganet pink hangers. Innumerable designer labels were thus innocently displayed and sizes too— some of the latter were slightly surprising to Jemima's inquisitive eye. Was everyone really size 10, or the equivalent American size 8, these days? Some of the jackets looked quite large. Perhaps an elegant size 10 or 8 label came with the designer label itself.

At all events, here in the Planty changing room, gazing at the linings of Saint Laurent, Armani, Valentino, with the odd Jasper Conran and Joseph, you could certainly tell the fakes for what they were; safe on their owners' backs, you simply had to guess. In the same way Jemima noted that of the rows of pretty light high-heeled sling-back shoes beneath the suits, some were Chanel—and some were Chanel-style.

"The P.P.T.—don't you love it?" gasped a very pretty but distinctly plump dark-haired woman of about Jemima's own age. She had entered the room at a run, and now threw down her Chanel—or Chanel-style—navy and white jacket on the floor. (Jemima was not surprised to see that it was a size 10.) Seeing Jemima's air of polite incomprehension, she elaborated: "The Pink Plantaganet Tournament, no, the Pretty Pink Tournament, no, well, I guess it doesn't matter. The last one before the holidays. We're all wearing pink favours in our hair—I got Kenneth to make up something special, a kind of wreath I guess it is. How the hell do I *serve* with that on? Costa keeps telling me to *concentrate*." A ravishing concoction of pink roses was exhibited. "Anyway, that's why I'm so late. Then there's a salmon mousse, pink champagne." She removed her navy silk blouse, revealing a splendid brown bosom barely contained in a lacy bra, and donned a bright pink T-shirt which itself included enormous shoulder pads.

"Adriana, you are always late," pronounced Lady Manfred, accompanying her words however with an indulgent smile. "The roses, darling, are nothing to do with it."

Jemima, preparing to add her own Chanel shoes (three years old but *real*) to the row, turned to her in alarm: "Jane, this is a tournament? You never warned me."

"A tournament? At my age? Certainly not," replied Lady Manfred haughtily. She touched the heavy pearls which swung in her ears: they were presumably her tennis pearls, since she had worn them on the previous occasion of their play. "Tournaments are for children, like our little Adriana here." She gave Adriana, now panting as she struggled with the zip of her shorts, an even more gracious smile before turning back to Jemima: "We are playing a doubles with Dan and Alix Carstairs—Dan plays with me of course but you will find Alix a perfect partner, with your long legs you do not need a man—" Yet another smile followed in which triumph as well as geniality could be detected.

"We shall play on the Royal Court. Since all the other courts are taken up by this children's tournament."

In view of the immense regality of Jane Manfred's bearing, there was no doubt a good argument for her playing on the Royal Court, thought Jemima. For herself, on the other hand, she dreaded the idea of being divided from interested watchers in the bar merely by huge plate glass doors up to the lofty ceiling. Gloomily, Jemima predicted that the attention of the spectators would be fixed on their game: which, as it turned out, was a singularly accurate prophecy if not exactly in the sense in which she meant it.

In spite of Lady Manfred's smiles, poor Adriana was looking increasingly unhappy. "It's for charity, the P.P.T., not for children," she floundered indignantly. Jemima, deeply relieved at being let off the tournament herself, could only sympathise with her. First to have to play and then to be insulted!

"I know it is for a charity, darling," replied Lady Manfred imperturbably. "A children's charity. I myself flew the salmon down from Scotland in our private plane." It was a measure of the strength of her personality that for one mad moment, Jemima had a picture of Lady Manfred herself at the controls of the plane, pearls swinging under her aviator's helmet . . . "Let us hope you win, darling. If you are not too late that is. How pretty those roses are!" She swept out, leaving a trail of her peculiarly strong musky perfume behind her.

It was not only the devotion of its members to a cause—health in this case as well as charity—but also something about the high arched roof of the Planty, the lofty glass windows opening onto the river, that put Jemima suddenly in mind of that other more ancient site of devotion, Taynford Cathedral. Were health clubs in fact the modern equivalents of cathedrals? The Plantaganet Club in the late twentieth century replacing the Taynford Cathedral of the Middle Ages. It was a bizarre thought: but then what were health clubs about if not worship—worship of the body . . . And that was certainly a cult these days.

Jemima said as much to Jane Manfred, forgetting the proximity of

Taynford Grange to the cathedral. Jane swiftly reminded her of it. Clearly regarding Jemima's comparison of the Planty to Taynford Cathedral as somewhat distasteful, she observed:

"Ah, the beautiful cathedral! Max and I bought the Taynford Globe when it came up for sale last year. Gawain said we should do so and we did . . ."

"The *cathedral* Globe?" It was Jemima's turn to be shocked: she had a vision of the Green Knight prancing round the historic Globe in admiration before placing it reverentially in the Manfreds' library.

"Of course." Jane Manfred patted her shining black busby of hair beneath its white tennis visor, which on her had the air of a crown. "When we presented it back to the cathedral, the Dean made a most touching speech. Max had it printed. I shall send you a copy."

Seeing that Jemima was suitably humbled, Lady Manfred once again radiated geniality as she had done to Adriana.

But as they reached the bar area her geniality disappeared. It was clearly the presence of Charlotte Lackland, with a racket in her hand, which disconcerted her. Furthermore Charlotte, quite apart from being dressed for tennis, had no pink roses in her hair and thus showed no signs of being included in the P.P.T. tournament. Beside her, towering over her in his navy blue track suit (no Planty pink for Handsome Dan) her husband looked thunderous. Alix Carstairs, fully accoutred in pink, with a massive pink bunny-girl bow secured on a comb in her flowing red hair, appeared to be equally angry.

"Oh no, Charlotte, I'm not upset," she was saying with icy politeness, her words contradicted by her expression. "It really doesn't matter one bit. I can, after all, play anytime. And with Dan too." This last was said even more politely. "But one just would like a little bit of warning. First of all Dan asked me to drop out of the Pink Tournament and make up a four. Which I did and now—well, of course it doesn't matter; apart from feeling an absolute idiot in this bloody bow, I just run the Club—" Her voice rose as Alix Carstairs began to tear at the vast bow, tears starting in her eyes. Players on the tournament, passing through the bar area between matches, were beginning to regard the scene with interest, as Alix, control gone, tears by now spilling down her cheeks, dashed in the direction of her office.

"Now darling, you really should have telephoned—" began Dan to Charlotte. The thunderous expression had been smoothed away. He used a special tender tone, which Jemima, now that she had seen more of him, had an awful feeling he kept for just this kind of occasion. But Charlotte now looked as if she too was going to burst into tears.

"But darling, I did telephone," Charlotte wailed. "I thought you said we were going to play today. I'm sure it was today. Then I telephoned late last night and very early this morning on my way to the shop. And when I didn't get an answer—Dan, I'm terribly sorry, darling, if you'd said—" This was so evidently a domestic minefield, that Jemima did wonder how that Houdini Handsome Dan would break free. But it was in fact Lady Manfred, in her most charming manner, who rode to his rescue.

"Now my dears," she said. "Please indulge an old woman and allow me to have my little game of tennis. It is already—" she inspected a tiny diamond watch, "seven minutes past the hour. But, Charlotte, what good news that you are playing more now. That adorable shop used to take up so much of your time. Which reminds me, I have to give an order the moment we stop, for my dinner party tonight, my lovely Mrs. Parsons forgot. But you won't neglect the shop, will you? Where would we all be without Charlotte's Cakes? And you're such a practical, down-to-earth person, I think you would miss it."

"Actually tennis is rather my thing these days," replied Charlotte bravely. She had recovered her poise with the disappearance of Alix. "Now that the shop is going so well and I've got this dishy American student—Dan is quite mad about her—who can actually do our accounts on the computer without bursting into feminine tears every five minutes." Was this a dig at Alix? Charlotte rattled on: "So Costa took my game utterly to pieces and hopefully put it back again." She turned to Jemima. "I bet you're jolly good."

Lady Manfred now indicated that Dan should open the side door to the Royal Court for her; he also, without being asked, picked up her racket and a tennis bag looking to be worth a Plantaganet king's ransom. Lady Manfred herself, unencumbered by anything more than a tiny white handbag, hanging on her shoulder by delicate gold chains, swept through.

At the start, it could only be described as an unequal match. Charlotte's new enthusiasm for tennis—her attempt perhaps to woo back her husband from the influence of Alix?—did not really survive the impact of those powerful swinging forehands from Lady Manfred. Moreover the latter's determined immobility (which had been a marked feature of her previous match with Jemima) was no disadvantage at all, given that her partner was Handsome Dan Meredith, who simply covered the remaining seven eighths of the court. As for Dan, his speed and agility made it quite obvious why his figure remained as slim and muscular as that of the tennis idol Jemima remembered fancying as a schoolgirl. Seen from afar, Dan might have been almost the same age as the current young stars of Wimbledon; it was only after a while that Jemima realised that it was more cunning than bravura play which enabled him (and Jane Manfred) to win so easily. Much of Dan's game consisted of brilliant placing—both of himself and the ball. In this way, he was somehow always right on the spot to retrieve a ball without effort, only to dispatch it himself to the tennis equivalent of Timbuktoo—or anyway somewhere where it was strictly irretrievable by either Charlotte or Jemima. In this way both of them were probably covering about twice the ground covered by Dan himself.

"Jolly good shot, darling," panted Charlotte, as having just managed to get to a wickedly sliced ball at the front of the court, she had then been lobbed in the far corner of the trams right over her head. Jemima found herself on this occasion reduced to the role of helpless spectator: but she did wish Charlotte would swear at Dan instead of congratulating him.

Would Dan have been so deliberately teasing to Alix? Jemima doubted it. She herself would probably have done much better partnered by Alix in any case: a much bigger girl—woman—altogether, a good seven or eight inches taller than Charlotte, with a strong frame; more of a Steffi Graf to Charlotte's Chris Evert . . . although on reflection size was hardly relevant, since the latter had had her fair share of victories, as had Billie Jean in the past. Lack of inches did not necessarily mean lack of strength.

Jemima prepared herself gloomily to serve in the first game of the second set, having lost the first 6:1. (It seemed to be her fate to be heavily defeated at the Planty; really, she would have to reconsider the question of membership!) Her nifty serve in the past had had its admirers, notably Cass Brinsley, who had praised its ability to probe certain weak backhands—but what was the point of doing that when there were no weak backhands on the other side of the net? The best she could do was to send it out of Jane Manfred's reach, hoping to get the satisfaction of the "you-with-your-long-legs" look. But her nifty serve, like the rest of her game, was failing her as her confidence became whittled away by defeat.

It was somewhere in the middle of this set, with Dan and Jane having their original 4:love lead cut down to 4:3, that Jemima realised the atmosphere had changed. At first she fondly imagined it was due to the unexpected renaissance of the aforesaid nifty serve; with Jane Manfred "aced" three times in a row, if you liked to put it like that, as Jemima certainly did. Even Dan dared to call out "Bravo" the third time, while Jane Manfred, who was stationed several feet from where the ball had landed, looked predictably pained and leant for a moment, all vulnerability, on her racket.

Then Jemima discovered a surprisingly powerful backhand of her own, to be ranked with Lady Manfred's own. Jemima's backhand under normal circumstances was a chancy affair—"I'm afraid it's liable to go off like milk," she had once had to confess to a stranger partnering her in a country house game—and she was only playing in the left-hand court because Charlotte vowed that her own was even worse and Dan did not disagree. So Jemima could not imagine to what she owed this welcome, but novel, apparition. Yet here it was, in the hour of need. Had she somehow managed to blow Roland's magic horn at Roncesvalles and bring it to her rescue?

Best of all, Jemima was now, in direct contrast to the first set, managing to be everywhere the ball was, as opposed to everywhere it wasn't . . . Unlike Charlotte however. It had to be admitted that although poor Charlotte continued to chase every ball with the gallantry of a demented terrier after a much faster rabbit, her own game was not actually improving.

It was at this point that Jemima's eyes were opened. She understood suddenly what was really happening. She was not so much playing better as being made to play better—and by Dan Lackland himself. He was carefully, subtly, teasingly, but undeniably, orchestrating the whole thing. There was no further time to analyse the situation as Jemima, breathless and flushed but happy, found herself not only playing the game as never before but also enjoying it as never before. Neither Jane Manfred nor in effect Charlotte, although she continued to pursue every shot with undiminished energy, were part of what was becoming something of a private game. Other strokes were discovered in her repertoire under Dan's implicit tuition; inventive little manoeuvres of her own were executed; it was Jemima who increasingly covered for Charlotte when she missed a ball, and Jemima who dived forward at the net—a seemingly impossible shot—and under his unspoken encouragement smashed the ball triumphantly just beyond Dan's reach, so that he flung his racket in despair, half laughing, half cursing, yet at the same time obviously almost as pleased by her triumph as she was.

The score was now 5:4 to Jemima and Charlotte.

"You've taken five games off us in a row! What cheek," said Dan to Jemima as they changed sides; they were level at the far side of the net. Jane Manfred was busy touching up her makeup with a lacy handkerchief by the chairs on the other side and Charlotte, her head turned away, was sipping something from a pink plastic glass. A small knot of people in the bar area were watching the game. Jemima no longer cared about their presence. In fact she was even secretly rather pleased: since she was certainly never going to give this dazzling display again, there might as well be witnesses to it.

"You know, you could be really good," added Dan, giving Jemima an approving little pat, "with a little coaching, perhaps, preferably from me! You've got a wonderful eye."

"You mean I could have been a contender?" replied Jemima.

"As far as I am concerned, you are a contender. A serious contender." Their eyes met; for a second, the lightness of it was gone. I just hope we're still talking about tennis, thought Jemima; maybe he's never seen *On the Waterfront*.

It was in the course of the next—crucial—game, which might give the set to Charlotte and Jemima, that the final revelation came to her about what was taking place; as a result she found herself annoyed and amused in about equal proportions—with perhaps just a dash of excitement thrown in as well. As she swooped down on Jane Manfred's service and delivered a sizzling low backhand in her direction only to find that Dan himself was at the net volleying, and yet in the nick of time Jemima managed to get that back too, but Dan was there once more . . . her own willing participation, her eagerness, the fun, the invention, the sheer pleasure of it all, what did all this remind her of, frankly, but making love? And finally what was Handsome Dan Meredith doing to her now, from his strange vantage point at the other end of the net, but seducing her?

It might be a rather strange method of wooing—the image of Richard III seducing Lady Anne over her husband's bier came to her—"was ever woman in this humour woo'd?"—since she had seen the play at the Barbican the night before with Cass, with its merry opening references to Mistress Shore's "cherry lip, bonny eye and passing pleasing tongue." But who was to say it was an ineffective one? "Was ever woman in this humour won?" the crookback future king, as played by Anton Lesser, had concluded. Well, Handsome Dan had not exactly won her, had he? They were still playing the game. On the other hand, if she was to go ahead and, with Charlotte's help naturally, win the set . . .

The score was now 15:40 with Jane Manfred taking an unconscionable time to deliver what might well prove the last serve of the set; she had already insisted on adjourning to the side to mop her seemingly ivory brow with the lacy handkerchief once more, and then one of the famous pearl earrings had threatened to come loose. Charlotte, ready to receive the serve, was hopping from one toe to another, her head bent slightly forward, her lips parted open, as though willing this to be *her* mini-triumph by which she would at least send the return which would end the set in victory. (It was in fact this scheduled delay which had given Jemima the breathing space in the course of which the bizarre but not altogether unpleasing notion of a from-over-the-net seduction came to her.)

At last Jane Manfred served. In spite of the delay—or perhaps because of it—she looked as poised during her delivery as she was presiding over one of her own famous dinner parties. It was a good strong deep serve, precisely aimed at Charlotte's backhand, which, as its owner had correctly explained, was still "a bit feeble in spite of all that wonderful Costa has done." Nevertheless Charlotte flung herself at the ball, which was springing away onto the tramlines and just managed to get there. She returned a soft crossing shot to where, inevitably, Dan at the net awaited it. He killed it, and there was nothing anyone—not even the new Jemima Shore—could do about that. 30:40. Now Jane Manfred was due to serve to Jemima. Her serve to the left-hand court was not nearly so strong, although it could be testingly deep.

Jemima, waiting, caught Dan's eye at net. But he did not, as she had half expected, give her that little complicit grin. On the contrary, he appeared uncharacteristically abstracted from the game. A moment before the ball finally coursed past his ear in Jemima's direction, he had actually looked briefly over his shoulder towards the bar area. Then a great many things happened at once.

The serve was indeed quite deep, down the centre line, but not so deep as to defeat Jemima. She decided to attempt a lob high over Dan's head to the far corner of the court, a position from which she knew that Jane Manfred, on her usual form, would not even try to retrieve it. Jemima sent her lob soaring upwards and—oh joy!—judged it perfectly. Just as she had anticipated. Dan, despite his height, could do nothing and Lady Manfred, immobile at the other side of the court, did do nothing . . . In a moment, the set would be theirs . . .

What she had not anticipated was what followed. Just as the ball was about to bounce—or perhaps had just bounced, since at the time it was never quite clear and afterwards nobody but Jemima ever cared—a woman rushed onto the court, not through the little side door used by the players, but directly through the enormous glass doors which formed the barrier with the bar area. She was screaming something, which, with her mass of long black hair, made her seem to be some form of Maenad. "You *muddler!*" was what it sounded like to Jemima, who was standing, unable to take anything much in other than the fate of her brilliant ball.

The yellow ball landed—or just did not land. The woman then caught it—or just picked it up and hurled it in the direction of Dan Lackland, who had turned right round to watch the trajectory of Jemima's shot. The knot of spectators in the bar area had grown, many of them players in the P.P.T., with roses or other pink objects in their hair. One of these spectators detached herself from the group and dived after the intruder into the court. The streaming red hair, with the large bunny-girl bow back in place, alerted Jemima to the fact that it was Alix Carstairs even before the intruder turned on her and shouted again.

This time Jemima could hear quite distinctly what she said and so could all the spectators, whose numbers had increased still further as though word had spread throughout the club that there was some extra sport to be watched on the Royal Court quite apart from the traditional game of tennis.

"You red-haired bitch!" the woman was shouting, "I bet you're having it off with him." The intruder, in a thin white blouse and long Laura Ashley-style flowered skirt, was thin almost to the point of emaciation so that her collarbones were visible sticking out of the blouse's neck like two huge knuckles. But as she flung back her hair, her resemblance to Nell Meredith, give or take the lines on her face and her haggard expression, was sufficiently marked for Jemima to realise that this must be Dan's ex-wife, whom she had wanted to meet, if not exactly like this, even before Dan Lackland had put his arm around her and said in that special tender voice: "Now, Babs."

Babs Meredith shook him off and moved towards Charlotte, who had reached the net. Then she started to shout again:

"Murderer!" she was saying, "Your husband's a murderer. The man you took away from me is a murderer! How do you like that? He killed that poor old butler—"

This time Dan behaved more firmly; the arm he now tightened round Babs Meredith's shoulders was less comforting than restraining and the voice a good deal less tender as he said: "Now, Babs, you're making an exhibition of yourself. To say nothing of me and my guests." Babs Meredith, struggling in his grip, did try to make her own comment on this—it sounded remarkably like, "Fuck your guests—" but Dan was by this time masterfully hustling his ex-wife away through the side door and in the direction of his office. "Come and sit down and we'll talk," were his last audible words, the tenderness beginning to return to his tone as he approached the welcome sanctuary of his office.

The silence which had prevailed temporarily in the bar area, due possibly to embarrassment but more likely to an intense universal desire to take in absolutely everything that was happening, came to an end. In the excited buzz of conversation which followed, Adriana's plaintive voice could be discerned: "Did I miss something? What happened? Will someone tell me just what happened?" Since at the crucial moment she had most unfortunately chosen to go back to the changing room in order to adjust Kenneth's magnificent but by now woefully lopsided wreath of roses.

On the other hand the group surrounding Little Mary, the famed gossip columnist of the *Daily Exclusive* (who notoriously doubled as Miss Mouse of the Mousehole column in *Jolly Joke*), were audibly if jocularly congratulating her. For Little Mary to manage to be personally present at the moment when the Cavalier Case encompassed sport—and in a sense a spot of sex—as well as all its other elements, was a considerable *coup*. Little Mary herself, eyes twinkling behind her rose-tinted spectacles (a nice if slightly inappropriate touch on her part), accepted the congratulations, while reflecting with satisfaction that her disguise in tennis gear in order to report the P.P.T. tournament at which she had believed, wrongly, royalty would be present, had fooled Handsome Dan Meredith, known to be on the warpath since Nell's revelations to the Press. Really, everybody did look alike in tennis clothes: she must bear that in mind for the future.

It was bad—or good—luck, depending on your point of view that the second round of the P.P.T. had just come to an end and almost all the players were now gathered in the bar area, beginning to avail themselves of the pink champagne before the start of the semi-finals. In the midst of this pretty feminine gathering—appropriately pink faces, high voices, squeals of laughter, delightfully modest denials of excellence, charmingly boastful claims of utter failure, pink favours everywhere, on the head, pinned on as corsages, at the waist—the Home Secretary, Stuart Gibson, cut an incongruous figure. He had just been playing with, of all people, Marcus Meredith—but of course it was not really so surprising given that Marcus was his P.P.S. The Home Secretary's face was red not pink and he was drinking Perrier not pink champagne. Marcus himself had vanished. Altogether the Home Secretary looked highly embarrassed at finding himself, like a large sweating Gulliver, among all these deliciously pink-favoured Lilliputians.

When Stuart Gibson caught sight of Jemima, he looked relieved; this was a face he did at least recognise without knowing immediately why (she had interviewed him two weeks earlier about the need for more black policewomen).

"Is that Lackland's wife?" enquired Stuart Gibson nervously. "Rather useful sort of wife to have, I suppose. I must train my own wife to interrupt when I'm losing—" The Home Secretary laughed to show that he was making a joke. Jemima smiled out of politeness; to her, the idea of the Home Secretary's wife, a shy creature who spent most of her time raising money for hospices, behaving in Maenad-fashion was less amusing than her husband appeared to think.

"I must say that for a moment my chap over there did think we were in for trouble—" The Home Secretary nodded in the direction of his detective, who once again, in his plain inconspicuous dark suit, managed to be clearly distinguishable from every single other person in the club. "But he relaxed when he realised that it was just a bit of domestic sport for spectators. What a wife to have! I must train mine—" In his embarrassment, the Home Secretary seemed to be on the verge of repeating his own joke.

"She's not actually his wife," said a nervous female voice at Stuart Gibson's elbow. "She's his ex-wife. Poor thing, she's not been very well lately—"

"Minister, may I introduce Lady Lackland?" Marcus Meredith, who had reappeared, seal-like with his wet hair sleeked back, was wearing the only other conventional dark suit in the club. But meeting Charlotte only served to increase the Home Secretary's embarrassment.

At the same moment, however, Jane Manfred, who in the midst of all the kefuffle, had paused on the court to inspect herself in a tiny gold pocket mirror, chose to join them. Now the Home Secretary's happiness was restored. Jane Manfred was after all the one person who continued to look totally recognisable, pearls and all, in her tennis clothes.

"My dear Jane, what a wonderful chance! Gillian and I so much enjoyed that amazing dinner and the young Indian cellist was such a special touch—" He hesitated. From Jane Manfred's expression, Jemima thought that the musician had been neither Indian nor a cellist although possibly quite young. Stuart Gibson plunged on: "I am sure Gillian has written to you."

Although Lady Manfred gave her own regal smile of acknowledgement to all this, she had, for the time being, other fish to fry. "What a pity, darling, we did not manage to finish the set," she observed warmly to Jemima. "Dan and I won the first set so easily but you were playing really well in the second set. We must play again sometime very soon."

Jemima, too dignified to enquire whether the famous last ball had actually reached the ground—in which case she would have the moral satisfaction of knowing they had actually won—but not too dignified to wonder about it, began to reply that she would love to play again, the sooner the better.

But Lady Manfred, with the air of recollecting something really important, had already turned back to the Home Secretary. "Now, Stuart," she said, "both you and Gillian are coming on to the board of my Euro-Opera 92 Appeal. We have the darling little Princess as Patron. No, I won't take no for an answer. Gillian told me in her very dear letter how fond you both are of the opera, and how work and the House of Commons too often prevents you . . . I shall change all that . . . my box . . . so easy . . ." As Lady Manfred moved imperturbably forward, outlining her plans for future large-scale opera outings for both Gibsons, the Home Secretary was left to mop a fresh burst of perspiration from his brow. It was related possibly more to his threatened operatic future than to his recent sporting past.

10

Seduction Of The Fittest

"I wonder what Decimus would have made of all this?" murmured Dan Lackland, who was lying across the enormous double bed in Jemima's Holland Park Mansions flat. He was gazing up at the Decimus portrait which Jemima increasingly thought of as her own (hence her removal of it from office to bedroom) although technically it still belonged to Rupert Durham. Jemima herself was also lying on the bed, partly cradled in Dan Lackland's arm. By "all this" Dan presumably meant the fairly tumultuous events of the last hour and a half, which had taken place in the bedroom under the portrait's soulful gaze.

"No ghost you," Jemima murmured in return, touching Dan's hard muscley thigh. The golden hairs on his body gave him, in the half-light, an extraordinary look of youth. He stirred under her hand and—for the time being—she moved it away. She felt both extraordinarily content and deeply sleepy. It was quite possible that this desire to slip, just for a moment, into satisfied oblivion was to do with an uncomfortable feeling, not a million miles from guilt, about these same quite tumultuous events. Had she really been seduced so easily? Was it indeed fair to regard the whole most agreeable episode in the light of a seduction? Had she herself not been a perfectly willing party to it all—seduction of the fittest, as you might say? (Richard III came to mind again: "Was ever woman in this humour *won*.") Better to sleep against the delicious comfort of Dan's upper arm, almost as hard and strong as his thigh, and his chest.

It must now be about five o'clock in the afternoon. The shutters of her Holland Park flat had already been drawn when Dan and Jemima arrived back from lunch; that was something the prudent Mrs. Bancroft usually did when she left at noon, as a barrier against the encroachment of the western sun high over the trees in the park. The hot weather had returned. Outside, Jemima knew that the sun was battering away at the shutters, high over the trees of Holland Park, without penetrating the secure womb-like dusk of the interior.

It was another happy coincidence, at least from Jemima's point of view, that *Don Giovanni* (Thomas Allen, naturally, as the Don) happened to be *in situ* on her CD player.

"A new experience." When was it exactly that Dan had said that? And did he mean listening to *Don Giovanni*? (Unlike the more socially craven Home Secretary, he had been frank enough about his usual reaction to the opera: "I'm afraid I associate it with long and boring evenings planning what I'm going to have for dinner but of course I know I'm wrong.") Or did he perchance mean making love to the sound of an aria? But perhaps the presence of *Don Giovanni* of all things on her CD was not quite such a coincidence after all; for why should Jemima find herself moodily playing this particular CD, late at night and alone, if not in some way brooding on the presence of Handsome Dan Meredith, that latter-day Don in her life . . .

The one thought which Jemima wanted to keep resolutely from her at the present time was where last night's encounter with Cass Brinsley fitted into all this. There was a sense in which Dan's move had been all too perfectly timed; as though his sportsman's instinct had instructed him exactly when to strike the blow, serve the ball, or whatever other ridiculous sporting metaphor she chose to come up with. That was the sense in which Dan Lackland had made his not-so-casual suggestion of lunch the very morning after Jemima had learnt that Cass was seeing his ex-wife—no, darn it, his *wife*, Flora Hereford, again on a regular basis.

"Does it make a difference?" Cass had asked carefully at dinner. "It shouldn't." It was so irritatingly predictable of him, Jemima thought at the time, that he should cook her a carefully studied ethnic meal—in this case Vietnamese, a new departure. She could write a thesis on the culinary efforts of Cass Brinsley in relation to his amatory exploits, or projected exploits.

"No, of course it doesn't. Why should it?" was what Jemima actually replied with equal care, her poise annoyingly shattered when she stabbed herself with one of the chopsticks Cass had thoughtfully borrowed from their local Vietnamese restaurant. When she recovered, she went on to speak with a greater degree of honesty than either of them had shown in the previous exchange: "On the other hand, if you were thinking of settling down again in, your favourite phrase . . . a proper relationship . . . now that surely would make a difference."

"You know, Jemima, I don't think anything in this world would really make a difference to how I feel about you." Cass sounded suddenly very sad. It was that sadness, more than anything he had actually said—including the fact that he had not answered her question—which told Jemima the truth. Not now, not immediately, not even very soon perhaps, but sometime in the future Cass would "settle down" again—very probably with the girl to whom he was still married: the girl whom he had left "because I just could not get you out of my system: it wasn't fair to her." Cass had told her that only the other night; up till then Jemima had fondly imagined, the wish being father to the thought, that there had been some basic lack in Flora Hereford herself.

Had he now *got* Jemima out of his system? Should she start feeling that famous allegedly feminine feeling of being "used" in relation to the events of the last reconciliatory few weeks? Honesty, another of Jemima's strong qualities along with curiosity, compelled her to admit that this would be a ludicrous suggestion. There had been no using on either side between Cass and herself, only pleasure freely given, freely taken. The truth was that his nature was as inexorably "settled," or at least prone to look for commitment, as hers was "free," or at least shrinking back from commitment. How ironical that in this way, but in no other, they reversed the traditional male/female roles! At least she, Jemima, was doing the world a favour by *not* settling down since the results were not likely to be satisfactory for either party.

And yet, and yet . . . Was it always to be so? Sad in her turn, Jemima recalled her favourite romantic melody from *Arabella*: "Aber *der richtige* . . . One day the right man—if there is one for me in all this world—will suddenly appear. He will stand before me and look at me and I at him, and there will be no doubts or questions . . ." It was of course the Straussian equivalent of "Some day my prince will come," but what was wrong with the plot of *Snow White* anyway?

It was in her public nature to accept defeat—if that was what it was—gracefully. Certainly there was a kind of defeat in the fact that Cass would no longer tolerate the easy sliding relationship of recent weeks, the relationship preferred by Jemima: Cass with whom she had everything in common, every taste (including how, when and where to make love), *her* Cass . . . That was no way to think about it all. Far better to be good-mannered and philosophical. A quick peck on the cheek to Cass at the end of the evening and she was gone from his flat, if not quite as yet from his life. (Dramatic statements were to be avoided at all costs, the one thing she had learned that distinguished the sophisticated thirty-year-old woman from the passionate twenty-year-old girl.) Cass had not asked her to stay—and she of course would not have stayed if asked.

None of this *really* explained, did it, the presence of Dan Lackland in or rather on her bed one late afternoon on a hot summer's day; something of which her cat Midnight for one, with his usual strong belief in territorial rights, certainly disapproved. He stalked into the bedroom, surveyed Dan, still with Jemima in his arms, and then, black tail held high, stalked out again. For one thing no-one could possibly pretend that Dan Lackland was "*der richtige*" for Jemima Shore, which once again was a delightfully fancy way of expressing the dear old concept of Mr. Right; not even Jemima herself.

That left open the question of why Jemima had brought Dan back to her flat in the first place, following a rather long lunch—rather too long—at the most expensive neighbourhood restaurant, the Kingfisher. (That had been Dan's suggestion: Jemima would have happily settled for the Plantaganet's local, the trendy and delightful River Cafe. But Dan had murmured something about "his own backyard"—not that the River Cafe was anybody's yard.) The lunch had one ostensible purpose and one covert one—leaving quite apart the whole question of seduction and whose purpose *that* was.

The covert purpose was to explain away—if it could be explained away—the highly embarrassing eruption of Babs Meredith into the Plantaganet Club and the scene which followed. Even if the word "murderer" had not been publicly shouted, the scene was embarrassing enough in its own right, and could hardly be ignored given that Little Mary had duly gone to town on the whole subject under the following titillating headline: THE CASE OF VERY CAVALIER DAN. Although the exact wording of Babs' shouted imprecation was obviously not repeated, readers were otherwise reminded of all the previous sensational details comprising the Cavalier Case, before being imparted the latest development.

"That bloody woman!" was Dan's only spoken comment on the Plantaganet affair to Jemima. For a moment she actually thought he was referring to his ex-wife—but for Babs, as opposed to Little Mary, Dan was back using his special tender tone. "She has her problems, but then don't we all? You know, when she *hasn't* had a drink, or taken too many of her pills, or both, Babs can be the most charming woman, so it's not fair to judge her by her behaviour when the drink's in her, she'll say anything and frequently does—"

His covert purpose accomplished—his ex-wife was a paid-up alcoholic, alternately hooked on tranquillisers, whose utterances must be gracefully ignored—Dan Lackland changed the subject to the ostensible reason for the lunch. As it happened, Jemima had two important appointments coming up with regard to her own unofficial investigation of the Cavalier Case. One was with the Taynfordshire police. The other was with Babs Meredith in her Ladbroke Grove flat. Under the circumstances, she did not try to dissuade Dan from dropping the topic of his first wife. The ostensible purpose for the lunch was to discuss the Cavalier Celebration. This had now officially replaced the Decimus Ghost programme as the topic which drew them together. Since Cy Fredericks was cruising off the coast of Turkey in Baby Diamondson's yacht—whence periodic and generally incomprehensible telecommunications proceeded—the whole ghost series had still never been officially cancelled. On the other hand the disappearance of its cameraman, Spike Thompson, to shoot a highly lucrative Californian commercial for the ecology called "Back Green for Life" (known to his friends as "Back Greenbacks for Spike") was hardly insignificant.

Jemima, who frankly now had nothing else to do with her summer, the Decimus programme and Cass Brinsley having disappeared more or less simultaneously, was thus delighted, if slightly surprised, when Dan formally invited her to enact the role of Lady Isabella Clare in the Celebration. She did not wish to spend her summer thinking about Cass—with whom she had been contemplating a Paxos holiday in September—and this new role would help her to do that; besides, playing the part would also enable her to pursue her investigation from the inside as well as the outside.

"I accept!" said Jemima hastily before he could change his mind. It only occurred to her afterwards that she was thus supporting the establishment of the Lackland Court Country Club: but then it was too late to change her mind, wasn't it?

"Lucky Decimus! With you as Lady Isabella." Dan toasted her with a second glass of champagne (it seemed at the time to Jemima mere politeness to agree to a second): "You've got exactly the right colouring and we're copying the dress from the portrait, though we'll spare you the lamb." But I haven't got the Page Three figure for that Restoration décolletage, thought Jemima, well, not quite. But, I expect I'll manage somehow.

Then Dan Lackland began to describe the casting of the rest of the parts. Acting, it turned out, was not of the essence. The actual narration of a text written by a historian—not, she noted, Zena Meredith—would be done by a professional actor.

"We think someone like Jeremy Irons would do the trick," explained Dan Lackland. "He'd look good in the Cavalier clothes, sweeping off a plumed hat and all that romantic bit. You need a bit of style for that and I gather he went to a public school. Someone else suggested Bob Hoskins but we weren't quite sure about his accent, the plumed hat element. What do you think?"

"They're both very good actors," replied Jemima. It was her private opinion that neither of these stars would actually be available for a one-night son-et-lumière production in Taynfordshire, in aid of a new country club, regardless of their education; but you could never tell.

"But we're not really bothered about that," Dan went on, "because I gather you can always get hold of one at the last minute."

"An actor, you mean?"

"Yes. Apparently they never really know their plans in advance. It's not like the tennis circuit."

Once again Jemima, while suspecting that Jeremy Irons and Bob Hoskins did generally know their plans in advance, forbore to comment. He'll end up with someone like my old friend Charles Paris, she thought; and that will teach him.

For the non-speaking roles, it was hardly surprising that the Meredith family had been heavily pressed into service, given that their services could be had for free, leaving all available money raised to go to the new country club. Charlotte for example was to play Olivia Lackland, which was appropriate enough in a way even if, judging from the portraits, Zena, so much darker and taller, would have been a better match. But Charlotte would play the "Victorian" Olivia of The Petitioner pictures very well, modest and feminine, softly courageous. Then Nell was going to play Decimus' only child, Antony Decimus, even if she was both the wrong sex and the wrong age—by a good many years.

"Charlotte had the ludicrous idea that Dessie should play the boy! Dessie, I ask you. No quicker way to turn the Celebration into a wake—or at least chaos. No, we're going to give Little Nell a treat. Zena tells me in her bossy way that we've all got to pay her a lot more attention. At least all that unkempt hair will come into its own. Why Babs lets her go around like that, but then Babs herself these days—she used to be so pretty, so well turned out—" But Dan evidently decided not to elaborate on that painful subject yet again. He turned back to the Celebration itself, as a result of which Jemima learnt that Marcus Meredith was being cast as Sir Bartleby Potter, the Puritan M.P. from Taynford Grange. That was another appropriate choice in a way; especially since Jane Manfred, exercising a *droit de seigneur* over the role of "her" ghost or at least the previous owner of her house, had graciously endorsed it.

Jemima did not recognise most of the other names—mainly young neighbours, she was assured—but they did include several members of the Smith family (but not the egregious Dave). Through all the listings, however, she took it for granted that Dan himself would enact the famous "poet and Cavalier." She got a shock therefore when Dan announced quite casually:

"And then Zena will play Decimus. She's got the looks. As she never fails to point out. Once again it's not a speaking part—all that poetry will be spouted where necessary by the narrator—so the female voice doesn't matter."

"And you? What will you play? Will you play the ghost?" She hesitated. It had been intended as a joke. "You are having a ghost I take it." She remembered Dan's ambivalent reactions in the early stages of their acquaintance in which he had half pressed forward on the subject of the ghost programme for the sake of the publicity for Lackland Court, half hung back as if finding the subject of the ghost more unsettling than he cared to admit.

"Yes we are having the ghost, and no, I shan't be playing him. I'm leaving that to Zena too. You see, I had to make it up to her for not writing the narration. She did have a go but we wanted something a little more popular, downmarket."

"And you've got—" But from Dan's slightly embarrassed look, Jemima knew the answer already.

"Dave—D. J. Smith. Zena had so many theories of her own—no Lady Isabella for her for example—but she'll just have to keep them for her book, and what's more she's so bloody argumentative, Jesus, no wonder Cousin Tommy called her the Schoolmistress—and then we tried that chap at Cambridge—your friend—and he was totally involved with that television programme of his all the girls watch. So then there was Dave, who's, let's face it, always available and Gawain, who's acting as our director—Jane Manfred arranged that for us—he positively *loved* Dave Smith's script. I have a feeling he may have loved the odious Dave himself. Be that as it may, we went with Dave—well, we live in the real world."

Or not, thought Jemima, considering Dave Smith's way with history. But at least she understood the enormous number of Smiths represented among the lesser members of the cast.

So far, so good. Or at least so interesting. But she was still left with the problem—if problem it was—of explaining to herself that strange process by which a practical lunch at the Kingfisher on the subject of the Cavalier Celebration had somehow led on to the offer of a glass of something further on her own delightful balcony, so conveniently near. And on arrival at the flat, one thing had inexorably if pleasingly led to yet another, the sunshine on the balcony, a brandy for Dan, the shaded bedroom, the music . . .

What are all these excuses? Jemima admonished herself sternly amid the wreckage of her bed. It happened. It was great. Admit it. You'd probably do the same thing again—that is, if you had today over again. But you won't do the same tomorrow. This is it. This *has* been it. Enough is enough, et cetera and so on. You may be going to enact Lady Isabella Clare at the Cavalier Celebration—in aid of the Lackland Court Country Club! Really, Jemima. Oh well, I suppose it's also to do with *him*. She looked in the general direction of the portrait. But you are definitely not going to be Lady Isabella Clare to his Decimus. What was it he said? I've always wanted to fall in love with a clever woman! Really, in 1988 . . . He'll be telling you that his wife doesn't understand him next; in fact I have an awful feeling he did say something of the sort, or perhaps it was his first wife, or *women* who didn't understand him. Plenty of those about, that's for sure. Quite a few Lady Isabellas already, including, I suspect, that red-haired number at the Planty. To say nothing of his two Olivias, difficult Olivia the first, devoted Olivia the second. In the meantime, how the hell do I get him out of here? Postponing the problem, which seemed the only course temporarily open to her, Jemima went back to sleep yet again; from which she was awakened sometime later by Dan himself.

"Christ, I'm supposed to be playing tennis at the Planty at six o'clock," was what she heard him say. After that there was an astonishing rush, the demingling of garments previously rather eroti-cally mingled on the floor and elsewhere round the room at high speed, last swift kisses, last swift words from Dan which to Jemima's horror rang in her memory afterwards something like this: "I'll come back. I've got to make love to you again . . . and again . . . and again . . . On my honour, I'll return. Love and Honour, don't forget, the family motto."

The door of the flat slammed. Jemima wandered thoughtfully back into her large white open-plan sitting room in the direction of the CD player. She removed *Don Giovanni* and put on *Arabella,* for the sake of *Aber der richtige . . .* This was to remind her. Not only was Hand-some Dan Meredith not Mr. Right, but he must never be allowed to come here again, at least not alone, since she had proved herself to be such a tower of weakness.

"I have just made a major mistake," Jemima said aloud; Midnight, directing one of his heavy leaps onto her lap, began to make himself comfortable there; his purr was loud and even raucous under her chin. Love and Honour! The family motto indeed, she ruminated, in a mixture of amusement and crossness. Where there is no love, where can there be honour? I loved Cass, that was different. And for another thing, where does this leave my investigation? She addressed the top of the head of the now somnolent black cat.

"For God's sake, I may have been in bed with a murderer. If there's any question of the butler having been killed—and I shall know more, I trust, from Pompey's contact in the local police tomorrow—then I suppose Dan has to be a suspect. No, wait, he was up in London, said he was going back up to London. I've got to think this thing through, that was my promise to Zena."

It was a result of thinking the thing through, if sometime later, that Jemima took another decision. "Since this will definitely not happen again and since he is definitely not coming back this evening I had better get on with making that clear." Determined not to let more time pass before she put her positive decision into practice, Jemima rang up the Plantaganet Club. She would leave a message at the desk, crisp and to the point, since Dan, she knew, would be playing somewhere on court. First of all both Plantaganet numbers were engaged—the club was clearly very busy this evening but then Dan had told her that six o'clock was the most popular time—and then the second number rang for an extraordinarily long time before anyone answered. A woman's voice answered: Jemima had a feeling that it was not the voice of the usual receptionist.

"A message for Lord Lackland," said Jemima briskly. "Miss Shore has to leave London this evening for meetings over a new programme series and will be in touch further about the Cavalier Celebration on her return." The voice, according to Planty custom, duly repeated the message back to her. To her dismay, Jemima recognised the voice: it was Alix Carstairs. There did not seem to be anything she could usefully add to her message to defuse it still further: she just wished that it had not been Alix who received it.

II

What The Butler Knew

Jemima Shore went to her off-the-record meeting with the Taynford-shire constabulary the next day in a chastened mood. The constabulary was actually personified by one Detective Inspector Mike Spain, and the contact had been provided by Jemima's good friend Pompey of the Yard, a.k.a. Assistant Commissioner John Portsmouth, with whom she had shared a good many investigations—and a good many jars—in the past. The agreeable exterior of Mike Spain, who revealed himself as having played tennis "for the Met" in bygone days, was however not quite lost on her. Among other things, Mike Spain's tennis-playing abilities meant that he would surely have a special interest in the Cavalier Case, in view of Handsome Dan's participation. Besides, he was not only nice looking but also on first impression a nice fellow: it remained to be seen whether he believed in keeping his mouth shut, in which case Jemima might have to rethink his niceness.

They met in fact at the Lackland Arms just outside Taynford, a pub with a lawn sloping down to the River Tayn, where a couple of swans had the air of having been hired to advertise rural tranquillity as they sketched their endless silent circles on the surface of the water. Fortunately for Jemima, Mike Spain, if anything, seemed to be yearning for the metropolis—and the Metropolitan Police—given his transfer to the country following his marriage to a Taynfordshire girl (photographs of "our two little Spaniards" duly produced). He certainly applied himself with generous enthusiasm to a problem pertaining to the Cavalier Case as set him by Jemima: whether under the circumstances of the butler's death, with the consequent Press attention, Megalith Television could legitimately proceed with a programme based on the forthcoming Cavalier Celebration.

Jemima wasn't quite sure, as a matter of fact, whether Mike Spain believed her cover, or whether he wasn't aware all along that she was intending to conduct her own investigation. He certainly gave Jemima a very favourable reception as, unlike Pompey, he quaffed his alcohol-free lager (Jemima drank Perrier). Mike Spain told her for example about the funeral of the late Albert Edward Haygarth. And his will.

"We kept a discreet eye on all that. Wanted to see if any relations turned up out of the woodwork. In view of the will, that is."

"And did they? What about the will, anyway?"

"Left it all to her, didn't he, in trust for the girl." Mike Spain disclosed with an air of triumph. "Not to his family at all—if they existed. Wife dead. No children. No sign of a relative at the funeral. No sign of anyone very much except his Lordship of course, correctly dressed in a very dark suit, tennis racket left at home, and her little Ladyship. Plus her. Not the girl, of course, they wouldn't let her come, you can understand that."

Jemima felt completely baffled. "Her?" she repeated. "The girl?"

"Mrs. Babs Meredith. Her Ladyship number one, as you might say, except of course since he didn't inherit the title till long after the divorce, she isn't a Ladyship and never has been. Merely Mrs. Babs. I got the impression that's yet another grudge and she's a lady who would appear to have quite a few. In trust for Little Nell Meredith, the hysterical girl who says she saw some nasty ghosties all over the place. And what he left wasn't rubbish either. Would you believe it? What the butler saved. A substantial sum in a building society, plus a seaside boarding house somewhere in a southcoast town. That's worth plenty these days."

"Does she know? Little Nell Meredith, I mean, not the mother. Obviously the mother knows. Nell was very friendly with Haygarth: she told me the other day that she used to spend a lot of time at Lackland virtually alone with the old Lord and the butler. He might have told her what he was going to do. And why."

"Her father says not only does Nell not know but she's not going to be told till she's eighteen. He's explicitly forbidden Mrs. Babs to tell her." Mike Spain paused. "Now how do I know that? Because our man at the funeral, nothing in uniform mind you, just another nice dark suit, we detectives know how to dress, our man witnessed the scene. He could hardly help it, he said, there they were coming away from the churchyard, lovely old place, yew trees, tombstones, the lot, and this Mrs. Babs rushes up to Handsome Dan, ignores the little wife, and starts screaming out things like: 'Haygarth knew! *He* knew!' Then the cousin, the local M.P., pompous fellow, dead boring speaker, but good in this kind of crisis, dragged her off."

Jemima thought she recognised the style. "What did he say in reply? Handsome Dan himself."

"Very calm, apparently. Well, he must have match temperament, mustn't he, and I don't suppose a first wife yelling at you at a funeral is much worse than facing Roscoe Tanner's service." Mike Spain, the tennis buff, chuckled.

"All he said was: 'You are not to tell our daughter, Babs. I forbid you to do that. Is that understood? I forbid you. Until she's older and better able to handle these things.' Later we questioned him, part of our routine inquiries apart from the butler's death, safety precautions on the roof and all that sort of thing, and he was quite open about it. Didn't think Nell, already upset and hysterical about finding Haygarth's body, a nervous teenager at the best of times, would be able to handle the information. So: no breaking the happy news till the age of eighteen."

This was a new twist. Jemima decided she ought now to probe Mike

Spain further concerning Mrs. Babs Meredith—especially since she was due to meet the grudge-ridden lady herself the next day. She wondered whether Mike Spain had yet heard about the incident at the Plantaganet Club or at least read about it in the *Daily Exclusive*.

But Mike Spain had yet more to offer on the subject of Albert Edward Haygarth's will. "And he made it quite clear, very clear indeed, why it was all done. In theory it was all a tribute to the old Lord's memory. Something about 'in token of the particular affection the late Lord bore for Mrs. Barbara Anne Meredith and her daughter Olivia Nell Meredith': but there was something more about 'their present difficult and restricted circumstances.' Pretty, wasn't it? A kick in the pants for Handsome Dan, administered by his own butler, for treating his first wife and daughter badly, *and* from the grave where nothing more could be done about it."

"But Haygarth wasn't Handsome Dan's butler," Jemima could not help pointing out. "It was a purely temporary arrangement. His retirement was all set out in the old Lord's will."

"All the same, no chance to kick back where wills are concerned," concluded Mike Spain merrily. He seemed thoroughly (and democratically) delighted at the thought of the butler's revenge.

"Honestly, I don't think people go around kicking their butlers these days . . ." Then Jemima recognised the danger; she *was* somehow being partial to Dan and she must stop now. "But how would I know?" She gave Mike Spain in return her own most delightful smile, the one that experienced politicians had learned to dread when she was interviewing them.

Mike Spain repaired to the bar indoors for further alcohol-free lager for himself and Perrier for Jemima. "What a wonderfully puritanical pair we are!" she thought, "here in a country pub on a summer's day with a river and swans . . . this is the late eighties for you, I suppose." Then her mind went back to the Cavalier Case.

No, Dan didn't exactly kick his butler, but there wasn't much love lost there, was there? she reflected, this time with greater honesty. What about the way he tried to stop me talking to Haygarth in the first place, *then* he gives me permission because Haygarth is retiring, and *then* what happens . . . Bingo, Haygarth goes over the parapet . . . She simply had to stop batting for Dan Lackland—a ridiculous idea when she was supposed to be conducting an investigation—and find out from this cheerful chatty tennis-playing detective what their private suspicions were concerning Haygarth's death: accidental, suicide, or what Zena had euphemistically called "the other"? That was after all what she was here to discover, give or take the swans, the designer drinks and the unexpected bonus of the revelation about Haygarth's will.

"I'll be frank with you," Mike Spain confided, by now consuming a smoked salmon sandwich with relish: his taste in food was not quite so puritanical. "There is a lot to suggest suicide. And yet we don't feel inclined—those higher up don't feel inclined to press for a verdict of suicide in view of all the rumpus it would cause, criticism of Handsome Dan and all that, unless we can really make a good case for it. The coroner might get the bit between his teeth, go for us for jumping to unwarranted conclusions and all that. The chief hates that kind of thing and what the chief hates," Mike Spain rolled his eyes, "we *all* hate, don't we?"

"At least one member of the family thinks it's very surprising that Haygarth committed suicide." Jemima, thinking of Zena, knew that she had to tread carefully if she was to air her suspicions without seeming to be unnecessarily sensationalist—or for that matter critical of the police, which, like a coroner's hostile remarks, "we all hate, don't we?"

"Ah, that poor girl again! Who thinks he was actually frightened to death—"

"No, not her. An altogether more reliable source." Jemima took a deep breath. "Mike, look, was there any possibility that it was neither suicide nor accidental death. But that *somebody*, not a ghost, a real live somebody, pushed him off those parapets?"

"Murder." To her surprise, Mike Spain, in pronouncing the word, sounded neither irritable nor dismissive. "Why do you ask that?"

"It just seems rather odd—this is what Zena Meredith, the sister, the writer, put to me—that an old man looking forward to retirement, in a perfectly happy frame of mind, no history of mental unbalance, I take it, should . . ."

"He *wasn't* in a perfectly happy frame of mind. That's one thing I can tell you. He was a worried man. His own words. Two independent witnesses."

Jemima maintained what she hoped was an encouraging silence.

"Number one, there was Cathy Smith, the girl gardener who found him. The first thing she said when we questioned her was 'poor old boy,' or words to that effect, 'I knew he was in a state but I never thought he'd go and do something like this.' He told her the day before when he was polishing the silver that he was a worried man. She told him something about the lawns and the grass and being worried, and he came back with being a worried man himself."

"And number two?"

"Her brother. We're less happy with his statement because you could say we're less happy with Dave Smith altogether; him and his stories to the Press. And he doesn't exactly love the police either. That type never does. At any rate Dave Smith, the historian or whatever he now calls himself—unemployed might be a better word for it—was up at Lackland Court a few days previously to see if he could do some oddjobbing. Since he was unemployed and thus broke. Despite his sister telling him they needed another pair of hands, Dave was given the brush off by the butler sharpish. As an observer of human nature—his own words—he, Dave Smith, thus concluded old Haygarth must be in a pretty panicky state." Mike Spain laughed. "Although you *could* say, that just shows how sane he was! That is, if you know Dave Smith."

Jemima thought privately that not only Dave Smith's statement but also Cathy's constituted fairly thin evidence of suicidal tendencies. No wonder the police were holding back on the subject. On the other hand, it was true that both accounts did fit with her own impression of Haygarth as a *concerned* man: she remembered his words to her about "something going on here."

"But murder?" she persisted. "If he was going to do himself in, why choose such a messy horrible death? And if it was accidental death, well, what was he doing up there in the middle of the night? Haygarth knew, if anyone knew, how dangerous it was."

"A noise, a banging door perhaps. He *was* a big worrier about the state of the house, always nosing about after intruders, everyone agrees to that, used to wander about like some bloody human burglar alarm, Lord Lackland's choice phrase." For the first time Mike Spain sounded just slightly impatient—or harassed. Then his manner changed.

"Look, I'll tell you," he blurted out. "There are, were, some odd features. The pathologist's report. Dreadful injuries of course, well you'd expect that. That's no bungalow up there, more of a skyscraper, not many old houses are as tall as that one. But some of the injuries just could have been caused before death, not on impact, or bumping his way down. We did find marks on the parapets indicating that he had bruised himself or grazed himself there, fibres from the dressing gown, that sort of thing. He didn't take the trouble to jump cleanly. And that is, was, odd. Suicides generally do. To get it over with, you might say."

"So then what did you do?"

"Examined it all very carefully all over again; took fingerprints—"

"And?"

"Nothing. That is to say, nothing you wouldn't expect. Lord Lackland. But he'd been up there quite recently to do with plans for his country club. Strange prints turned out to belong to the architect. The M.P. cousin went along on that expedition too, for some reason, he always seems to be hanging round the family place, and then there was the architect's assistant. But this is not an Agatha Christie murder. They can't have all been in it together. That's worse than the idea of the ghost doing it."

Jemima tried to recall who exactly had been in Lackland Court that night; information she needed to ascertain in any case. Mike Spain was happy to oblige.

"Quite a few, but then the house has quite a few bedrooms, doesn't it? You have the M.P. yet again for example, Marcus Meredith, but since this is his constituency, and he lives properly speaking in the next county, I suppose it's not so odd. And you have the writer sister, Zena, who according to you has her own views on the subject. Then there's the Lackland family, not only mother, kiddies and the nanny, but also of course, Little Nell, she of the rambling disposition. The one person you don't have is his Lordship. He turns out to have a different kind of rambling disposition. He went up to London quite late for some reason, but the butler was definitely still alive when he went. The Irish nanny, who luckily for us is not only Irish but extremely nosy, looked out of her window and saw them talking to each other in the forecourt."

"Could he—Handsome Dan—have come back? He must have his own keys." Jemima wished her voice did not sound quite so strangled. "I'm talking about the theory of the thing."

"In theory, yes. Anyone with keys could have come in. The front door is not barred, and what is more, anyone sufficiently determined could probably have got in without keys. It's a house where security is a total wash-out in our terms. The old Lord never bothered while he was alive and it's not yet been tuned up. You could have forced any of the ground-floor windows and even the side doors. Any outsider could have got in with ease. But as to Handsome Dan—" Mike Spain gave vent to another merry smile. "Perhaps I shouldn't be telling you this but he does have an alibi. Not that we put it quite like that, but he volunteered it. Said it would be highly embarrassing if it was known where he was, but it could be known. And the lady—naturally it was a lady—would back him up."

A lady. Jemima's thoughts went back immediately to the Planty: first, Alix Carstairs on that fateful morning following Haygarth's death, white-faced and distressed at the desk when Jemima arrived late. Then Babs Meredith on another equally distressing if not so fateful occasion, shouting not only "murderer" but then: "You red-haired bitch, I bet you're having it off with him." Alix as an alibi? Dan going up to London to spend the night with Alix, leaving Charlotte safely in the country? Only too likely . . . But there was a third possibility: Dan coming back stealthily to Lackland Court, still having the convenient Alix as an alibi. All this needed further consideration, to say nothing of investigation. She returned to the subject of Haygarth's corpse.

"No tell-tale fragments of material? Nothing clutched between his fingers?" suggested Jemima hopefully.

"Nothing like that at all." Mike Spain sounded quite sad. "Just an awful mess in the garden, and the very faintest suggestion—no more than that—that there could have been a struggle up there. It still could have been Haygarth's own struggle with himself. But if it was murder, you have to ask yourself about the motive. Butlers are an endangered species. Most people don't have them, but if they do have them, they don't kill them. Who on earth would want to kill poor old Albert Edward? And why?"

Later: That is exactly the question I'm going to ask Mrs. Babs Meredith, thought Jemima, as she drove herself back to London. Not so much who, since rightly or wrongly, she's already publicly accused her ex-husband, but why. I wonder what she's like in private, away from the Planty, that is, and not in the throes of a hysterical screaming fit. She sounded perfectly calm on the telephone, thank God.

As a matter of fact, the woman who greeted Jemima at the door of her top-floor flat just off Ladbroke Grove did at first sight appear perfectly calm. It was Jemima who was panting slightly from the steep and quite lengthy ascent.

"No lift, I fear," said Babs Meredith. "But I do have a very good view to compensate." It was true. You could hardly compare the view over the roofs of Arundel Gardens towards the Portobello Road with that fabulous view from the roof of Lackland Court towards the winding willowed River Tayn; nevertheless in its urban chimney-potted way, taking in the odd church spire, this was certainly an interesting vista. Jemima did not particularly want to make the comparison but the second point which struck her was the extent of Babs Meredith's safety precautions compared to those at Lackland Court. Some considerable care had been taken to see that no-one could fall from the roof terrace; even self-precipitation would be quite difficult. There was a good deal of netting as well as quite high iron railings curving inwards and a parapet.

Paradoxically, the very extent of these precautions made Jemima feel rather uncomfortable; under the circumstances it seemed impossible to ignore even for a moment the danger implicit in a roof—any roof. Yet she herself lived perfectly happily with a roof terrace, even if it was not quite so vertiginous as that of Babs Meredith, without any of these morbid imaginings. True, Jemima did not have a resident child, but Nell Meredith was a teenager not a toddler.

Babs Meredith followed the direction of her gaze.

"It does look a bit like Colditz, doesn't it?" she admitted. "But after poor old Haygarth's death, Nell began to sleepwalk and generally wander about at night—well, she's always done that since a child but it got worse—so we didn't want to run any chances of a second tragedy, did we?"

In one way this flat statement on the very subject she had come to discuss made it easy for Jemima to plunge in. On the other hand her inquisitive eye was still busy roaming round Babs' sitting room and trying to form some estimate of its occupant's character other than the various *aperçus* she had had from Marcus Meredith and Dan Lackland himself—to say nothing of the Planty incident.

"How pretty!" she remarked politely, given that the flat was remarkably full of objects, mostly china. "Aren't those cats charming? I'm a mad cat-lover myself."

"They're for sale if you like them." In her denim shirt and long black cotton skirt, with some kind of ethnic belt tied several times round her narrow waist, Babs no longer resembled a Maenad, and her long hair was neatly spiked on top of her head with tortoise shell combs. She was composed and perfectly friendly; yet it was still as impossible to feel altogether at ease with her.

Was it her unnaturally steady gaze? Or perhaps it was Babs' physical emaciation which was the truly disconcerting element about her. Did women of her age suffer from anorexia? Then there was the excessive drinking at which Dan had hinted (which could lead to excessive thinness in women, unlike men). But there was certainly no sign of any drinking. Arriving at five o'clock, Jemima was offered Earl Grey tea, served in a large rose-patterned cup. Babs herself took nothing, merely saying: "I prefer a cigarette." Maybe cigarettes were to blame, given that Babs had started one cigarette when Jemima arrived, and had already lit up again.

"Everything in the flat's for sale," Babs went on. "I run this shop called Goldentimes, as you probably know, and I use the flat as a kind of overflow."

Since the cats in question were only fairly charming and that in a kitsch kind of way, Jemima did not feel it necessary to go so far as to buy them. In any case she suspected that Babs was not so much trying to make a sale as challenging Jemima to understand her straitened circumstances. So she sipped her tea and ignored the question. The taste in which Babs' flat was decorated was assuredly nothing like that of Lackland Court, which veered between the shabby elegance bequeathed by time and Charlotte Lackland's few pleasant if Sloaney "improvements." Jemima reminded herself that Babs had never actually lived at Lackland Court, only visited it with Nell in the lifetime of Cousin Tommy.

"You know I've seen you a lot on television." Mercifully, it was Babs herself who decided to switch the subject away from the cats. "It's odd you should ring me up now like this because I've sometimes thought of ringing *you* up. On what subject? Oh, why do you ask?" Babs gave that disconcerting fixed look. "Grief, tragedy, *abandonment*, the whole damn thing, why women can't get over it, being left. That programme you did a while back: very good. I wanted to ring you up and say, 'Well done, for speaking up for us, the ones who get pushed aside.' What was it called? It's some time since I saw it but I can't get it out of my mind. 'Her story, his story.'"

The programme in question had been shown so long ago—in her pre-Megalith days—that Jemima, contemplating that new programme on socially unequal first wives only the other day, had forgotten all about it. Dreading the reappearance of the Maenad as she did, Jemima could not believe that Babs' retentive memory concerning this particular programme constituted a good omen.

"It was actually slightly different: 'Her story, his history.'"

"History!" The steady gaze was gone. "That's a good word." Babs began to tremble as she stubbed her cigarette fiercely into an ashtray: it was in the same kitsch style as the cats, made in the shape of a pig, surrounded by a litter of china piglets with blue bows round their necks. Instantly Babs lit another: from the packet, she was smoking High-Tar Rothmans. "I've got a good mind to come to their wretched Cavalier Celebration and *haunt* it, I'll give them ghosts, I'll give them history. When I think about the *history* of the wonderfully ancient and famous Meredith family, and all that fuss about Lackland Court and that boring eighteenth-century poet of Zena's . . ."

"Actually seventeenth century." Jemima made her second correction in a markedly cool tone, but Babs, now in full flow, with little beads of sweat on her pale forehead, paid no attention.

"What does all that stuff matter compared to *me*? I'm part of their fucking history too, aren't I? And a good deal more recent. I was married to him. I'm the mother of his first child, oh I know she's not a *boy*, a beloved Little Lord Fauntleroy of an heir, just a girl, that was left to Apple Charlotte to produce—that's what I call her, Apple Charlotte with her ridiculous rosy cheeks—and even then it was her third shot, was I glad she had two girls? I laughed! Then I *cried* when the boy was born, all the same Nell *is* his child and I *am* his wife. That's history, too."

"Ex-wife. You're his ex-wife." This third time Jemima corrected her very firmly indeed. Babs had begun to bang her chest with her clenched fist in a way which suggested that yet further hysterical outpourings were on the way.

Jemima now understood why she had felt disconcerted by Babs' original composure: she had sensed the abyss of suffering lying just beneath the calm surface and found it painful. "Listen, Babs," she continued, "I'll grant you the whole thing. The desolation of abandonment. I've just been left myself as a matter of fact . . ." Making the confession gave her first a pang, then an odd sense of relief. "But you've got to help me. Why did you call Dan a murderer at the tennis club? Why on earth should he kill the old butler? Yet it wasn't just some kind of random insult, was it? Let's face it, if every unfaithful husband was a murderer . . ."

Babs gave a convulsive shudder like a dog shaking itself on coming out of the water; she put up a hand to her face as if to wipe away the beads of sweat. Jemima noticed that her hands were strong and even muscular, at odds with the frailty of her appearance; the fingers, unsurprisingly, were heavily stained with nicotine.

"I know that Haygarth was very fond of you and Nell too." Jemima looked around for ways to encourage her. "I even know about the will. Some unpleasant remarks in it from Dan's point of view, but that's not a reason. I doubt whether he even knew about the will in advance. Did he?" Babs shook her head. Then she stared at Jemima for a moment in silence. When she next spoke, her voice was once more calm; the frenzy—at least temporarily—had abated; the demon of loss which drove her had—if only for the time being—absented itself.

"Haygarth thought there was something odd about Cousin Tommy's death. Someone was there that night who shouldn't have been there. When I went there to pick up Nell directly following the death, he never suggested such a thing; he must have worked it out later; he mentioned it to me another time when I was dropping her, and Dan—typically ignoring our specific arrangement—was away in London. Haygarth had realised then that it wasn't 'a natural death,' those were his words. Someone hastened on the death. And who could that be but Dan? Handsome Dan?" she ended bitterly, but not hysterically.

"Always so expert at his silent mysterious comings and goings. The thing I remember best about our marriage, oddly enough. His ability just to disappear. One moment there, smiling, charming. Then you'd turn round for another smile, another kiss—and he'd be gone. Maybe all great athletes have that talent? I wouldn't know."

Sexual athletes maybe, was Jemima's (unspoken) thought. Her other equally unvoiced sensation was one of sheer relief that she had ended her brief personal involvement with Handsome Dan Meredith so rapidly. She had managed to avoid his telephone calls since that steamy afternoon, deputing Cherry to leave an obviously artificial message about her absence "in Manchester" instead.

"Hastened on the death. A good phrase." Babs lit yet another cigarette and tracked her way through the ornament-ridden room; its fussiness seemed increasingly cloying. Babs stood with her back to the room looking out over her own urban vista, or perhaps at her own Colditz-type security precautions. "That's probably the truth of it too. He wouldn't have thought of it as murder the first time, just a game that he was in danger of losing and that he had to win fast. The second time, well, that was different. But by that time . . ." Babs shrugged her thin shoulders. "You know what they say about the first step. Like the first time I caught Dan out with another girl, after we got married, he was so terribly penitent, at least I thought he was, but the second time . . . And then Charlotte, Apple Charlotte, letting her get pregnant, and telling me it was going to be a boy, so I must divorce him. I'll never forgive him . . . although I suppose Charlotte might have invented the bit about the boy, she's capable of it."

"But *why?*" burst out Jemima, terrified that Babs would pursue the topic of her marriage yet again while at the same time noting that Dan had married both his wives due to pregnancy—which did not seem to soften the bitterness of wife No. 1 one bit. At that moment the handle of the florid roseate cup came off in her hand, leaving the cup itself to shatter on the ground, with a little debris of Earl Grey tea-leaves.

Babs turned round. She ignored the fate of the cup. "He was desperate. That's why. Not so much Handsome Dan as Desperate Dan by then," she said flatly. "Desperate to get his hands on the inheritance before it was too late. He needed money desperately—he wasn't even paying my alimony regularly let alone Nell's school fees, which was rotten of him—and Dan never had any money. He was a tennis star at a time when nobody made big money out of it, you see. Expensive new family." Babs raised her eyebrows. "Expensive things like nannies. *I* never had a nanny for Nell. But *she* has a nanny. Then he was desperate to get proper backing for the Plantaganet Club. There was some question of having to buy a new lease, and that ghastly old bag, Jane Manfred, was just playing with him, wouldn't say yes, wouldn't say no; above all the bank was restive, threatening to grab the club if he didn't reduce his enormous overdraft. How do I know? He told me himself, appealing to me to be patient about my own payments; came round here, all charm once more because he wanted something; he even, I let him . . ." Babs stopped. With some embarrassment, Jemima could guess at what was being hinted.

"Yes, he really needed Lackland Court and the estate all right to keep the bank quiet," Babs continued. "Not only that, but he was frightened that the vital inheritance was secretly being whittled away. He suspected that piece by piece, things, valuable things like books, were being sold. Yet Cousin Tommy, whisky bottle and all, frail as he might be, continued to survive. 'I believe that damn whisky is keeping him alive, I've got a good mind to poison it.' Dan actually said that once, in front of Nell, which was foolish of him, wasn't it?"

When Jemima did not comment, Babs rushed on: "You see it was an odd situation. The house and estate were entailed and had to go to Dan as the male heir, but for some odd reason, you know what lawyers are, the position about the contents wasn't nearly so clear. Of course no Lord Lackland had ever tried to sell things before, so it had never been tested. That was because the title had always gone down directly from father to son, ever since it began. But Cousin Tommy didn't have a son, and he didn't particularly love Dan . . ." Babs sounded now more triumphant than hysterical. "Especially following his treatment of me."

Jemima remembered that she first heard about such possible sales from Dan himself on her original visit to Lackland Court, although it had been put rather differently. That was before Zena mentioned the subject.

"Was it true about the old Lord selling things?"

"Of course it was. He was already doing it. And he was going to do it on an even greater scale in the future. Good luck to him says I!"

"Babs, you sound very sure . . ."

"Of course I'm sure. You see I'm the one who helped Cousin Tommy do it." Her satisfaction was now quite open; given that vengeance is never particularly attractive to contemplate from the outside, Jemima found herself almost preferring Babs' previous mood of frenzy. At least that had its own pathos. Now there was an air of menace about her, reminding Jemima all too vividly of that old adage about a woman scorned. If not exactly a fury, Babs could certainly be a dangerous enemy.

"I had contacts," Babs was saying. "Contacts through my own trade. Upmarket contacts. You could say that it was a pleasure to help out. And do you know, Jemima, that Dan, for all his boasted love of the family history, the family place, never even noticed? It was Zena who spotted what was going on, Zena who told Dan. And that decided him. The need to pacify the bank was the real reason, but the selling off of his precious belongings—as he saw it—that was what really drove him mad."

Babs advanced towards Jemima, her foot crunching the pieces of the fallen cup.

"Now, Jemima, don't be shy, wouldn't you like to buy the china cats? Not to make up for breaking the cup of course—that doesn't matter a bit, it's a silly old cup, far too big—but because I know you really liked them."

Jemima bought the cats.

12

Smelling Of History

The words hardly made any impact just because they were being transmitted through a loudspeaker. It took time for the blur of inordinate noise to distribute itself into proper sense. Finally Jemima Shore, standing next to Charlotte Lackland at the Taynford Grange fete, understood what was being said to be: "Lady Manfred has found a body." Charlotte Lackland had evidently understood to the same effect and at roughly the same moment. She gave a little scream, swayed, clutched Jemima's arm as though for support, and then repeated: "A *body*! Here!" in obvious shock. Her next words were: "Where's Dessie?"

How ironic to recall that Charlotte had actually apologised in advance to Jemima for "dragging" her to the Taynford Grange fete on the grounds that she would find it "so terribly dull"! Whatever else could be said about the Taynford Grange fete, it certainly did not turn out to be dull.

In any case Jemima was not quite so reluctant to be dragged to Taynford Grange as Charlotte imagined. At the time, it provided quite a welcome distraction. Her visit to Lackland Court had been ostensibly arranged via Zena Meredith to discuss the forthcoming Cavalier Celebration and her own role in it, but Jemima intended at the same time to take her investigation further; it would be useful to inspect that roof again in the light of Haygarth's death. Her arrival, however, was liable to be tinged with slight embarrassment, given that she had not actually seen or spoken to Dan since the notorious day of the Kingfisher lunch.

Jemima did not flatter herself that Dan would take his polite dismissal—via Cherry's message—all that much to heart. It was just that she herself was left with a faint honourable sense of uneasiness at having to firmly discourage what she had once—let's face it—rather passionately encouraged. Given her own training in public poise, whatever the circumstances, and given Dan's excellent manners, she had only to get over the first moment of the encounter and all, she was convinced, would be well. As she drove across the forecourt and looked up at the magnificent facade of the house, the date "1600" proudly carved over the high front door, and the words *Amor et Honor*, it was Haygarth's ghost, the old but still active man who had come down the steps to greet her on that first visit, which haunted her, not that of Dan—or for that matter Decimus.

In view of her admirably rational approach to the whole matter, Jemima was annoyed to find that she experienced a small but distinct pang on hearing from Charlotte Lackland that Dan was not actually there. Nor planning to be there.

"He scooted off this morning to play in some friendly match in Hertfordshire which he'd completely forgotten. He's desperately sorry!" Charlotte was looking remarkably pretty in a white-spotted blue dress with a wide white collar and straw boater with a pale blue ribbon round it on her long fair hair. Was the style just a bit too girlish for the mother of three children? But then Charlotte was herself so girlish-looking that she could get away with it. She was suitably and gracefully apologetic; well, she must have had a good deal of practice at covering up for her wandering husband, thought Jemima rather acidly.

"Zena's here, of course, who knows far more about the Celebration than I ever will; but Dan really should be here, shouldn't he? And on top of it all"—Charlotte pulled a face—"there's this fete. I've promised to take you, just for five minutes. I'm afraid we absolutely *have* to go. Zena too."

It turned out that the real force in persuading Charlotte that "we absolutely *have* to go" was the owner of Taynford Grange herself, Jane Manfred. "She'll be furious with Dan for skipping it but she'll forgive him. But she'll be even more furious with me if I don't come—and she *won't* forgive me. Luckily, bringing you makes up for everything in her opinion. You're such a star! You won't mind signing autographs, will you? Oh dear, I know I'm being dreadful, dragging you off like this. Apart from anything, it'll all be so terribly dull."

"I'm sure I shall find it all totally fascinating." And so, of course, in its own macabre way, it all turned out to be. You could even go further and say that well before the booming news over the tannoy transfixed those present, the fete itself, that peculiarly English social function, had aided Jemima by casting various people, involved one way or another in the Cavalier Case, in an interesting new light . . . but that she would only come to realise much later.

Marcus Meredith, for example, exhibited quite an unexpected side to his character. It might be going too far to describe his demeanour as positively jolly—there remained something slightly lugubrious about him, dark-suited as ever, sporting the tie of some impeccably respectable club even on this hot day, and the reek of his gentleman's hair lotion was to Jemima as powerful as ever—but he was certainly far more cheerful than usual and looking as a result a good deal less hunched. His wide smile and warm handshake to all and sundry as he ranged through the various stalls and sideshows came indeed as a considerable surprise to Jemima (as did the kiss-on-both-cheeks Marcus bestowed upon her personally) until she remembered with amusement that he was of course the local M.P. Even if the rather dour figure encountered previously was his true self, and the extrovert Marcus Meredith she witnessed not only shaking hands but shying coconuts and buying sponge cakes was proof of hitherto unsuspected acting abilities, it was still a welcome apparition.

The sponge cakes in question, as with a whole host of other

elaborate and delicious-looking cakes, buns, breads and quiches, had been contributed by Charlotte Lackland herself in the name of her shop, Charlotte's Cakes. Jemima, fresh from her encounter with the frenzied and neurotic Babs, looked at Charlotte with new interest. She no longer wondered just why Dan had chosen Charlotte of all people to marry since Babs had told her bitterly of Charlotte's pregnancy. But she still wondered if he had been in love with her at the time. (Supposing he knew the meaning of the word.) It was clear—very clear—that he was no more faithful to Charlotte than he had been to Babs. Now perhaps she understood. Charlotte gave Dan the kind of domestic tranquillity he sought as a base of operations (that was something Babs could surely never have provided). And of course Charlotte provided the deep unquestioning adoration he also sought. Babs herself had been clear—if malicious—on the subject.

"He *hates* being criticised," she had told Jemima. "Just can't take it. Especially by women. All those fans, screaming girls and so forth, years ago, *ruined* him. I should have kept my mouth shut, I suppose, if I wanted to keep him. But then how could I?" It was a reiteration of what Marcus had told her in the Chinese restaurant at Taynford. Charlotte, on the contrary, knew how to keep her mouth shut. She had even apologised to her husband for turning up at the Planty in what was surely an arrangement botched by Dan's extra-marital carelessness, not her own inefficiency.

Jemima was directly reminded of Babs by one of the stalls which contained a plethora of china ornaments in which kittens in blue bows appeared to predominate. She could have donated her own recently purchased china cats to the stall—except that Midnight, in an unparalleled act of clumsiness (unless it was purposeful good taste) had swept them off the kitchen shelf with his strong black tail. But the uneasy, even sinister, impression left behind by her interview with Babs was not so easily swept aside.

Babs—a woman of strong personality and convictions if unbalanced—as the Decimus Ghost? A ridiculous idea. But was it *possible*? She herself had derided "them and their ghosts, their history" to Jemima: but that could be a cover-up. Anyone could come and go at Lackland Court—the police had made that clear—and in any case in the old days Babs had been a welcome visitor. On the other hand, the thing made no sense. It was true that no-one, but no-one, was going to be automatically eliminated from Jemima's investigations. But if you took the death of the old Lord Lackland, Babs had so clearly been the loser by the end of the old regime. Coming to the butler, what about Haygarth's money, now in trust for Nell, as a motive for killing him? That made no sense either: you certainly didn't go to such dangerous lengths to secure a nest-egg for your daughter a few years early, and it left the old Lord's death—by which Babs and Nell lost a valued patron—unexplained. When it came to motives, Babs had some right on her side when she pointed to the one person with a strong motive for both deaths (if they were linked): her ex-husband, Dan.

Nell: no doubt it made sense for Nell to cling to Zena's side from the moment they arrived at the fete, if only to distance herself once more from the "babies"—her step-siblings—but Jemima had the impression that Nell was at the same time seeking to avoid any conversation with her personally. Did she regret those confidences in the cathedral? Another potentially sinister thought crossed her mind. Was Nell too frightened to talk further? Was Nell being threatened in some way? She had hinted to Jemima she might have some idea about the identity of the Decimus Ghost. Once again, this line of argument led far away from the notion of Babs, as the ghost-murderer. "I recognised it and yet I didn't recognise it"—wasn't that something to do with the smell? Why try to frighten her daughter at Lackland Court when she had total control of her most of the time at home?

Yet it was Nell's reluctance which first suggested to Jemima that beneath the surface of this apparently innocuous outing there were certain new tensions. This was no longer the outwardly happy family of that first summer lunch party; but Haygarth had been alive then, he had served the food to the outwardly happy people at the outwardly happy lunch, and the Cavalier Case had not begun in earnest. Today Zena herself was in an odd mood. It was Zena, after all, who had begged Jemima to conduct her investigation, "whatever she found"; this afternoon she was thoroughly out of sorts for some reason and not even particularly warm in her welcome. Suddenly, she had the air of one who regretted having invited Jemima to investigate dark doings within her own family circle.

It was the plaintive voice of Louisa (or was it Emily?), one of Charlotte's little girls quaintly got up in a miniature version of her mother's clothes, straw boater and all, which gave Jemima the clue.

"Where's Daddy? I want to sit with Daddy, it's my turn," wailed the little voice.

"Where indeed, Louisa?" commented Zena from the middle seat of the big estate car, in her sharpest tone.

That was the measure of it. All these females were in their different ways reacting to the unexpected absence of the central male figure in their lives, including his independent-minded sister. Marcus was the only other male in this family circle (Dessie had a few years to go yet before he filled the role) and Marcus too seemed in a curious way in perpetual subordination to the personality of his glamorous older cousin. Even his pursuit of Zena could perhaps be seen in the light of Zena's own obsession with her brother. Furthermore, it was noticeable that the "extrovert" Marcus was only emerging on his own ground as the M.P.—and in Dan's absence.

Only one member of that original lunch party was apparently oblivious to all the tension. Jane Manfred glowed. Unlike the Meredith women, young and old, Jane had taken Dan's defection in her gracious stride.

"Oh, that wicked Dan!" was all she said; the swift frown which creased her remarkably smooth olive brow was as quickly dismissed. She was wearing a green dress, the colour of some remarkable ancient liqueur and, for all Jemima knew, the roughly cut objects dangling in profusion round her neck were actually emeralds; unlike Charlotte Lackland (and Charlotte's small daughters) she did not wear a hat; thus the startlingly black sheen of her hair in the sunlight had its greenish tinges too.

Was it the self-confidence of great riches which gave Jane Manfred that air of sensuality, unabated by middle age or the fact that Jane Manfred was not even, strictly speaking, beautiful? She was too fleshy altogether, not only her figure, but her features also, for the photogenic standards of modern beauty (Jemima had seen a terrible photograph of her recently in sweetly spiteful *Taffeta*, sagging in every sense of the word on the arm of Dan Lackland, at a charity cocktail party held at the Plantaganet). Or you could look at it quite differently: it was Jane Manfred who had the sensuality in the first place and the great riches had merely enabled her to hang on to it a little longer than most women—and, maybe, to gratify it from time to time.

The Green Knight was at Jane Manfred's side, attempting—as usual—to discuss something to do with the famous north-facing conservatory (all the same, rather an odd moment to choose, Jemima thought). But Jane Manfred's radiance was entirely directed towards the man presently destined to open the fete: Stuart Gibson, the Home Secretary.

Stuart Gibson greeted Jemima with a remark about the splendidly dry and sunny weather: "They couldn't have known *I* was coming—otherwise they'd have sent rain." Who were they, she wondered. Whoever they were, he liked the remark enough to repeat it at least four times within earshot. Otherwise he praised the house lavishly— "What a perfectly delightful situation you've got here" and "Good to get all this fresh country air after Westminster"—in terms which irresistibly reminded her of Duncan arriving chez the Macbeths: "This castle hath a pleasant seat." Duncan too had praised the good fresh (Scottish) air: Jemima trusted the Home Secretary's fate at Lady Manfred's hands would be kinder.

Gillian Gibson, on the other hand, a slight and nervous figure compared to a husband both bonhomous and bulky, made a series of intelligent and informative remarks about hospices, albeit in a very low voice. It then transpired that the fete was actually being given to raise funds for a local hospice and not, as Stuart Gibson somehow implied by his solid presence, the Conservative party. Jemima meanly asked herself whether his forthcoming speech would also reflect that fact.

She was never to find out. For it turned out next that Gawain's presence at Lady Manfred's elbow, jabbering away about his conservatory, was not quite the intrusion it seemed. On the contrary, one of Jane Manfred's characteristic little plots was in progress. Before the Home Secretary was allowed to make his speech, political or not as it might be, he was first of all to watch Jane Manfred ceremonially dig the first sod for the foundations of the famous new structure. With attendant Press photographers, of course, and a few words from an important botanical person.

"A little surprise, dear Stuart, dear Gillian," murmured Jane, taking each of them by the elbow. "We shall go round the corner of the house, seeing the new layout of the late summer garden on the way—we didn't allow that to be used for the fete, I'm afraid, any more than we opened the swimming-pool—this is not Cliveden," threw in Lady Manfred sternly. "But you too, Stuart, are a gardener"—the Home Secretary looked startled but pleased—"you will understand— and you will find it so much cooler round the north of the house as well. A botanist of great distinction is here for the occasion, a good friend of our dear Gawain's, giving up her Saturday, such an enthusiast for what I am going to do. For with Gawain, I am planning a most extraordinary botanical treasure house . . ."

It was now Gillian Gibson's turn to look bewildered but delighted: "Is Jane building a hospice *here*?" she enquired of no-one in particular. "How absolutely marvellous of her!"

"No, she damn well is not." Marcus Meredith, who had been as he supposed on the point of introducing the Home Secretary to the crowd, looked thunderous. "Sorry, Gillian," he added. "But really, when Stuart has come all this way, and you too, of course, it's a bit bloody much. Never mind that poncey decorator. Sorry," he threw in once more.

All the same, Marcus moved off in the wake of the Home Secretary and Mrs. Gibson, who had themselves moved off obediently in the wake of Lady Manfred. The only person who showed any sign of independence from her imperious will was in fact Stuart Gibson's detective . . . Jemima could only assume that the words being babbled into his small black intercom were as unflattering in their own way as the general reactions around her. Zena's was the most outspoken.

"Do we have to go and watch *that*? Jane making a travesty of the original plans of the house." She was tight-lipped and angry. "Jemima, let's take the opportunity to nip into her library; she's got some wonderful things, if you can forgive the curtains. Pelmets! Absolutely the wrong date. Nell, you stay here with Charlotte and the children."

"I won't stay here. I want to watch the digging." Nell, evidently resenting Zena's sudden attention to Jemima, scampered off after the retreating official party.

But to Zena's further fury (although it seemed to Jemima herself not unreasonable in view of the large concourse of strangers present) the doors of the big house were firmly locked. Unlike Lackland Court, Taynford Grange was also remarkably secure so far as its other ground-floor entrances were concerned.

"What a lack of style!" exclaimed Zena, finally accepting that she was to be frustrated. "As if we were all thieves or spying on her. I was longing to show you her bedroom, among other things. Gawain and Jane between them went really quite mad: a sixteenth-century Polish warrior's campaign tent, erected at vast expense to block out all the light in that wonderful bedroom. They say that Max Manfred took one look at it and turned on his heel, saying 'Here I could never sleep.' But then again that may have been the point . . . So where does one go to the loo, for instance? Jane thinks of no-one but herself."

All this took some time. Finally, the pair of them returned rather crestfallen to Charlotte Lackland, standing roughly where they had left her—except that she appeared to have lost all three of her children.

"The loo is in that awful tent over there," she observed drily. "I've already taken Dessie three times and now he wants to go to the Gents."

In this way, Jemima, Charlotte and Zena were standing all three of them side by side when that remarkable and—at least to Charlotte—distressing announcement came over the tannoy. A moment later, Nell raced up, even faster than she had departed. She grabbed Zena's hand, ignoring her step-mother (and Jemima).

"Come on, Aunt Zena," she panted. "Come *on*. You've simply got to see. It's ghoulish. It's grisly. Like a horror movie. And did she get a shock? You'll love it."

The three women, at a pace dictated by Nell, advanced rapidly towards the north side of the house. The first sight which struck Jemima was neither ghoulish nor grisly in the slightest. It was, however, pathetic. Jane Manfred, her shoulders in their liquid green silk cradled by Gawain, was sobbing convulsively. She did not even put that tiny lace handkerchief to her eyes, but something large, plain and masculine-looking, which surely belonged to someone other than the Green Knight—Marcus maybe or even the Home Secretary? Her weeping did not even stop when, after a while, she gulped out some words; as a result it was impossible to tell even what language she was speaking. Gawain on the other hand could be clearly understood.

"But Jane, my angel," he was saying. "Don't be upset, it could be such a *feature*."

Jane Manfred stopped crying. She glared at him.

"Haf you no heart?" she demanded. Her accent—whatever it was—was unusually strong. "You silly little man with your talk of features. There must be a proper burial naturally. For this poor, these poor—" she hesitated and cried a little again.

"I think one's first sight of death is so upsetting." Gillian Gibson's intervention—from a distance away, her view blocked by the substantial form of her husband—was undoubtedly well meant. But it had the effect of turning Jane Manfred's disdainful gaze from Gawain in her direction.

"My dear, of what do you talk? I have seen death many times, and not in your comfortable hospices either. But this is not a body, these are bones. Someone is dead here, long ago I think, someone buried here secretly, and it is for this I weep. For these poor bones never found before. And now we have caused them with our clever plan to be disturbed. It is for this I weep. I am a foolish old woman. I should not have made this plan." She put the masculine-looking handkerchief to her eyes again.

It was true. The tannoy had been inaccurate. Lady Manfred had not found a body. She had found a skeleton.

Would Charlotte have been quite so upset, Jemima wondered, if she had known that it was not so much a body that had been discovered as a skeleton that had been dug up? The word "body" conveyed something recently dead—a corpse in fact. But the body in question had been dead long enough to disintegrate into bones, even if these bones had preserved something of their anatomical shape as they lay, so that to an amateur glance, the human nature of the skeleton was not at issue. And the skull, seeming to stare up at them with sightless eyes and large grinning teeth, clinched the matter.

Afterwards, Jemima would recall with a certain embarrassment that she had virtually pushed her way to the edge of the grave—as the open trench before Lady Manfred now proved to be. On second thoughts, it was surely strange how well preserved the bones were: perhaps it was something to do with the soil? Jemima noticed that the soil was surprisingly sandy: but then she realised how close to the river Taynford Grange lay; the lie of the land concealed the fact that the house was in effect built high up on the bank of the river, even if the main facade faced away from it (and south).

Had there been a coffin? There did not seem to be any traces of one. How long ago had the body been buried? Was this another matter for the police and Detective Inspector Mike Spain? All these questions ran through her head as she gazed at the bones. Another surprise at her feet was a sheet of transparent polythene: how on earth had that been provided so quickly?

"It's a man," said an aggressive (male) voice in the little knot of close spectators. The accent was what Jemima privately thought of as working-class public school (or vice versa: that is, the owner of the voice might be socially mobile in any one of two directions). "At least we know that. Been dead for centuries, too. I realised that immediately when I dug the old geezer up this morning, skull and all." Jemima looked again at the skull: it was a macabre and dominating sight. She felt a pang either of pity or revulsion, she was not quite sure which. Lady Manfred's distress—it later turned out that the skull had been the first object she disinterred—was the more understandable. "Alas poor Yorick," went on the authoritative voice, "and all that. I nearly spouted the whole speech, I can tell you."

"How do you know it's a man?" another (female) voice. It was Nell Meredith, leaning forward over the trench with an expression Jemima could only describe as gloating. For a moment, Jemima even wondered . . . Nell . . . some kind of practical joke . . . she was interrupted by the aggressive male voice.

"Look at the pelvis. Quite different. To say nothing of the skull. I remember my biology from school. Don't they do biology at private schools? Besides, I take an interest in the past, don't I? Bones are part of history, if you like."

It was Zena Meredith who exclaimed: "Dave Smith! For God's sake! What on earth are you doing here?"

"And Cathy?" Charlotte added, rather more politely.

"And Cathy!" repeated Zena.

Dave Smith and the young woman next to him who proved to be Cathy, the girl gardener from Lackland Court, were both, unlike the Home Secretary's little party, wearing jeans. They also both had rather loose thin fair hair of about the same length and were roughly the same build and height. But where Dave Smith's expression was a mixture of impudence and amusement, Cathy looked nervous and rather upset.

"I was doing the digging, wasn't I? At the request of him," Dave Smith indicated Gawain. "And she's the botanical expert. Cathy. Lady Manfred wanted one. She got one." He nudged his sister. "And now I'm covering the event for the local paper, and other newspapers of even greater renown. I bet this is an important historical event. And I'm here to report it." He laughed. "We Smiths do have a lucky touch! What I mean is, we have quite a talent for stumbling on unexpected corpses, don't we? Ms. Meredith," he added after a pause. The appellation gave the impression of being more cheeky than polite.

From somewhere within his skin-tight jeans, Dave Smith produced a small camera and proceeded, before the eyes of the stunned assembly, to photograph various conjunctions of bones, Home Secretary, Lady Manfred. As a result of this, at least one mystery was cleared up, leaving the greater mystery of the skeleton itself intact. It was now explained, what had just begun to puzzle Jemima, how Lady Manfred's single ceremonial dig of her spade had managed in some way, at once magic and macabre, to turn up an entire corpse—correction, an entire skeleton.

Dave Smith had in fact been deputed by Gawain, with the aid of his sister Cathy, to dig everything necessary for the ceremony carefully in advance; thus Lady Manfred would be able to perform some kind of conjuring trick, turning over a single sod. Now, with the nonchalant confidence of one about to break yet another fascinating aspect of the Cavalier Case to a wider world via the media, Dave Smith outlined what he had in fact done.

He had happened on the first bones by accident, but had subsequently taken much trouble to uncover the entire skeleton in its surprising state of preservation. With the aid of Cathy—sworn to secrecy—he had then mantled the skeleton in clear polythene to protect it from the ceremonial spade. This explained, surely, the extraordinarily neat way in which the bones were laid out, even though Dave himself denied it.

"No, of course I touched nothing, moved nothing. I'm a historian, aren't I? I'm not some kind of ghoul." Zena Meredith gave a little snort. "I thought it would be just great for her Ladyship to uncover it all. Lovely publicity! Lovely pictures! No offense, Lady M, certainly didn't mean to distress you. Not for one minute. I mean, he knew all about it—skull and crossbones and the whole lot—the whole thing would look so adorable—his very words—sort of framed among the floorboards." Once more Dave Smith, a.k.a. D. J. Smith local historian (and gravedigger), jerked his thumb in the direction of Gawain.

"Now, Jane darling, I can explain—" began the decorator. "An adorable Memento Mori was what I had in mind." His voice sank to a whisper. Jemima thought: his chief client! He's been in a corner before, no doubt, but not much tighter than this one, I suspect.

"Look here, young man—" began the Home Secretary, suddenly aware that D. J. Smith was not only the centre of attention, reasonably enough, but had also somehow assumed a mantle of authority to which he surely had no right. "Do you realise that this might be a case for the police? Marcus?" But the dutiful P.P.S. was already at his side. "Faraday?" He looked for his detective, who was already in conclave with the bystanding policeman. "What's the procedure here?" he went on, followed by: "What happens about my speech?" And lastly: "What do we tell the Press?" It was the unmistakable voice of the politician.

After that Jemima could hear words like "coroner" and "Coroner's Rules" repeated several times and then "Chief Constable" and "our pathologist"—the latter spoken first doubtfully then with increasing authority—emanating from this particular conversation. Marcus' baritone (his extrovert mood had entirely disappeared in favour of a discreetly helpful stance) could be heard far less than the Home Secretary's bass: quiet enough on private occasions, Stuart Gibson somehow deemed his House of Commons boom to be appropriate to the recent dramatic turn of events. He was definitely booming at Dave Smith, who stood, arms akimbo, in what Jemima supposed was a characteristic attitude when faced with an angry force of authority. Cathy, on the other hand, cowered at his side.

From the other little huddle, as represented by Jane Manfred, Gawain, and, at her own volition, Zena Meredith, very different scraps of conversation emerged. Jane Manfred, recovered from her initial shock, tears finally dried, was clearly very angry. The phrase "an adorable Memento Mori" excited her particular disgust, especially when she discovered that Gawain had envisaged the skeleton lying

displayed on some kind of rich velvet bed—"burgundy I thought"—
beneath a pane of glass set into the floor of the new conservatory. (As
Dave Smith had correctly indicated.)

"Has death no *privacy?*" she asked sternly.

Jemima suddenly remembered visiting some stately home near
Cambridge when she had been an undergraduate. She had gone with
a party of friends—surely Rupert Durham had been among them?—
and they had been shown a skeleton of a nun, a pre-Reformation
inhabitant of the place, which you peered at through a glass window
in the wall. She entirely agreed with Jane Manfred. Then as now it
had seemed a curious invasion of privacy; although Rupert—yes, he
had been there, it was the summer of their romance—Rupert had
brushed aside her qualms. He started instead to talk about the social
consequences of the Reformation: "That nun, you know, played an
important economic role . . ." She had still shivered. She shivered
just a little now.

The formation of the two rival groups in earnest colloquy left a third
group among the little knot of spectators around the grave to create
itself. This consisted of Jemima, Nell, Charlotte Lackland, who had
by now re-acquired Dessie and was holding him firmly by the
hand—and by default the Home Secretary's wife, since neither her
husband nor anyone else had seen fit to include Gillian Gibson in the
first group. Nell was hopping up and down in an excited state which
bordered on the hysterical. Her behaviour was all the more striking
since alone of the spectators—unless you counted Gawain before Lady
Manfred took him to task—she greeted the discovery with unalloyed,
even gleeful, enthusiasm.

"Does it *smell?*" she asked at one point, leaning over the grave to get
a better look. "I bet it does, I bet it smells."

"Oh shut up, Nell, for God's sake." Charlotte in contrast still
looked rather sick as when the announcement of finding the so-called
"body" had come over the tannoy; although she now had the missing
Dessie firmly by the hand.

Dessie took up the chant "Nell says it smells" with some delight.

This quickly became "Nell smells, Nell smells," until Nell herself lunged at him to shut him up.

"If it smells of anything, it smells of history," threw in Jemima hurriedly, to keep some kind of family peace. Happily the mention of history—that new buzzword in Nell's life—distracted Nell from her step-brother's impertinence. As a matter of fact, there was no smell at all, not even newly turned earth, since Lady Manfred's expensive musky perfume effectively drowned all other scents, including the more delicate lily-of-the-valley perfume Charlotte and Zena held in common.

"It's important to get all the details right. You see, I'm going to write all this up for the school magazine," she pronounced. "I'm a historian now like Aunt Zena." And like Dave Smith. And like Rupert Durham, for that matter. There are a good many of them about, one way and another, thought Jemima. All the same, much was to be forgiven Nell. That, at any rate, was Jemima Shore's conclusion, long afterwards, thinking back on the whole intricate web-like course of the Cavalier Case. Because it was Nell and Nell alone, like the child who called attention to the Emperor's obvious lack of clothes, who thought of asking the obvious question:

"Who is it?" asked Little Nell Meredith, future historian. She added in her faintly whining voice: "I mean, it must be someone. A crusader or something."

Thinking it over afterwards, Jemima felt fairly sure that she herself would not have acted as she did now if Nell had not put that— admittedly obvious—question. For it was a question which took her back to her obsession with Decimus, the fact that now more than ever—Cass vanished from her life, no Mr. Right on the horizon, let alone closer—the dark-eyed poet-in-the-portrait facing her (now singly occupied) bed so dominantly had begun to haunt her dreams again. Alas, these dreams were no longer erotic as they had sometimes been during her reconciliation with Cass—to his annoyance.

The dreams now owed more to the convolutions of her new investigation than to sex—or history. This was a phenomenon Jemima had encountered before in some of her previous investigations. It was not exactly a case of the solution being discovered in a dream—that would be far too neat a way of expressing it—and anyway it was never the full solution of the mystery which occurred to her in this manner; more a question of some detail or aspect of a case, hitherto confused or embedded deep in her mind, coming to the surface, as it were, in sleep. In the morning certain things were infinitely clearer than they had been the night before: as though the sands of the horizon had been reshaped under cover of darkness by some strange night wind, to lift up a new prominence.

Of course exactly the same process also took place with her television work: she would never forget waking up *knowing* what the first shot for the Sri Lankan brides programme should be (and it wasn't the one that Spike Thompson, the cameraman, thought it was going to be, either).

Two nights ago she had had a rather horrible dream about Decimus, which she knew simply tied in to the fact that his portrait faced her bed. Nevertheless it had upset her. So far as Jemima could remember, Decimus had stepped out of the portrait (like the Decimus Ghost was supposed to do at Lackland Court?) and as he did so, issued some command to the big dog beside him. At which the big dog—breed still unknown—had rushed at Midnight with his enormous teeth bared and begun savaging the beloved black cat, who had been lying curled in his familiar position at the bottom of Jemima's bed. Jemima had screamed and dived at the dog, trying desperately to protect her pet. At the same time she shouted at the poet: "Stop him, stop him, can't you see, he's going to kill him . . ."

"I can't," replied Decimus. "I can't. You see, I've lost my fingers." And he held up his left hand, the one hidden in her picture (and in the National Gallery version but revealed at Lackland Court). She saw the mutilated white hand, but with a single finger—the forefinger—extra long and menacing in her dream, ending in a curving predatory fingernail. Jemima had woken up shaking, to find

Midnight buffeting her face and shoulders, a furry claustrophobic presence, demanding in his own way to be let out of her bedroom.

It was the sudden recollection of that dream which caused Jemima now to say, slowly, to Nell Meredith:

"Nell, you can see the hands quite clearly, can't you?"

The girl nodded. She was once again kneeling by the graveside.

"Those phalanges, I think they are called, the bones of the fingers. How many bones, fingers really, are there on the left hand?"

Nell bent forward further—the skeleton had been once more covered in its polythene—as though to trace the outline.

"No, that's the right hand; the left. Do you see what I think I see? But contrast it with the right hand: they're absolutely different, aren't they? Look, Nell, and Charlotte—" Jemima herself knelt down and stared intently into the grave. After an instant, Charlotte, pushing Dessie also down on his knees as though they were in church, joined her. As Jemima knelt there, concentrating on the disarticulated bonework of the skeleton and wondering desperately if she was imagining what she saw—all the fingers missing? a kind of odd blunted bone structure in place of fingers?—she was aware of being joined by Zena Meredith, and then immediately afterwards by Dave Smith, who had both abandoned or been released by their respective groups.

Nell scrambled to her feet and grabbed Zena's hand. "Aunt Zena," she cried. "It's absolutely brilliant. Jemima says the fingers are missing, just like in the story you told me, do look—"

"Decimus?" The name itself was first pronounced by Zena in a soft, wondering voice. "Here? It can't be."

It was left to Dave Smith to exclaim, much less softly, much less wonderingly: "Yes, it bloody well can be. Do you realise who lived here? Christ, just let me look at this." He shoved Charlotte—and Dessie—roughly aside, knelt down himself, pulled back the polythene, and began to gaze intently into the earth. He put his own finger forward. "No phalanges, and even those metacarpals tapering away. Quite unlike the right hand. No other sign of disturbance. It can be, it is, it bloody well must be," he muttered.

"Don't touch anything, Dave Smith." It was Zena again, now very fierce. "You've no right to touch anything. This is *our* history."

Charlotte, outraged at her treatment by Dave, and busily brushing down her pale blue spotted skirt, joined in. "If it is Decimus," she said firmly, "then we must get hold of Dan immediately. He is the head of the family."

But it was Gillian Gibson who had the last word. Really, Jemima reflected later, she was a very nice woman. Twisting a pair of navy blue fabric gloves in her hands, she spoke for the first time since the drama of the skeleton's discovery had began to unroll.

"Whoever it is," she began nervously but with the sound of proper determination in her voice, "I think we should all say a little prayer for him. For the repose of his soul. Wouldn't that be the right thing to do?"

13

Late That Night

That night Handsome Dan Meredith, the tennis player victorious in his tournament, came back to Lackland Court. And the Decimus Ghost came back too. Jemima Shore, alone in her four-postered bedroom which overlooked the forecourt, heard Dan Lackland's car. Or rather the car she thought was his. She did not see—or hear—the Decimus Ghost. Although the ghost took note of her presence.

When Jemima heard the noise of the car—it must have been nearly midnight—she went and looked out of the high embrasured window. The action was, as she knew in advance it would be, a mistake. The car was Dan's Mercedes, but it barely stopped to debouch the occupant of the passenger seat—Dan himself, leaping lightly out, easily visible in his white shirt and linen trousers. There was a quick kiss to the driver and he was running with equal lightness up the broad front steps. Did he glance up as he went at the words engraved on the front porch? Love and Honour: the perfect motto for the successful tennis player.

The driver of the car, equally, with her great loose mane of red hair, was recognisable even at a glance as quick as Dan's parting kiss: Alix Carstairs. Love and Honour? His tennis partner in the "friendly Hertfordshire match"? No doubt. Jemima went back to bed.

The four poster itself was much as it must have been in Cousin

Tommy's day, with its thick tapestried hangings of a vaguely Jacobean nature: hardly original, but nevertheless they badly needed renovation. The sheets and pillowcases on the other hand were new, delicately shadowed with flowers, and edged with frills: Charlotte's taste. Either the stifling feel of the tapestried ceiling above her head—memories of Edgar Allan Poe's sinister story of a descending ceiling lurked in her mind—or the slight stiffness of the pretty new sheets, or maybe the tumultuous events of the day itself, prevented her from sleeping. She felt extraordinarily restless and strongly tempted to wander herself in the old creaking house, as Haygarth must once have done . . . Was the ghost abroad? A foolish thought. I *must* go to sleep, Jemima told herself. Who knows, perhaps a dream, another illuminating dream will come . . .

It would be foolish to pretend that by the time the Lackland Court party left Taynford Grange earlier that evening, all possible doubt concerning the identity of the newly discovered skeleton had been eliminated. That of course would be for various official processes to establish in the future: including, crucially, the approximate dating of the bones by the Home Office Pathologist. But so much could now be deduced from a skeleton, or parts thereof, as Jemima was aware, in view of modern technology, modern instruments, modern machines, that sooner or later not only the age and sex of the subject, but also the approximate dating *would* be known. And even, it was suggested by Zena (who like Dave Smith had done some research on the subject—for one of her books), the actual manner of death, had it been violent.

So that *if* the skeleton proved to be that of a mid-seventeenth-century male in his thirties, missing all the fingers on the left hand for many years before death but who had received wounds in his head and thigh at the point of death (that would be the final clincher— "Heaven's True Mourning" being explicit about the wounds, "first still on his charger, reached by many hands, then, falling amid the hooves of his own horse, in his arm, in his very head") *then* the evidence of this being Decimus Meredith, lst Viscount Lackland, a body already

known to be missing, would surely be very strong. Before you got on
to matters such as teeth and dentistry—it was explained that teeth (or
the lack of them) and dentistry (of a sort) could help as far back as the
seventeenth century.

That was Dave Smith's contribution, supplementing the information given by Zena. One of the weird effects of this dramatic discovery
was to draw Dave Smith and Zena Meredith together into a new
alliance of the knowledgeable. So that it was in fact from a combination of their two accounts—for once not in angry opposition—that
Jemima pieced together the meaning of Dave's enigmatic exclamation
at the graveside: "When you think who lived here!"

Later Jemima would see this as the vital element in the story—the
strange historical link which gave her the solution to the Cavalier
Case. But at the time Jemima merely cried out in shock:

"Lady Isabella! I don't believe it." Then, feeling almost affronted in
some way: "It's not true! What about that famous Puritan? Sir Bartleby
Potter. Lady Manfred's elusive ghost, who was killed at the siege of
Lackland. *He* lived here."

"Sure he was living here in 1648, but this wasn't Puritan
country . . . ," began D. J. Smith, local historian. There was a smug
suggestion of "I told you so" about him: for it was after all Dave (not
Zena) who had all along held to the theory of Lady Isabella removing
the body. Then Zena herself, future biographer of Decimus, took over.
It had the air of the lecture, something already prepared, or at least
thought out.

"In 1645, the year in which Decimus was killed, this was Lady
Isabella's house, or rather her husband's. Her second husband, Sir
Ludovic Broughton, the Royalist soldier who was killed himself the
next year. She was married three times, you know, no, four, and
despite what we may euphemistically call her hyper-activity, never
had any children. So Bartleby Potter got hold of the house after
Ludovic Broughton's death. Then he tried to marry Lady Isabella into
the bargain. As well as trying his luck with Olivia. Both of them at the
same time. They were both widows at that point. Rather tactless of

him—but then Sir Bartleby was probably not into tact where marriage was concerned. The real point was that they were also both of them heiresses, except Olivia had a son and Isabella didn't. Which of course made Isabella a more attractive proposition as a wife. Even to a Puritan. Money, you might say, made up for morals."

"No kid to inherit her loot," put in Dave.

Zena continued: "Lady Isabella simply said no. But it was Olivia who gave Sir Bartleby that famous brush-off about not subjecting her son to another man's corrective rod."

Jemima thought Dave Smith was working on some witticism on the subject of Lady Isabella and a man's corrective rod. Instead he contented himself with observing:

"Yeah, everyone wanted to marry Lady Izz, wouldn't you know it, big eyes, big tits and best of all, big bucks." This left Zena to plod on at some length through Lady Isabella's family tree, explaining just why she was an heiress—"the last of the ancient English family, no, not the Irish one as you might think . . . ," where Jemima frankly could not follow her.

One point, however, in all this was fully established. At the time of the Battle of Taynford, late in 1645, following the Battle of Edgehill, Lady Isabella Clare—either for convenience's sake or in tribute to her fortune, her maiden name was generally used for this much married lady—had unquestionably been living at Taynford Grange, home of her second husband, Sir Ludovic Broughton. It was then that D. J. Smith rose to the occasion.

"And all this time, hubby was away!" he shouted. "That's rich, isn't it? Plenty of local nookie up to the time of the battle for her and our Decimus. Romantic tryst-in-death, love you forever, you're mine not her's (the wife's) ever after."

Zena frowned; not so much at her new ally's choice of language, it turned out, as in genuine historical doubt.

"Ludovic Broughton? Are you quite certain? Surely he must have fought at Taynford?"

"No way, listen I just checked it out for the Cav. Celeb." (even this abbreviated reference passed without troubling Zena). "He was off with the King, probably just outside London at that point. Mind you, we could bring him back for the Cav. Celeb., and the King too, Charles One, that's always a good part, sort of small and stammering and terribly terribly dignified, then with hubby around we get jealousy, cuckoldry. Take a few liberties—"

"No, no, we can't do that. It didn't happen like that." But Zena's tone was patient as to an over-eager child. "Decimus!" she went on. "Here! So it was true. He did love her. That awful red-haired trollop."

"All we know so far," corrected Dave, "is that *she* loved *him*. He had no say in this body-snatching bit, did he?" Zena paid no attention.

"This changes my whole book, my whole approach," Zena went on dreamily. "A study in Love and Honour," she murmured, "that was going to be the sub-title of my biography—but it would have rather a different connotation, wouldn't it, if all the time Decimus was betraying Olivia, as the gossips suggested . . ." Zena looked round, as though expecting to see John Aubrey, Samuel Pepys, or some other seventeenth-century gossip writer instead of two twentieth-century families—her own and the Smiths. "The three of them, his death, Isabella's daring in taking the body—if true . . . I have to say that it would all make the most wonderful story . . . After all, historical fiction can do things . . . 'Recreation in the proper sense: an enviable gift'—some reviewer said that. Also an academic inciden-tally. Love and Honour," she murmured again. To Jemima, it already sounded like the title of Zena Meredith's next historical novel.

"I saw this mini-series called something like that. It was great. She was an aristocrat in the French Revolution and he was the local guillotiner—sent to chop off her head, but instead he fell in love . . ." That was Nell. She was interrupted by Dave at his most cheerful.

"Plenty of good fiction in history—" he began. But this time he had gone altogether too far.

"Not in my history. And in *my* fiction, there's plenty of good history as well." Zena's sharpest tone had returned. The temporary alliance was over.

As Jemima tossed and turned—and maybe slept fitfully—the creaking silence of Lackland Court was disturbed by more than one door being gently eased open. The first door was that of Nell Meredith on the upper floor and she was able to open it very quietly since it was not entirely closed when she went to bed.

Nell was frightened. She thought that after all it was no fun being at Lackland Court for all its grandeur, now that Cousin Tommy and Haygarth were both dead. Daddy was always away and anyway Daddy—but that was a subject she didn't want to think about. Daddy not loving her, Daddy *never* loving her, Daddy loving the others, especially Dessie. And the other thing, the horrible thing. Better after all to get back to Mum and home. Mum was really stupid the way she behaved to Daddy, even Nell could see that, all those ghastly scenes, who needed it? Not Daddy. But at least Mum wasn't frightening. You could feel safe in that awful flat with its dreadful bunnies and whatever. No-one would get you there.

At Lackland Court Nell no longer felt safe. She was frightened that someone was trying to get her as they had got Haygarth. Not the ghost—Nell no longer believed in the ghost *as* a ghost and wished she had not spouted all that silly childish rubbish to that ghastly woman from the *Daily Clueless*, everyone would tease her about it next term in school. (Everyone at school read Little Mary's column in the *Clueless* even if they read nothing else their whole lives.)

The ghost was a person—a person who might kill you if they knew what you knew.

Nell also wished she had never talked to Jemima Shore Investigator about her suspicions. That too could be dangerous. She hadn't said very much, had she? She couldn't have. Because she hadn't realised then what she now realised . . . it was the costume actually. That odd costume she had found, the Cavalier costume which shouldn't have been there.

At least she hadn't strictly speaking found it, because it wasn't strictly speaking hidden, it was just in among all the other costumes, which was quite a brilliant way of hiding it.

And Nell wasn't supposed to be checking through all the costumes either, which is why she had to do it secretly, late at night, knowing where the baskets were. The reason she did it, she had to do it secretly because no-one would understand, no-one ever did, just a boring cry of "Oh Nell, you look fine"; she did it because her costume as Antony Decimus, the young Cavalier, was just embarrassing it was so tight across her chest and showing all her legs which ever since she had overheard Daddy, Daddy! the traitor, horrible, treacherous Daddy, saying one night to Cousin Marcus, even more horrible Cousin Marcus, in the dining room when she was prowling about:

"What a pity that my eldest daughter hasn't got her mother's legs! The one good thing you could say about Babs, she did have the most fantastically sexy legs. And Nell hasn't inherited them." That was Daddy.

"Poor Little Nell. I can never understand why girls like that *will* wear mini-skirts. It looks grotesque." That was Cousin Marcus.

So Nell was looking for another costume, maybe she would even decide to be a girl after all, not a boy, depending what was available, make boring Decimus have a daughter not a son—why not? Dave Smith was making it all up anyway, the boy she was supposed to play had been a baby—and she found the list from Leaviss, the costumiers, as well. And then there was this strange costume not on the list. And she started to try it on. And she was very surprised by something. And the boots. The boots really clinched it. And then, suddenly, the *other* thing fitted, the thing she told Jemima, everything fitted. This evening. Nell thought about everything that happened. Everything she knew. And Nell became very frightened.

She was going to escape, go back to Mum, she had some money, she had been given money for the fete and luckily had had no time to spend it, what with all the excitement. She would get out of the house as quietly as possible, hitchhike to London (or even perhaps to

Taynford station for an early train), one way or another get to Mum's flat, and be *safe*.

"Wait," thought Nell. "I know what I'll do. I'll leave a note. Yes I will. That makes it even safer. Something about being homesick and needing to get back to Mum. Not that anyone cares *what* I do, but sooner or later, they'll find it. That way the *person* won't suspect—" She wrote the note in the laborious childish handwriting which, like many of Nell's characteristics, was the despair of her expensive school, and fastened it to her pillow with a safety pin, rummaged out from among her somewhat tattered wardrobe. Then she took off her torn cotton nightie and put on a pair of jeans.

Nell went carefully down the first flight of stairs from the top floor, something she had practised, although luckily boring bossy Nuala was away. Jemima, still wooing sleep and half-embraced by it, did not hear her.

The person who was the ghost did hear her. That was the second door which opened at Lackland Court that night. The person who was the ghost decided to follow Little Nell.

"I should go straight out, get away," thought Nell to herself. "Make a dash for it." But already her courage was waning just a little—not because of the darkened house, so familiar to her from her night-time prowlings, but because of the whole idea of leaving Lackland Court, losing it forever and going back to boring old Mum. As her courage waned, so commonsense—or was it?—returned. What she suspected, had suddenly *known*, could it be true?

It was at this point that Nell decided to have just one more look at the Cavalier costume . . . Just to make sure. She passed, a small silent wraith, into the deserted back quarters of the house.

At a discreet distance, the person who was the ghost (but very far, at present, from being dressed as such) went after her.

It was some time after that, that Jemima, awake once more and furious with her wakefulness, decided to act on her own kind of impulse. It was perhaps a decision she would not have made had it not been for insomnia *and* witnessing Dan's return *and* suddenly thinking all over again about Cass, which she hardly wanted to do, better to brood about Lady Isabella Clare, best of all to let thoughts of investigation take over.

She got out of bed—unlike the chaste teenager Nell, Jemima always slept naked—and pulled on the baggy navy blue cotton jumper and white knee-length Bermuda shorts which she had brought to play tennis in the next day on the old Lackland grass court (shortly to be swept away). It was her intention to make her way up onto the roof. The air was still balmy as it had been at the fete—and the Home Secretary had acted the genial Duncan. Earlier that evening Jemima had been in the Long Gallery with Zena and Marcus while Charlotte put the over-excited children to bed—what ghouls children were! Here were three blond cherubs gloating over the discovery of a skeleton. Young Penny Smith, that further member of the egregious tribe, who sometimes acted as nursemaid in Nuala's absence, had not turned up to help her. Penny had sent instead a message via yet another even younger Smith that the news about the discovery of the body—sic—had greatly upset her, and under the circumstances she would be staying home with her Mum instead of spending the night alone—sic once more—at Lackland Court.

This message did at least have the effect of uniting all the Merediths present in a universal condemnation of all the Smiths, Zena concentrating on Dave (their brief alliance quite forgotten), Charlotte on the defaulting Penny, and Marcus, for some reason, reserving his ire for Cathy the girl gardener.

"We should really look at the Smith situation," he said at one point. "I believe their influence in the village is considerable, and not necessarily for the good. That's the trouble with a family which doesn't have family values." Jemima thought privately that the Smiths probably *did* have family values—they certainly displayed family unity—but they were unfortunately just not the kind of family values Marcus Meredith had in mind.

"Anyway," concluded Marcus rather huffily, "I will not have Cathy Smith calling me Marcus. I will not have it." He turned away and, kneeling down, started feeling for the key to the spiral staircase which led to the roof. His physical deformity, which he concealed so well in his well-cut conventional suits, was startlingly apparent in this position. At their feet, he might have been some latter-day Quasimodo. For the first time—it was a distasteful thought—Jemima wondered how much of Zena's rejection of Marcus was due to sheer lack of physical attraction. One did not have to delve into the depths of incest to realise that Zena had been brought up with a paradigm of the healthy athletic male before her eyes in the shape of her brother. Maybe poor Marcus—as he was so often described—had never quite measured up?

Then Jemima noted exactly where Marcus found the key—by the skirting under one of the imposing floor-length portraits of bygone Merediths. It was in fact a portrait of the chaplain, the Rev. Thomas Meredith, the presumed author of "Heaven's True Mourning." She also noted exactly where Marcus put the key back, a moment later, having changed his mind about an expedition to the roof. "Ever since poor old Haygarth took his header, one hasn't felt quite the same about the roof."

"Oh Marcus, you're so pompous!" exclaimed Zena in that tone, half-way between irritation and affection, which she seemed to reserve for her cousin. At the same time she shot Jemima a questioning glance as though to say: Was it a header? Did he take it? In short, to remind her of her mission.

"I believe Marcus used to rather fancy Cathy," put in Charlotte brightly. "There was a time when he always used to be lurking about the gardens. When she first started here."

"What were you after, Markie?" went on Zena in her teasing voice. "Conversations about old-fashioned roses? Or was it family values?" All the same, despite the teasing, Jemima had the impression that perversely Zena was just a little bit annoyed. In a rather whey-faced style, Cathy Smith was really quite pretty. Zena might not find Marcus' devotion totally acceptable—because she did not fancy him—but she was not necessarily prepared to let him go. For some reason Jemima's mind leapt to her conversation with Marcus in Taynford: how he had himself "madly fancied" Babs in the old days, and how it was Zena who had insisted on Dan marrying her: "I have to say she probably thought Babs wouldn't be a rival." Maybe Zena, consciously or unconsciously, had had more than one motive in bringing about the match: no rival with brother Dan—and an end to the possibility of Marcus' going after her.

What a contradictory character Zena was! Her relationship with her family veered from the independence which made her appeal for an investigation "whatever you find," to an obsession with them which focussed so many of her thoughts—perhaps too many—on her brother and involved her in an endless but presumably unconsummated relationship with her own first cousin. Perhaps it was an obsession with her own family history which was at the root of the whole thing—she could not or did not want to get away from these Merediths, then or now.

At this point Jemima, feeling her way through the darkened gallery, was taking, had she but known it, much the same route that the ghost used to take in the old days, and was even employing the same method of guidance by counting off the vast pictures. (Although unlike the ghost, Jemima had paused to admire the portrait of Decimus, lit up at the head of the stairs; she gave the dog in the picture a firm look.) It was by counting and calculating that Jemima finally reached the particular portrait of the Rev. Thomas Meredith, as lugubrious and correct in his white bands and long dark robe as Marcus Meredith M.P. ever was in his twentieth-century dark suit. She found the key quite easily. But the door was not in fact locked: Marcus, riled by the thought of Cathy Smith, must have forgotten to lock it before replacing the key.

The gallery seemed quite eerily dark to Jemima because the moon had risen sometime after she had gone to bed; so that the garden outside lay bathed in cold white light, enormous shapes of hedges and topiary seen quite clearly, while inside the gallery, in contrast, it was difficult to discern anything. It was also very warm. These long windows were evidently never opened. The moon must be right above the house, since no shafts of silver were streaming in through the long windows to bisect the floor.

Jemima ascended the narrow spiral staircase. As she reached the roof, her thoughts should by rights have been with Haygarth—in what frame of mind had he taken his last journey, pursuing what chimera of noise, or perhaps after all intent on self-destruction? But the theatrical splendour of the sight before her eyes—Lackland Court and its gardens laid out in the moonlight, with the moon itself, almost full, high above the sixteenth-century turreted chimney pots—momentarily drove all other thoughts out of her mind.

She stepped forward, put out a hand to steady herself—and found herself touching something warm and moving which was actually, she realised an instant later, a human face . . .

Jemima screamed. She then stepped backwards as though to seek again the sanctuary of the narrow staircase. But the door banged shut in her back as it had done when she first inspected the roof with Nell, either in the wind—there was far more wind up here on the roof—or perhaps someone coming from below had shut it behind her, shut her off up here—shut her off with—at the mercy of . . . Now the thing crouching beneath her on the roof rose up high above her, towered over her blackly, she saw a white hand stretched out towards her. As in her dream, she knew that it was mutilated, that it was—

"Darling, don't be frightened, darling, it's me, Dan," said the owner of Lackland Court in his most soothing voice, drawing the shuddering Jemima into his arms and holding her. He hugged her thus for a while in silence until her involuntary shudderings had finally come to an end. All the same Jemima still clung to him.

"I must say you gave me quite a fright too." Dan still spoke in that easy soothing voice, and still maintained his arms tightly round Jemima. "For a moment I really thought you were the Decimus Ghost come to get me."

After that it seemed quite natural at the time to let Dan's soothing quasi-paternal embrace turn into something more passionate and in this, her mood heightened by her previous fear, Jemima's response was certainly quite as whole-hearted as Dan's. They began to kiss, hungrily like starving people.

"Oh God, how I want you," she thought he said at one point, as kisses gave way to more urgent embraces, his voice muffled in her hair. All Jemima could think—without speaking because there was no need for words—was: I want you too—now.

Afterwards Jemima knew perfectly well that she would never have resisted Dan at the last moment—it was not in her nature to do so, any more than it was in his to draw back. Where they had been lazily, slowly, sensually in tune that hot afternoon in her flat, now they were as one in a far more violent rhythm of possession and surrender. Much more difficult to know was what the final outcome of it all would have been. Regret? Embarrassment—after all her good resolutions? Or a new twist to the Cavalier Case, with sex becoming as prominent as history and sport?

Like the contents of the Home Secretary's speech, the question of Jemima's regret or otherwise was never to be resolved. A loud shout from down below caused them both to freeze. The door to the staircase, Jemima realised, had fallen open again.

"Dan! For Christ's sake, Dan, where are you?" It was Marcus. He sounded either very angry or very frightened or both. He seemed to be at the end of the gallery or at the head of the stairs.

"Dan!" Marcus shouted again. "Where are you?"

Dan released Jemima, pulling at his clothes as though to knot some non-existent tie; he was in fact wearing an open-neck dark shirt and dark trousers. He stood a little way apart from her and called out in a loud perfectly measured voice: "I'm up here, Markie, on the roof. Getting some air. What's the matter, old man?" But Jemima was still close enough to him to realize that Dan, for all his measured voice, was panting, even trembling, much as she had been earlier.

The gallery below flooded with light.

"It's Nell, Little Nell." Marcus' voice came up hoarsely from below.

"There's been an accident, the most ghastly accident. Dan, you must come."

It was extraordinary how coolly Dan still managed to speak, although Jemima could feel that he had not stopped trembling when he put his hand out to her again, this time as though seeking reassurance.

"How bad is it?"

"Very bad, I'm afraid." Marcus had reached the bottom of the staircase; Jemima could see him gazing upwards at them both.

"I'll come at once." As Dan went rapidly, lithely down the spiral without making a sound, Jemima realised that Dan was wearing dark rubber-soled trainer shoes.

14

Death Rehearsal

"She'll live. In fact she'll recover almost completely, they think. She's conscious now and ever since she recovered consciousness, began to recognise people, she's got better all the time."

Perhaps it was appropriate that it should be Alix Carstairs—in the pinkly chic surroundings of the Plantaganet Club—who broke the news to Jemima. Because it was Alix Carstairs who had also kept Jemima in touch with Nell's progress—or rather lack of it—during the terrible days following her "accident" in the back quarters of Lackland Court.

"Charlotte's been wonderful," added Alix generously. "Wanted to stick by her all the time. And Marcus too. He coped with Babs as well, who's been totally hysterical of course—well, you can hardly blame her for that, poor thing"—another burst of generosity. "It was Marcus who kept Babs off Dan's back."

"How is Dan?" Jemima had not seen Dan Lackland again since that forever-interrupted idyll on the roof, except carrying the apparently lifeless form of his daughter across the hall in his arms, before the ambulance came. She heard Marcus say something about not moving her, how it was dangerous to move someone with head injuries, and heard Dan himself hiss back over his shoulder: "I'm not leaving my daughter there lying in a pool of her own blood." Charlotte was at his elbow, trying to calm him; Dan shrugged her off equally fiercely.

"Zena had to cope with Dan. Zena and Jane Manfred between them." Perhaps that too cost Alix something to admit. "I—I've scarcely seen him. He's hardly been here." Alix looked extremely strained as she had done once before on the morning when the news of Haygarth's death arrived to disrupt the tennis match. Come to think of it, she had also looked strained and unhappy in advance of her hysterical outburst on the day of the tournament. You simply assumed that someone of Alix's fresh appearance and robust athletic build—she was really quite plump in places, with an unfashionably voluptuous bosom for a tennis player—was naturally good-natured and full of equanimity. It was not necessarily so. At Jemima's original visit to the Planty, Alix had greeted her in quite a hostile manner beneath the conventional politeness due to Jemima's celebrity status. Really, to be the girlfriend of a famous womaniser—frankly, that was Dan's other career—was one worse than being his wife; all the same opportunities for torturing jealousy, none of the comfort of the public position. A further warning, as if she, Jemima, needed one . . .

Of course Alix Carstairs had had to endure a further ordeal beyond the prolonged absence of Dan at his daughter's bedside, with his wife, with his sister, with his ex-wife (as little as possible), with Jane Manfred, in short with anyone except Alix herself. The last days and weeks at the Planty must have been testing in themselves when this latest development of the Cavalier Case—as it was inevitably seen by the Press—brought still greater attention to the club. Stories like MIDNIGHT MERCY DASH DRAMA OF CAVALIER CASE TEENAGER brought comfort to few—except of course the numerous readers of the *Clueless*.

"What happened exactly?" Jemima felt she must ask Alix. Although Marcus Meredith had given her his own account, so far as it went, the next morning at what was a highly subdued breakfast in the Lackland Court dining room: with even young Dessie silent. Jemima had tried to establish if there was anything she could helpfully do, before she left for London.

"No, no, nothing, nothing," cried Charlotte in visible distress. "Unless you could stop Jane Manfred coming over. She's just rung up—Dan must have rung *her*—"

"I'll settle her," said Zena Meredith grimly, stalking out of the room before Jemima could say anything. Then a pale young girl appeared who proved to be the missing Penny Smith; she took charge of the children. Charlotte went off to the hospital. That left Marcus to explain to Jemima how he had stumbled—literally stumbled—over Nell's inert body on one of his nocturnal rambles: "One just can't sleep in the heat, sometimes, can one? Perhaps you find that too?" The question was put quite casually. At the same time Jemima recognised her cue. She too had some explaining to do, to Marcus at least. (She did not think anyone but Marcus had realised that Dan had not been alone on the roof.)

"Oh, absolutely, one sometimes finds one just needs to spring up—" To her annoyance Jemima found she was slipping into Marcus' own faintly ludicrous impersonal style. "And then when one did get up onto the roof, Dan really gave one quite a fright"—she must stop this, she sounded like Princess Anne. "One minute later, one, no, I, no, *we* heard your shout." (That should make everything very, very clear, should it not? What was more, it was the truth, and nothing but the truth; it was not the whole truth—well, not quite—but what had happened between Jemima and Dan during that one minute, it was really not much more, was definitely none of Marcus' business.)

Marcus had little else to tell her at that point and certainly no clues as to how Nell fell and caused that massive injury to her head. Nor, in the days which followed, according to Alix, were any further definite clues discovered. The floors of the back quarters were both uneven and stone-flagged, but an accidental fall in itself would not be enough to cause such major damage. The most likely theory was based on the fact that the cupboards in the room where Nell was found went right up to the ceiling. There was evidence that she had been trying to reach the very highest shelf: a pair of high rickety wooden steps lying on the floor.

In the dark—there was no light bulb in the single ceiling light hanging from a flex—Nell must have overbalanced, failed to save herself, and fallen, bringing the steps crashing down with her. In that way, she would have hit her head on the stone floor with great force; quite apart from all the debris lying about in the room, old croquet mallets, one with the head missing, one with the handle broken in half, and so forth—the detritus of country-house life over years. Then there were all the wicker baskets full of seventeenth-century costumes waiting for the Cavalier Celebration. Some of these had been hired, some lent, some were family costumes. All in all, the room was in chaos.

"Mysterious things, head injuries," ended Alix. Jemima could not but agree.

Leaving Nell's injuries aside, there was the problem—also so far unsolved—of what the girl was doing in the back quarters in the first place. It was fairly clear what Nell was doing up and dressed in the middle of the night: she was running away from Lackland Court to "home," that is, her mother's London flat, on the grounds that she was homesick. A note to that effect had been found pinned to her pillow. There was however much family surprise, reported Alix, that Nell should reach a sudden decision and implement it in this manner— after all, who on earth would have stopped her going home anytime she wanted to go? The truth was: absolutely no-one. Alix did not need to amplify the reason.

"But Nell's always been rather hysterical. And a bit of a fantasist. Think of all that stuff about the ghost she told the Press, *she* started the whole thing off and *we're* still living with it. Gets it from Babs, I'm afraid." Alix's newfound generosity was waning.

But her trip backstairs? No-one could explain that although oddly enough Louisa, Charlotte's elder daughter, did contribute the fact that Nell was always poking about there. "And she chased us out, she was horrid, although it's our house not hers, she told us to go away, she had a secret there I think." Emily corroborated her sister's story: "She used to dress up. All by herself. That's rather silly, isn't it? And we weren't supposed to touch all the dressing-up things. But she did."

Now Jemima learnt from Alix that even Nell's recent return to consciousness had not resulted in further light being cast on the whole bizarre near-fatal episode. On the contrary, the story was now more baffling than ever. The first thing Nell did was to announce quite firmly, for all her weakened state, that she had absolutely no memory whatsoever of the events leading up to her accident. She did not remember falling and hurting herself. She did not remember going to the back quarters of the house. She did not remember getting out of bed and dressing. She did not even remember writing the note found on her pillow.

When the note was presented to her, Nell looked for a moment puzzled, abstracted and then read out the words: "Homesick for *Mum*," with exactly the same note of amazement as they had been read earlier by her father. Direct if short-lived questioning by Dan, gentle prolonged questioning by Charlotte, tender and even more prolonged questioning from her Aunt Zena—none of this produced results.

"It does happen. It's not all that uncommon with head injuries. The doctors say that. Concussion, etcetera. You remember the past but not the immediate past. She remembers the fete and all about the skeleton being dug up—yuk, Jemima, was that awful? Dan says if it is Decimus, it's got to be properly buried, by the way, by his family, not left at Taynford Grange—but she doesn't remember anything later. Not even getting into bed, let alone getting out of it."

Jemima was at the Plantaganet Club (of which she was now a member) not entirely to keep in touch with the Cavalier Case. She also had an appointment to play tennis with Cherry. Since the disappearance of Cass, Jemima had concentrated on her P.A. as her sounding-board for her thoughts on the Meredith family, Lackland Court and the Cavalier Case in a way which reminded her of successful investigations in the past—the pre-Cass era in fact. But times changed. And Cherry, Flowering Cherry of Megalith Television, as she had once been known admiringly for her deliciously well-endowed figure, had changed too, as she quickly reminded Jemima.

In particular the former Flowering Cherry had seen a film called *Working Girl*. It would not be fair to say that Cherry totally identified Jemima with the unsympathetic boss-woman role played by Sigourney Weaver in the film, any more than she totally identified herself with the Melanie Griffiths part of the secretary, an amalgam of innocent glamour and streetwise intelligence who gets to defeat her jealous boss, ending up with both her job and her man . . . It would be fairer to say that Cherry, forgetting Jemima, simply identified herself with all the more positive aspects of the Melanie Griffiths character (and there were no negative aspects).

One of the first effects of this creative piece of self-identification was Cherry beating Jemima at tennis. Their singles at the Planty got off to a fine start when Cherry appeared in an abbreviated pink Planty tennis dress with a pie-frill of a skirt and—on her—a plunging neckline—"I think I bought the wrong size," she said complacently—which was surely cheating under *Working Girl* rules. Stuart Gibson, perspiring heavily at the bar as he swigged his eternal glass of iced water after a work-out with his new Under Secretary—a younger more upright version of Marcus Meredith—failed to notice Jemima but did take in Cherry. His Under Secretary took in both and began to make some appreciative sotto voce suggestions about mixed doubles. Cherry gave the Home Secretary a blatantly admiring glance—she was into power these days, she had told Jemima—but ignored the Under Secretary. Jemima ignored them both.

After that Cherry, tripping rapidly about the court looking like a bunny-girl in tennis shoes, revealed herself as a ruthless player with shots which had something of the power of Jane Manfred's, plus a great deal more mobility. After two sets—both 6:4 to Cherry—Jemima panted: "We must do this more often." The sub-text was: "You bet we must, but not until I've had a coaching or two with Costa." She was particularly infuriated by the failure of her famed accurate lob to dismay Cherry in the slightest; Cherry had simply raced to the back of the court, reached the ball with surprising ease and hit it back, accurately, over her head.

Discussion of the Cavalier Case—in discreetly lowered tones—in the bar area of the Planty after the game found Cherry, similarly, with a new confidence. Maybe she even overdid it a little, like her wild smashes, most of which—they at least—had gone wide of the mark. For example, she threw out so many theories about the Cavalier Case and in so many combinations that in the end Jemima lost count of them. The wildest smash of all concerned Zena—Zena and Charlotte.

"They're having an affair, have been having an affair all along—this is the late eighties—" This time Jemima had to burst out laughing.

"Look, honestly, Cherry, they're both straight, I assure you. At least I'm quite sure Charlotte is—it may be the late eighties for you, but Charlotte has eyes only for Dan, lives only to please him in the most unreconstructed way—and as for Zena, if your argument is that any unmarried woman of forty *must* be a lesbian, that's equally ridiculous. She's a bit of a mix-up if you like, too bound up in her own family, has a rather pointless on-off affair with her cousin, frightened of marriage even, but not gay. You might just as well say Zena's having an affair with *her*, her brother's girlfriend." Jemima nodded in the direction of Alix, too far away fortunately to hear.

Seeing Cherry prepared to discuss that one too, Jemima hastily transferred the discussion to the subject of the "Decimus" skeleton. Nell's accident had thoroughly overshadowed its discovery. Nevertheless "Decimus" information was filtering through by degrees, put together by various forensic experts under the auspices of the Home Office Pathologist. The fact that the Home Secretary himself had been present at the discovery of the skeleton had concentrated the official mind wonderfully on the subject—including the mind of the police. After all nobody could be quite sure when Stuart Gibson, prompted by Gillian Gibson with her kindly interest in a "proper Christian burial" for the unknown, would not choose to make yet another enquiry on the subject.

"You getting on with finding out about them, those damn bones?" He would ask this (not, of course, in his wife's hearing) in a tone which was really rather short-tempered for a man so normally bland. But then "those damn bones" had ruined the delivery of one of his finest "human face of the politician" speeches in recent years. So perhaps he was entitled to a little crossness.

The first thing known was that the skeleton was, as Dave Smith had pointed out, male. Within a few days it was also known that this male had been, like Decimus, approximately thirty years old when he died. Then chemical analysis of the nitrogen content of the bones made the skeleton itself over 300 years old, probably about 350 years.

The confirmation of the injuries suffered by this male before death were, to an outsider, even more surprising. There was the matter of the fingers of the left hand, severed so many years before their owner's death that the remaining bones had had time to waste and taper off into points (as Dave Smith had once more pointed out). Since Decimus' tiltyard accident had occurred in his rash youth, this too was a help towards identification. Then just before death, it was established, the thigh bone had been cut—presumably while the victim was still on horseback—following that, the lower arm and finally "fractures of the vault of the skull"—injuries sustained lying on the ground. All of which tied in closely enough with the account by the Rev. Thomas Meredith, in "Heaven's True Mourning."

There was, however, no direct evidence to point to who placed Decimus in his unmarked grave and why. No clues, no plaque, certainly no love note which had miraculously survived three hundred years of interment; the survival of the skeleton and its fortuitous discovery was miracle enough. That put the onus back on the contemporary sources, of which there were two; Clarendon for all his eloquent tribute to Decimus on his death as "a gentleman of great hopes, of a gentle and winning disposition, and of very clear courage" being silent on the subject of his body's disappearance.

"Heaven's True Mourning" on the other hand was silent throughout on the subject of Lady Isabella Clare. But that was scarcely surprising;

since Thomas Meredith was a clergyman, he would no doubt align himself heavily on the side of seventeenth-century family values. Then, since as a result the whole book emerged as a monument to the devotion, perfect wifeliness and ideal love of Olivia Lackland for her husband, a love fully and completely returned, the presence of Lady Isabella in the story could only have constituted an awkward, nay gross, intrusion . . . So "Heaven's True Mourning," whilst honest enough to recount the abduction of the body, took refuge in the tradition of Parliamentary vengeance. It was left to John Aubrey, bored by the subject of Olivia Lackland's wifely virtues (although he praised her learning), to relate with gusto the story of Lady Isabella's body-snatching.

Balancing these two opposing accounts, you could at least say with some certainty that the discovery of the "Decimus" skeleton at Taynford Grange made the "Heaven's True Mourning" story rather unlikely, since the house had been a Royalist stronghold at the time, with Lady Isabella as chatelaine.

"Gutsy!" That was Cherry's verdict on Lady Isabella's behaviour. It was a historical word that might have endeared her to D. J. Smith, even if Cherry herself, her fancy turning towards Home Secretaries these days, would have had little use for Dave himself.

"The power of love," mused Jemima more tenderly; she was not giving up her romantic picture of Decimus without a struggle. Which of them had been his soul-mate, the learned perfect Olivia, or the sexy imperfect Isabella? And who inspired all those "Swan" poems? She was now inclined to transfer her custom to Isabella, especially since she was about to play the part.

Cherry paid no attention. "Now, Jemima, mind you play her as one strong lady," she went on. "It's rotten you've got that prune Zena Meredith as Decimus. All those soppy books full of fainting maidens! Handsome Dan would be so much more fun. Come to think of it, isn't it a bit peculiar, a woman in drag? Are you sure that Zena isn't . . . ."

"No, Cherry, it is not odd," replied Jemima firmly. "First of all it's a good old tradition, the principal boy. Then she doesn't have to

speak. None of us speak. We're figures in a landscape. Look . . ."
She had an inspiration. "You can see for yourself. You can come to the
rehearsal, I'll fix it. We're supposed to be having a rehearsal actually
here at the Planty: sort of dress rehearsal before we ever get to
Lackland Court, London being more convenient. But God knows if
it's still on, and if it is, God knows who will now play the boy, Antony
Decimus: that was going to be poor Little Nell's part."

"I'd love to meet Handsome Dan Meredith." It was good to know
that Cherry had not changed altogether.

Ten days later, you could legitimately use the term "a bit peculiar"
for the dress rehearsal of the Cavalier Celebration, thought Jemima.
The club was deserted. Since there were no people, there were no
flowers. It was the annual closure for staff holidays and renovation
(surely the exquisite Planty needed no renovation!). If there were
ghosts in the changing rooms and empty courts, they were the ghosts
of the smart women and important men who generally inhabited
them. But Adriana was in her villa on the Bosphorus and Stuart
Gibson with his boys establishing family values on the lower slopes of
the Cumbrian fells. You could not otherwise expect a highly modern
and modernised club to be haunted: this was no Lackland Court.

All the same, the deserted courts did have their own special
disconcerting atmosphere: if not exactly eerie, there was something
unsettling about being there alone, particularly in Black Prince, the
last of the four main courts. It was after seven when Jemima arrived
(the rehearsal was due to begin at eight) and dusk was not yet
approaching outside. Yet in Black Prince, to which Jemima had
wandered out of idle curiosity to fill in time, the light was already quite
bad. There were no windows here to the river, only a series of
skylights. You would need the big arc lights overhead if you were
planning to play tennis.

She had just decided to return to the bar area and have a drink or
sort out her costume or both—an empty court in the evening was just
a little too spooky to linger in—when the big lights in the Crecy court
next to her abruptly flared out. Jemima heard footsteps. Somebody

had entered—two people. The couple, whoever they were, were standing quite close to the heavy green plastic partition between the two courts. She heard murmuring, then much louder and clearly audible, a man's voice.

"Don't do that, don't put your arms round my neck, don't even touch me. It's over. Can't you understand? It's over. You . . ." There was a brief silence. "You *horrify* me." The voice was instantly recognisable. It was Dan's. But this was a Dan speaking in a way that Jemima had certainly never heard before. Gone was the tender seducer, the charmer of the tennis court, the gracious host of Taynfordshire. Jemima froze. The depth of disgust expressed by his tone made Jemima try to imagine what he must look like—the fair open Robert Redford face of Handsome Dan contorted with anger or sheer cold hatred.

Who on earth was he speaking to? It became imperative to find out. Jemima heard a sob, a muffled sob. Beyond the fact that it was a woman in Crecy—which where Dan was concerned told her virtually nothing—there was no further clue to the sobber's identity. If the unknown woman did say anything further between sobs—Jemima thought she probably did—Jemima could not make out the words. She began to tip-toe towards the plastic partition; she intended to gaze through the small celluloid-covered window at the side which acted as a spy-hole when play was in progress.

When she reached the window however, Dan Lackland was alone on the court. The plastic curtain leading to Agincourt and the Royal Court was still twitching slightly as if someone had just left. Dan himself was gazing somberly out towards the river. After a moment, he himself walked in the direction of the exit.

Jemima waited a discreet moment, walked on into Agincourt, and inspecting the Royal Court (where the rehearsal was to take place) through the spyhole, chose to enter when Dan was busily engaged in conversation with some man, the back of whose head she vaguely recognised. She joined the throng of Cavaliers, Cavaliers' molls, musketeers and musketeers' molls which made up the heterogeneous body of those in the Cavalier Celebration. The fact that there were numbers of women present made it further impossible to guess who the mysterious female, so coldly rebuffed by Dan, might be.

Alix Carstairs—the obvious candidate? Yes, but what could she have done to horrify Dan? For what it was worth, Alix looked rather more collected than she had done of late; she was wearing a rather pretty black dress with a plain broad white lace collar which set off her colouring, and a white cap; rather improbably in view of her age she was to play Dame Alice, the old nurse who watched over the dying Decimus.

The most agitated person present was undoubtedly Jane Manfred. (Since she was not billed to appear in the Cavalier Celebration she was not wearing fancy dress; rather more usefully she had purchased most of the tickets sold, so far as Jemima could make out.) Jane Manfred's agitation was, however, entirely due to the non-arrival of the gourmet snacks which she had promised Dan to provide for the players.

"Why is the roulade so late?" she demanded. "The traffic is not heavy." She might have been checking out the non-arrival of a royal personage at a gala.

"One will just have to eat cake, Charlotte's cakes." That was Marcus, looking suitably sober as Sir Bartleby Potter, the Puritan M.P. It was not clear whether he was making a joke or not, since Charlotte's elaborately decorated cakes were at present the only visible nourishment.

Fancy dress might not necessarily be a ludicrous garb for consenting adults but it certainly looked odd in the surroundings of a tennis club. These people might really be ghosts, so out of time were they in their costumes, in a decor in which tennis rackets and tennis balls or combinations thereof played such a prominent part. It occurred to Jemima that sooner or later the Lackland Court Country Club would take over the ancient mansion with its new atmosphere and its new demands. Then would the original inhabitants of the house—not only Decimus himself—come out to haunt it, drifting soundlessly in their velvet and lace on lawns now reverberating to cries such as "Good shot" and "Sorry partner"? A favourite line of Cass's—a cricket freak—came back to her: "O my Hornby and my Barlow long ago." This Hornby would be a Cavalier soldier, this Barlow his grieving wife—or mistress.

She was on the side of the ghosts. Zena was right. It was all very well taking refuge in clichés like "marching with the times," but it was outrageous to rob Lackland Court of its proper history—

Jemima was interrupted in these romantic reflections by the sight of Zena herself. In the costume in which Jemima had once seen her at the top of the stairs, she looked magnificent. And handsome. And poetic. In short she looked exactly like the Decimus portrait. To complete the resemblance, she wore a black gauntlet, and had hidden her other hand, in keeping with the known mutilation of Decimus's fingers. (Although Zena, being left-handed, had actually hidden the right hand, in order to manoeuvre her horse more easily: so even the historically minded Zena was subject to some practical consider-ations.) There was no actual horse on the tennis court but Zena did have an enormous dog at her side, hired from some expert in "show business pets." The animal, called Kylie—it was presumably female—looked amiable enough at the present time, if prolonged slobbering was a sign of amiability. All the same, Jemima, remembering her dream, decided to give it a wide berth.

Zena's expression was the only flaw in her appearance: outraged was the best way of describing it. But that was understandable in view of the presence not only of Gawain, as director (she had after all known that in advance and decided to go with it), and Dave Smith as author of the narration (of whom the same could be said), but also of he who was actually to pronounce the narration. Although a less disturbing surprise than that snatch of overheard dialogue in Crecy Court, the identity of the narrator still took Jemima momentarily aback.

Oddly enough neither Jeremy Irons nor Bob Hoskins had in the end proved available for this important dramatic role. Since ticket holders had been promised "a star," Dan had then turned off his own bat to television (about which he knew a great deal more than about the theatre, since he regularly watched the former and never if he could help it attended the latter). Once again however there had been a surprising degree of unavailability, such diverse and diverting characters as Melvyn Bragg, Magnus Magnusson and Sir Roy Strong proving to be otherwise engaged. But Dan had finally secured that linchpin of the new madly popular series put out by Titan Television—*Bunk Or History?*—none other than Dr. Rupert Durham.

Jemima had indeed recognised the curly head and exaggeratedly attenuated figure of her Cambridge contemporary, briefly her lover, now her friend—and the owner of her Decimus portrait.

"Women love him," Alix Carstairs explained. "Well I do, and so do the coaches at the club, everyone talks about him, it's that terrific mop of hair, I just want to run my fingers through it." Jemima resisted the temptation to retort: "You will, Oscar, you will." She joined instead the group where Rupert Durham was engaged in crossing out large chunks of Dave Smith's narration and writing his own words over it, very fast, without paying any attention at all to Dave's increasingly indignant remonstrances. Rupert Durham's expression behind his unfashionable horn-rimmed spectacles (which he was rapidly making fashionable again) remained as mild and distracted as ever and he nodded several times as if in agreement. Nevertheless, he continued to slash and write.

Jemima, despite the fact that she had not yet caught an episode of the series (known as *History Is Bonk* to Rupert's old friends), not even the one about Stonehenge everyone was talking about, had no doubt that she was looking at a star. So did Gawain; unlike Dave, he was gazing at Rupert with open admiration.

Jemima's impression was only confirmed when she found out what Rupert was up to. It was several minutes before he recognised her, several minutes more before he found her correct Christian name, although the kiss he then bestowed upon her was charmingly enthusiastic.

Jemima naively imagined that Rupert—the erstwhile scornful dismisser of Lady Isabella's pretensions to a proper relationship with

Decimus—must now be busily eliminating her own role, Zena's "red-haired trollop," from Dave's melodramatic narrative. And she had been rather looking forward to her simulated night ride at the head of her daring men to do a spot of body-snatching! Just as she rather fancied herself in her corn-yellow silk dress, a lighter shade of her own hair colour, with its green taffeta cloak and the large globular false pearls at her neck and ears which reminded her of the sort of thing that Lady Manfred wore to play tennis.

Jemima—and Dave—had reckoned without the true mettle of the trained historian turned television star. No, Jemima's role was not in danger. It was more that of Charlotte as Olivia which was imperilled, being altered and cut before their very eyes. At least Charlotte accepted it all without a mew of protest: she had the proper cast-down eyes to play Olivia, even if her lack of height meant that she did not quite manage to achieve the dignity, for all her heavy velvet costume and her own ropes of false pearls. It was in fact Zena who strode across the court to the rescue, between ranks of seventeenth-century extras. (Who were they all, neighbours? tennis players? For Jemima had suddenly recognised one of the Planty coaches, looking very fetching in breeches and doublet, with her hair in a ponytail.) It was Zena who tackled Rupert Durham.

The big dog, Kylie, followed obediently behind and put its huge wet muzzle into the nearest available hand—which happened to be Jemima's. Although she managed not to scream, the feel of it gave her an uncomfortable reminder of touching Dan's face on the roof. Today she had exchanged no words with him at all, beyond the most conventional polite greeting, and a kiss no warmer than that he planted on the cheek of every lady or girl present. That, however, was the way she wanted it to be—and this time she meant it.

Zena began a speech invoking the memory of "my ancestress Olivia": but its development was completely swallowed up in a huge wave of unexpected enthusiasm from Rupert himself.

"Zena Meredith! Don't you look terrific? You've got to come on my programme looking just like that. The trans-sexual thing is so important in the seventeenth century—how on earth can we understand Shakespeare by just going on about rent boys . . ." Rupert rattled on. At one point he even touched one of Zena's long legs in their high black boots to illustrate a point.

Jemima waited for Zena to return to her theme in full spate of excoriation. She waited in vain. Instead, before her amused eyes, she saw Zena melting just a little, succumbing just a little more to the famous (since Cambridge) keep-on-talking-and-talk-them-into-it technique of Rupert Durham. Really, D. J. Smith had tackled Zena quite wrongly from the start.

Only Marcus Meredith, standing close to Jemima, breathing heavily in his stuffy Puritan's costume—rather like the dog now snuffling at their feet—joined Dave in indignation, if for a different reason.

"I don't know what Dan wants with the woolly-haired fellow," he muttered crossly. "That television programme is a disgrace. Did you hear his language about the Druids? It may be history, it's still utter filth." But Jemima suspected that it was in fact the groping hand of the dedicated historian on Zena's thigh which had enraged Marcus.

For all Marcus' annoyance, for all the interested spectators, for all the need for the rehearsal to get under way, there was no certainty that Zena would have called the situation to a halt. But there was now a ripple of talk and an excited buzz and finally a sight which caused even Rupert to suspend in mid-flow, even Zena to turn her eyes away from him. It had been arranged for little Louisa Meredith to play the part of the boy Antony Decimus, since Nell was obviously *hors de combat*. The role called for some horsemanship, but Louisa, in spite of her youth, was a good rider; probably a rather better rider than her step-sister, if the truth were told, since more care had been taken to teach her.

But now, standing at the big open glass doors to the Royal Court, looking infinitely pathetic and at the same time gallant, the large bandage she wore round her head only partially obscured by an ill-fitting black wig and red velvet hat, stood Nell herself. Her mother was standing just behind her. But all eyes were on Nell as she said in the silence: "I've come to play my part. This is the Dress Rehearsal, isn't it?"

Her characteristic high slightly whiny voice was carrying enough. All the same, for one ghastly moment, Jemima thought Nell had said: Death Rehearsal. Then all other feelings were swept away in a pang of mingled pity and admiration for the stumpy determined little figure: surely Dan's daughter in this expression of her will to win—or at least to survive—if nothing else.

15

Thunder As Forecast

An obsession with history ran through the whole thing. Jemima knew it. Then questions came. Whose history? The Merediths' history, that was clear enough. But whose version of Meredith history?

She was lying awake—as she so often did nowadays, a maddening new development in her life—on the eve of the Cavalier Celebration itself. The eyes of the Decimus portrait seemed to mock her inability to solve the puzzle; the hidden left hand stood for her ignorance of things about the Meredith family which still remained hidden. A re-run in her mind of the events of the dress rehearsal brought no real enlightenment beyond that one brief exchange with Little Nell which had come about purely by chance. And even that was more puzzling than helpful.

Jemima had found Nell sitting alone in the third of the four courts—Crecy—since it was thought to be quieter than the bustle of Agincourt where the rest of the cast were now assembled waiting for their cues. Nell was huddled on a white plastic spectator's chair, a cloak round her costume; her hat with its feather gave her the look of a bedraggled bird with its feathers puffed up in self-protection. The swish of Jemima's heavy skirts made her look up. Nell looked for a moment frightened, then relaxed.

"I shouldn't really be alone but Mum's just getting me some orange juice," she said rather vaguely. Then she added without further ado, answering the question which had not in fact been put to her, "I really don't know what happened to me. Everybody has got to believe me." The sing-song note in her voice was very apparent.

"I do believe you," Jemima had assured her.

"And did you believe her?" asked Cherry. They were sitting comfortably on the balcony of Jemima's flat, sharing a bottle of Jemima's favourite white wine; Cherry had brought strawberries. It was hot and slightly sultry. The weather forecast on TV for the next day had been "very warm and dry but with occasional outbreaks of thundery rain"—the kind of indecisive forecast to drive you mad, said Jemima, if you were about to parade about in fancy dress at some outdoor event the next night.

"I believed her because she told me about the one thing she *did* remember. Nell decided to trust me, I think, on the basis of our conversation in the cloisters. She knew I kept my word and didn't tell the police. All Nell did remember was that there had been something bothering her about a costume . . . A costume and some boots . . . She had an idea she had been looking for a costume, 'a special costume' were the words she used, which had somehow worried her."

"Her own costume?"

"Probably not. But she thinks she must have tried it on. Or at least noticed some odd feature about it."

Unlike Jemima, Cherry definitely did not see the Cavalier Celebration as reflecting an obsession with history. She told Jemima confidently that she looked at it all from the psychological point of view. At the dress rehearsal, Cherry, armed with a clipboard, had introduced some vital order into the burning issue of who wore what when (the extras—in particular the numerous young members of the Smith family—certainly needed a touch of Cherry's whip). Now she had some pertinent observations to make on the suitability of role to character.

"That M.P., Marcus, he really is one of your dirty old Puritans, isn't he? Seething with it all under his codpiece. And I can't stand the stuff he puts on his hair—he ought to be made to leave it off for the sake of history."

"He didn't wear a codpiece, that was his breastplate."

"Whatever it was, I reckoned he'd lose his wig peering down my neckline, hunched over me like that. And I'm sure he was longing to make a grab at that little blond girl in seventeenth-century hot pants. He was hunched over her too. Luckily she had her pitchfork to hand." That must have been Cathy Smith or her younger sister Penny.

The person who did win Cherry's approval, oddly enough, was Jane Manfred: "What style! I'm going to be just like that when I'm old." Since Cherry's observations on old age were not overheard but she *was* the one who located Lady Manfred's missing roulade, languishing for some extraordinary reason in the gentlemen's sauna, a warm friendship was struck up which boded well for Cherry's future.

"I must talk to our darling Cy about you," Lady Manfred murmured approvingly. "No-one else understood how important it was . . . a *real* roulade . . ."

But Dan Lackland himself disappointed Cherry. A curiously distanced figure throughout the rehearsal—in which he had after all no official role—he only came to life to hug his daughter Nell from time to time.

Jemima got out of bed, switched on the main light which illuminated the whole portrait—she wanted no nightmares tonight—and began methodically to run through her mind everything she had learned about the Cavalier Case, as though it were television film which needed editing.

Oddly enough, at exactly the same moment, the person who had been the ghost and expected never to be the ghost again, because there would be no need, was thinking about Jemima Shore. Perhaps Jemima's own concentrated thoughts had awakened the person— perhaps there was something in psychic energy after all. Since the person had no reason whatsoever to believe in ghosts. And in any case the person no longer felt in danger from Jemima as the person had once done.

Jemima, who also did not believe in ghosts, continued to run the mental film. It was after she had been doing this, patiently and relentlessly, for so long that the dawn of the day which would end in the night of the Cavalier Celebration was beginning to break, that she began to see the pattern. Certain remarks, remarks by all sorts of people including innocent bystanders such as Cherry—that ridiculous conversation they had had, with Cherry's wilder and wilder theories— remarks by Babs, remarks by Nell Meredith, began to weave themselves into these patterns. And then there was love, the power of love—the obsessive love which had led Lady Isabella to abduct the skeleton of Decimus.

The costume. Love and the costume. Why should a costume, any costume, be such a giveaway? The ghost's costume—that was the line of thought to follow—let us say it was the ghost's costume. Why strike down Nell for finding it? Once again, the film of the possible suspects was unreeled before her mind's eye. She considered them all, envisaged them all physically. The smell. Jemima suddenly remembered the smell, that was what Nell had said originally in her rather confused phrase: "I recognised it and I didn't recognise it." Jemima stopped the film.

Could it be? Was it possible?

It could be. And as to being possible, Jemima had learnt from previous investigations that where primitive emotions were concerned, anything was possible. She ran everything—the whole film— through her mind again for one last time. Then other things fell into place too. As Jemima pulled back the heavy shutters to go out on her balcony in the first morning light, she was surprised to find that in spite of everything her first feeling was of an unbearable sadness. It was only after that, that she was filled with anger.

And she still had to figure out how to bring the murderer to book—for there was no doubt now that just as there had been an unreal ghost as opposed to a real one, there had been a real, not an accidental murderer. Twice over, probably, and a third attempted murder. But this was a clever resourceful person with a position to lose, who would do anything to protect the truth from discovery, and

understood perfectly well the art of bluff. How could she go to the
police—the agreeable Detective Inspector Spain let alone Pompey—
with such suspicions? As yet they were converted into certainties only
by the nocturnal processes of a logical mind, coupled with an
instinctive nature.

She needed proof. Proof from Nell. At the Cavalier Celebration,
she would get proof from Nell, if it killed her. The familiar careless
cliché made her draw back. Jemima rephrased it: I must get proof so
that no-one else is killed. She had been right in her instinct.
Obsession of a sort did run through the whole thing.

At Lackland Court that same evening, obsession could also be said
to be running through the whole thing. But this was, in contrast, the
comparatively harmless obsession of all present, spectators, perform-
ers, directors and all, with the weather. Would there or would there
not be a thunderstorm? The heat was oppressive. The air was very
still. The horses which would be used in the Celebration—borrowed
from hunting neighbours and amiable local riding-schools—were
visibly sweating. To Jemima's nervous eyes, they looked enormous: she
had not ridden since she was a teenager in West Germany during her
father's last Army posting when she had had ambitions to be a
show-jumper. Horses, unlike policemen, seemed to have grown bigger
and older since those Dortmund days.

The horses were grouped together at the north side of the house;
this facade would not be used for the Celebration since it was about
the only place where there had been some ugly later renovation of the
brickwork. The spectators' stands on the other hand were grouped in
the forecourt, while the spectators themselves wandered, wine glasses
in hand, in the gardens to the south and west, waiting for the light to
fade. There was a big grey horse for Decimus (but then Zena was an
accomplished rider), a nice-looking bay for Charlotte which looked
rather high for her (but then she also rode a great deal) and a fat
skewbald pony for Nell. Jemima's own horse was another lighter bay,
about the same size of Charlotte's, with a beautiful flowing flaxen
mane. It was allegedly "so quiet you'll need a whip to get it to move

at all, let alone canter"; for some reason Jemima was not reassured by these words.

Jemima's horse—actually a mare called Jilly, for reasons it took a sudden flick of the flowing flaxen mane to work out—belonged to Marcus. He himself was already seated on the biggest horse of all, a vast sweating blackish animal, heavily built like his master but far more magnificent; it was apparently his own hunter. Otherwise the horses stood sweating, champing, occasionally stamping, blowing their nostrils angrily at the flies which persecuted them, swishing thick coarse tails with equal ferocity.

The horses were tense not only with the heat and the flies, but also perhaps the seventeenth-century bridles and saddles with which they were lumbered: research by David, greeted with rapture by Gawain, contradicted by Zena, finalised by Rupert Durham. The spectators moved happily about the gardens where rival local gardeners expressed public enchantment at witnessing "so much colour for late August" and private delight at seeing "weeds like it was a conservation area." They were probably not at all tense except for those repeated speculations about the thunderstorm.

"We could get seriously wet," Adriana informed Dan Lackland with great earnestness.

"There's always that possibility with rain," agreed Dan. "Don't worry, Adriana, I personally will give you a rub-down." Temporarily, Dan seemed more cheerful. It was perhaps the fact that Adriana, returned browner, plumper and bonnier than ever from her villa on the Bosphorus, had bought twenty of the best tickets, which prompted this offer of special service.

But the tension among the cast about the forecast of thunder was almost palpable. Darkness was finally beginning to fall. Soon the ticket-holders would be urged to take their seats like so many crows making their way to the rooky wood—in this case the wooden stands in the forecourt. Some of them quite high up, all of them rather rickety. Jane Manfred frowned as the delicate spindly heel of her shoe got stuck between two boards and had to be rescued in a gallant manner by Dan, who then, with mock chivalry, kissed the hem of her dark red chiffon dress; at this the frown lifted. The Celebration depended on darkness for its skillful execution so that each window could be illuminated in turn, according to the narrative, while the characters arrived at their destination, spotlit briefly on horseback.

In the first half of the Celebration the story of the Meredith family would be told up to the point of Decimus' mortal wounding at the Battle of Taynford in 1645: his marriage to Olivia, his romance with Lady Isabella; followed by his return on a kind of bier from the battle, his death scene—old Dame Alice (enacted by the much younger Alix) at his bedside; the abduction of the body by Lady Isabella's men; the distraught grief of Olivia. In the second half battle would commence: the siege of Lackland Court three years later by courtesy of many enthusiastic extras, more horses, and a good deal of recorded noise and gunfire. One climax was destined to be the death of Sir Bartleby Potter (a.k.a. Marcus Meredith). He was supposed to fall heavily from his horse whilst besieging the house, impaled by something or other flung from the battlements. At the tennis court Jemima had been privately worried that Marcus could manage such a feat without doing some further damage to himself. It was Zena who airily reassured her.

"Oh, Markie's much stronger than any of us," she threw off. "Has been ever since he was a child. It's often the way with people, don't you find? They compensate. He's not even disabled, really, is he? Poor Marcus." Zena changed the subject to her future—mimed—romantic involvement with Jemima. A conversation took place between the two women which, despite the fact it was punctuated with slightly hysterical giggles, might have seriously disconcerted one Cherry Bronson. Then Rupert Durham put an end to it by insisting on demonstrating (on Zena) exactly how Jemima the famed courtesan should receive Decimus' first kiss. They had certainly moved a long way from that Victorian picture of Olivia, eyes cast down, receiving her husband's kisses as though she would die on the spot. Lady Isabella was supposed to display a good deal of seventeenth- (or late twentieth-) century enthusiasm.

Even the roof was going to be used. That had been the subject of some awkward debate in view of Haygarth's really quite recent death. Gawain, in a green velvet suit which was mistaken by several of the cast for seventeenth-century costume, and otherwise called to mind his sobriquet of the Green Nightmare, had been frivolously obstinate on the subject: "Oh, darlings, only a *butler* fell." This remark was thought to be in bad taste by absolutely everyone. Furthermore such an observation was definitely not the way to preserve Lady Manfred's now rather fragile patronage. (Shortly after the revelation of Gawain's plans for the Decimus skeleton, she had been seen lunching with John Steff at Le Caprice; generally felt to be a public warning.) But then Rupert Durham backed Gawain up, casually but quite firmly: "Lead from the rooftops—a vital part of siege warfare. We'll have the country women melting it down."

"Why only the women?" asked the blond girl in seventeenth-century hot pants armed with a pitchfork, not for the first time. She was in fact yet another member of the Smith family: Jo, sister to Cathy, Penny and Dave. Rupert Durham ignored her.

Then the noise began. An extremely loud, quite unexpected and very frightening noise. But it was not, as everybody first thought, the long-heralded thunderstorm but the peculiarly loud rolling thundery sound of repeated salvos being fired from big guns, guns which gave the impression of being remarkably close. The audience, only just settled in their seats—Adriana in fact still standing up trying to reorganise the entire placement of her twenty-strong party at the last minute—were so unnerved that several of them started to scream. Somebody put up an enormous golfing umbrella on the assumption—incorrect—that heavy drops of rain must be now falling. The next boom and the next did at least bring home to the majority of the spectators that this was a deliberate if startling prologue to the Cavalier Celebration; the equivalent to the *trois coups* of the French theatre. But there was a good deal of anger about at the shock of it all.

Lady Manfred was certainly furious (it turned out to be her golfing umbrella) and she was furious once again with Gawain. But then it turned out that Gawain himself was furious, actually purple with wrath in his vivid green velvet suit, since far from having organised the cannonade, he was complaining that this unsolicited prologue was effectively drowning the long steady drum rolls "and the whole seventeenth-century bit" with which he had intended the performance to begin. The dog Kylie was either furious or frightened, since it bounded from Zena's side with a long howl, hurtled round the corner towards the stands, bolted through their midst to the enormous alarm of all and sundry—"Is it a Rottweiler?" cried Adriana—and vanished.

It turned out that Dan Lackland had privately organised the salvos with an Army friend. He was unrepentant. "None fired at my birth, alas, so I thought it would be amusing to have some now."

"If only we could have had something like that when Dessie was born!" put in Charlotte, with the intention, apparently, of defusing the situation.

"Dessie's not a bloody little prince!" hissed Nell, who was rapidly recovering her spirits.

It was at this point that the noise and violent weeping was heard coming from the audience. Phrases, incoherent but unfortunately not inaudible, wafted across the murmuring ranks of spectators: "More killings," "it never stops," "this horrible family" were some of them. It was only when Dan said curtly to Marcus: "You go to her, old boy, you're the one who said she should be allowed to come with Nell, you handle her. Tell her to shut up or get out. I mean it," that Jemima understood the hysterical voice to be that of Babs Meredith.

"If Mum goes, I go," said Nell bravely to her father. But Dan, much as Rupert Durham had ignored Jo Smith, the feminist pitchforker, behaved as if she had not spoken.

It was not an auspicious start to the spectacle. Nevertheless, when everything had, roughly speaking, calmed down, some pretty seventeenth-century music had come and gone, and Rupert's exquisitely sonorous voice had embarked on the earliest known Decimus poem from his special podium in the forecourt, some measure of order was for the time being restored.

It was convenient to the narrative that the first Decimus poem celebrated his home in childhood: "Young pilgrim was I in thy nurturing arms"—although it was typical of Rupert, being Rupert, that he actually recited "in *those* nurturing arms" (less harmonious to Jemima) since he specialised in discovering subtly different versions of well-known poems and then imposing them on the rest of the world. Young pilgrim . . . Zena must have taken the title of her prize-winning historical novel from the line.

But Jemima had more urgent matters to consider than seventeenth-century texts and titles and for that matter Lady Isabella herself. Part of her plan—the entrapment via Nell she had tentatively devised—was to get free from the main body of the cast and extras where they lurked, somewhat awkwardly, cavaliers and pitchforkers, on the north side of the house, awaiting their cues. She needed mobility and she needed invisibility—of a sort; what she did not need was the extremely visible sunflower-yellow dress of Lady Isabella, not the dress and not the vivid billowing grass green cloak.

Cautiously, she dismounted. Jilly, who had reacted a great deal less violently to the unexpected gunfire than most of the other horses—so perhaps her docility was not so legendary after all—stood patiently by. Jemima, unhooking her long skirts, handed the reins to one of the extras; she thought it was Cathy Smith, but in the semi-darkness could not be quite sure.

"I'm desperate, I have to go," she murmured: "Hold my horse." The remark, she realised, had a quaint "hold the front page" ring to it. On the other hand, since Dan Lackland, unlike Jane Manfred, had generously allowed Lackland Court itself—or at any rate the back quarters—to be used for the cast to dress, undress, make-up, wash, use the lavatories and so forth, it provided the best excuse for slipping away.

The next part of her plan was to find Alix Carstairs, who, playing an inhabitant of the big house, did not need to arrive by horseback. She would appear at a window, and then nurse the dying Decimus on the front steps, simulating the great hall. She must be somewhere inside. To Jemima's relief, Alix was sitting alone indoors in the furthest backstairs room, beyond that ground floor room where Nell had been found. The one thing which worried Jemima was the time scale of all this—and then there was the forecast thunderstorm.

All the lights had been switched off in the main rooms of the house in order that there should be no distraction from the illumination of the facade. But here, in this remote little room, beyond the rooms where costumes were kept, make-up had been applied, hair frizzled, the windows were heavily shuttered, and the light was on.

Alix, in her plain black "dame's" dress, hair bundled away under her white cap, was holding her head in her hands. "Listen Alix, you've got to help me. I'm terrified of horses, they make me feel so sick, in fact I'm feeling sick already, ghastly, I think it's an allergy, I used to have an allergy to horses as a child, please, please, can we change places? You'd be a wonderful Lady Isabella and I could have a lie-down before I come on as Dame Alice. We were both at the Death Rehearsal"—in her haste she actually made the Freudian slip—"We know each other's parts."

Alix looked at her sombrely. All she said was: "*You're* feeling sick. That's rich." But she began to pull off the white cap as if she hated it, had hated it all along, so that her hair—she really did have the most glorious hair—spilled down over her back and shoulders. Then she began silently to strip off the black fustian dress.

In spite of her silence, there was something deliberately challenging about the way Alix took off all her clothes down to a pair of white bikini pants and bra at least one size too small. Jemima, seeing her in tennis clothes, had realized already how heavily built, even plump, Alix was, far more of an Adriana than a Charlotte—but hey, wait a minute, how could she, Jemima, be so stupid? Alix was pregnant, visibly pregnant, and what was more, she was making sure that Jemima appreciated the fact.

"Nice for me, isn't it?" said Alix, giving Jemima one of those bright bird-like looks which reminded her of their first encounter. "As it turns out, it is nice for me. Soon I shan't have to pretend any longer.

But I don't mind telling you that at first Dan was absolutely furious, he was horrified. To be fair, this is the third time it's happened to him!" Alix laughed shortly. "I could even feel sorry for him—Babs, then Charlotte, then me—except that men like Dan always get what they want, don't they? And the women carry it out. So he must want it, deep down. But he did tell me to get rid of it at first. Naturally I refused: well, I'm nearly thirty-eight you know, nearly as old as Zena. Worse than that, my God, Dan can be a bastard, he actually suggested I should marry Marcus!"

Alix gave another not particularly mirthful laugh. "Desperate for a wife and children! That's what Dan said about Marcus. And the child would be a Meredith after all. He even suggested it to Marcus himself. Said *I* would like it! No wonder Marcus won't speak to me. Here, give me your dress. I don't want the world to see me like this—not just yet. Dan only changed his mind the other day."

Somewhere in the distance there was a long low rumble: not gunfire this time but thunder, unmistakable thunder if not yet much nearer than, say, Taynford Grange. All the same, thunder as forecast. Jemima knew that she had to carry out her plan, not only racing against discovery, but also, equally crucially, racing against the approaching storm. She left Alix with a quick grateful hug. Herself now with her hair bundled into the white cap, and wearing the black dress—the waist was much too big for her but she would not be wearing it for very long—she went in search of her proper guise of invisibility.

A few minutes later, as Alix vanished in the direction of the north court, the green taffeta cloak swishing through the door into the darkened hall, Jemima found what she was looking for.

Zena's "Decimus Ghost" costume was hanging, just as she had hoped, on a hook in the deserted costume store. Zena was not due to put it on for some time—she would play all the early scenes, and her death scene, in her own costume, and of course very different make-up. The "Decimus Ghost" costume had had some kind of theatrical phosphorescent stuff sprayed on it, with a view to making

Zena's second appearance that much more dramatic to the spectators in the forecourt. But it was just possible Zena could have taken the ghost costume upstairs to her own room. Applying the most ghostly make-up she could manage to her own face, Jemima wondered whether she need bother with the question of the "mutilated" hand of Decimus; in the end she did put her left hand into her pocket. She could always take it out and, unlike Zena (but like Decimus himself), she was right-handed. In any case, impression rather than detail was what was needed here.

There was another rumble of thunder, following a flash of lightning. The storm was still some way away. But it was coming closer. As Jemima, now invisible—in one sense—as the Decimus Ghost, passed, in her turn, through the connecting door into the darkness of the great hall, she felt extraordinarily nervous.

This apprehension was not due to the absence of light, although in the hall a total black-out was absolutely essential to preserve the quality of the *son et lumière* outside and that made her own costume glow in quite an eerie fashion. Nor was it due to a torrid atmosphere. Here, the sultry heat outside had hardly penetrated; the great hall of Lackland Court with its high ceiling was probably the coolest place in Taynfordshire. It was not even evoked by the prospect of her mission: for Jemima, having taken the decision to carry it out, did not allow herself at this point to think about what would happen if she failed (any more than she intended to digest at this point Alix's astonishing revelation—was she implying that Dan would marry her? Ah well, as Macbeth said, there would be a time for such a word . . .).

No, she was in thrall to some strange feeling of nervosity, compounded of the tensions within the Meredith family, the impending drama which would—if she had her way—tear it apart and certainly reverberate publicly in a way that would make previous public manifestations of the Cavalier Case seem tame.

Nevertheless she had to go on, and she had to go up to the roof. And she had to go soon. Marcus, as Sir Bartleby Potter, was due to ride by, down below, at the head of a posse of his Puritan men any minute; he would issue the first armed challenge to Lackland Court, on the eve of the Battle of Taynford. Jemima knew his time-scale only too well, and it was a time-scale which was vital to her plan. She had committed the whole of the action of the Cavalier Celebration to memory, not only her own part. And Marcus' first appearance had also been the subject of much discussion. In truth, Sir Bartleby Potter had not been in the Taynford area in 1645, nor had he fought at the Battle of Taynford.

"But we need to *establish* you, Marcus, so you can die later with some dignity," exclaimed Rupert.

"Go on, be a goody boy, Markie, get on your horse as told and die for your King and Country; I mean your Parliament and Country, but that's appropriate enough." That was Dan. Marcus had not acknowledged the intervention of either man. But he had finally agreed when Zena had pleaded with him, her sense of history dominated on this occasion, it seemed, by her need to please Rupert Durham.

Jemima had to be up on the roof before Marcus appeared.

She took out the torch she had brought from the car. The oddest thing about the great hall was the absence of the portrait of Decimus at the top of the stairs—or rather the absence of the picture light which normally illuminated it. The portrait itself had been moved. It was now established on an enormous easel in front of the great doors. With his public in mind, Dan had agreed to the move; and Zena, who might otherwise have demurred, was, as before, putty in the hands of Rupert. It was planned that at the climax of the Celebration—after the din and shouting of the Lackland siege assault—the great doors would be flung open, spotlights would play upon the portrait, and Zena, in her second role of the ghost, would then "emerge" in her glowing phosphorescent costume from the portrait, and come to the rescue of the beleaguered Meredith supporters.

"The ghost strikes back!" had been how Dave Smith had entitled that particular tableau.

All that was some time ahead. In the meantime the portrait, in its new position, lay in darkness. Jemima needed to find the door to the Long Gallery, which was shut—the cast members already on the roof had gone up, and would ultimately come down, by another staircase leading from the back quarters of the house. She shone her small torch quickly upwards: the gap left behind where the portrait had hung—for how many years? centuries?—looked cavernous. But it was of course only plain flat wooden panelling. She then speedily moved her torch away to find the door to the Long Gallery. There was a flash of lightning which lit the hall for an instant through the big windows, and almost immediately a further rumble of thunder. It sounded virtually overhead. But as Rupert's voice rolled on beautifully, sonorously, inexorably, through the loudspeakers—he was reading one of the "Swan" poems at this point to accompany Alix's arrival as Lady Isabella—the rain must have held off.

A second flash of lightning followed, in this case accompanied directly by its own mighty burst of thunder. It was at this moment, out of the corner of her eye, that Jemima caught sight of Zena, in her first Decimus costume, passing downstairs. She saw her rather than heard her, because the noise of the thunder—and some increased shouting from outside—effectively muffled the noise of Zena's footsteps. For an instant, Jemima was surprised—surely Zena must have made her first entrance by now, unless she had mistaken the entire time-scale of the Celebration. But then she saw that Zena had secured another dog—had replaced the vanished Kylie with an animal who looked in fact rather more like the dog in the portrait. Zena seemed to be holding his collar with her right hand. Jemima, who had no wish to be seen by Zena (or the dog), shrank back.

A moment later she was in the Long Gallery on her way to the roof. Ignoring the portraits, Jemima did decide to cast a quick look out of the long windows. Judging from the audience, who could be seen *in situ*, there was still, unbelievably, no rain. Would the storm really pass over and break elsewhere? The sinister rumblings continued. Oh, spirit of Decimus, she incanted, let the rain hold off till I reach the roof.

She found the key in its now familiar position beneath the aldermanic portrait and ran lightly up the spiral staircase. She knew who would be up there.

"The Ghost!" Nell Meredith's frantic scream, as she backed away from Jemima, looking with particular horror towards her silvery costume, her gloved black hand, occurred one second before the expected colossal downpour of rain began to swamp the ancient gutters of the roof with water as if this was some Taynfordshire monsoon. Below, the noise and confusion was appalling: drum beats mixed with the continuing sound of the thunder, the crashing of spectators trying to run out of the crowded stands, Rupert Durham's voice, still sonorous as he called through the loudspeaker for calm and orderly departure, while, most incongruously, the loud recorded jingly singing of the Psalms (in a seventeenth-century setting) to which Sir Bartleby Potter's men were intended to march in true Puritan fashion, suddenly came in on cue, giving a bizarre ecclesiastical twist to the whole nightmare.

Then the illuminations suddenly went out. It must have been the lightning striking the controls—but that was only realised later, when it no longer mattered. At the time many of the audience gave way to fruitless anger—even on the roof Jemima could hear their outraged cries, once the Psalm-singing had come to an abrupt stop. All the same, she had no time to spare for what might be happening down below. Across the now slippery roof, clinging to one of the turrets, she advanced towards Nell Meredith.

"So tall," said Nell uncertainly. "So tall—but you're not—" Nell put her hand to her head, pushing the velvet cap back so that the brave Antony Decimus feather curled over her eyes.

"The smell," she said. "It was you—*you* came—you hit me—*you* tried to kill me—" She screamed again, but this time, in the grip of the thunderstorm, no-one could hear, no-one but the other member of the cast there on the roof, the person to whom Nell had turned and whom she was beating with her fists.

"You," she kept screaming. "You, you, you . . ." The rain pelted down on her furious anguished face, a child's face transfixed with adult hatred. So fierce was her attack that for one moment Jemima thought that Nell would actually force her companion, in her weighty black velvet dress rapidly becoming sodden with water, over the edge of the parapet. Thus she would have gone to her death, grimly but appropriately, just as Haygarth had gone to his. And that in its own way would have been poetic justice.

It might also, leaving aside Nell's responsibility, have been the kindest solution to the future life—and punishment—of the murderess Charlotte Lackland.

16

Decimus Goes Home

The telephone rang in the Holland Park Mansions flat just as Jemima was getting out of the bath. She picked it up without thinking before the answering machine caught it. It was Cass. He was lucky—in the sense that she would not have returned his call had he merely reached the machine. All that was over, well and truly over, unlike the Cavalier Case itself, which was finished for her but in no way finished in the public imagination. First there was a trial to come. Then in that cheerful cauldron of speculation, fed by the *Daily Clueless* and even the magisterial *Jupiter*, details of the case would continue to bubble and bubble over for many years to come and maybe even generations.

It was after all a story that had everything: sex and sport (the involvement of Dan and Alix, his flame-haired tennis-playing mistress, had inevitably emerged), violence and the supernatural (there was no way that the Phantom Cavalier was going to be forgotten, even though the two witnesses to Jemima's final apparition—Nell and Charlotte—were both, if for different reasons, likely to be forever silent on the subject). Then there was snobbery—plenty of lords and ladies to play with, including a pretty young Viscountess who was up on a charge of murder—and last of all there was historical romance: if Lackland Court ever opened to the public, instead of existing as a country club, it was likely to prove a major tourist attraction. Yes, the

Cavalier Case really was the story that had everything. It might one day in legal terms be finished. But it would never be forgotten.

"That case of yours hit the headlines all right," said Cass. "Did she really do it all? The second wife. What's her name? She looked so tiny and helpless in the photographs."

"Charlotte. Charlotte Lackland. She was and is tiny. She wasn't helpless. But she's feeling pretty helpless now, not just because she's on a charge of murder but because he's turned on her. He'll get a lawyer and all that—play the gentleman, if you like—but he won't speak to her. And he won't let her children visit her. So then she made a full confession. Said she did it all for him, to save his family heritage. A sort of Lady Macbeth who didn't even let Macbeth know what was going on."

"Ah, she did it all for him—the handsome tennis player."

"Exactly. She was even inclined to point out how clever she had been, using the Meredith family history as she put it, the legend of the ghost and all that. She told him she got the idea from Zena—that's the sister—always going on about the Decimus Ghost. Then Zena had a Decimus costume, made for a fancy dress ball, which she liked to parade about in. That gave Charlotte ideas too. But she couldn't wear Zena's costume, let alone her boots—the two of them are about eight inches different in height, let alone the shoe size."

But Jemima did not really want to discuss the Cavalier Case with Cass Brinsley. He belonged—like the rest of the sensation-seeking public—to the outside world. For a time, a short but crucial time, she had been part of the inner world, the inner world of the Cavaliers—then and now.

One nightmare was the prospect of Charlotte's children in the future: those little blond girls, the blond ebullient little boy she had loved so much, tagged in the public memory forever by their mother's crime (or crimes). Yet there was always some prospect of natural elasticity where children were concerned: or one hoped there was. Dan would marry Alix, and in view of her pregnancy, marry her soon. There would have to be some kind of plea for a dispensation and a quick divorce in order that this ceremony could take place before the birth of the baby.

"You see, it's a boy. I've had a test. We're going to call him Thomas Antony Norton—Thomas is the real Meredith name, by the way, not Decimus, that was just a fluke because of that huge family, did you know that?" As Alix communicated this to Jemima, in spite of all the tragedies around her, she had a kind of creamy complacency. She rattled on: "And of course if he's not born within marriage, then he couldn't succeed to the title. Even if we married later." The words gave Jemima a terrible momentary pang. Was poor Dessie, the first son, not to inherit? Was there to be more violence? Then she relaxed. Alix, the loyal if occasionally neglected mistress, was certainly no Lady Macbeth. She had simply adopted the Meredith family history in her own way, as Meredith wives had done for centuries, and was making sure her own son was part of the (legitimate) family tree.

How quickly Alix had learnt! But she would surely act as a kindly step-mother to Charlotte's children, and even to Nell, whose brief love affair with her aunt Zena had been brought to an abrupt end by the latter's total involvement with Dr. Rupert Durham. Besides, Lady Manfred, in one of those swift elegant volte-faces which had enabled her to maintain her powerful social position for so long, had become charmingly enamoured of Alix.

"Those poor children. They need someone like that. So down-to-earth. So practical." (Jane Manfred had once used almost exactly the same terms about Charlotte.) "And of course Dan does too—not that he hasn't been a naughty boy." Jane sighed. "But I'm too busy, really, for all the attention a man like that needs. And darling Alix absolutely understands that Dan and I will continue our delightful *amitié amoureuse.*" Alix certainly did understand. Her conversation— she kept in touch with Jemima in a way that would probably not outlast the birth of her child—was now larded with "Jane Manfred says this" and "Jane Manfred says that." Furthermore Alix, the new Viscountess Lackland, had been placed on Jane Manfred's prestigious Euro-Opera 92 Appeal Committee (a project to which her other new protegée, Cherry, was also lending a good deal of voluntary assistance, it turned out). Besides, Alix's understanding—if it had been in any way lacking—was further helped on by the fact that Lady Manfred was at last going to make that long-needed heavy investment in both the Plantaganet Club and the future Lackland Court Country Club.

So you could argue, thought Jemima, that Handsome Dan Meredith, a.k.a. Decimus Antony Norton, 18th Viscount Lackland, had as usual secured everything he wanted through the agency of women. His wife had secured the death of the aged cousin whose prolonged existence, coupled with the sales of heirlooms, was ruining him; after covering her own tracks by the death of a suspicious witness, and an attack on her teenage step-daughter, she had then, no doubt perfectly correctly in legal terms, taken all the blame on herself. Whatever Charlotte had told him or he had suspected which caused him to repudiate her at the Planty rehearsal—overheard by Jemima— and subsequently decide to marry unhappy pregnant Alix, Dan had certainly not had foreknowledge of Charlotte's grand design, let alone the murders. What was more, he had ended up with a devoted new wife (with the prospect of a second son), one who would always be totally understanding of his outside activities . . .

Yet did Handsome Dan really bear no moral responsibility for it all? Even if he had been "horrified"—the word heard by Jemima behind her own kind of plastic arras on the tennis court. It was an imponderable question: how much ultimate responsibility for all the destruction should be borne by the spoilt charming man. But then who, how many women, had conspired to create this spoilt charming creature himself? That too was imponderable. What for example was the responsibility of Olivia and Lady Isabella for creating Decimus? A poet who happily wrote the same poems to two women.

Like Lady Manfred, Jemima sighed. Had she not herself agreed, frankly, to whatever Dan proposed, albeit briefly; including playing the part of Lady Isabella at the Cavalier Celebration? When she did not even support the notion of historic Lackland Court being turned into a country club. Just as Zena, who hated the idea, had also agreed to take part and play a leading role. Hadn't Zena too in a sense created Dan, from their shared childhood onwards? She was glad she was not the judge trying Charlotte either in court or for that matter at the Last Judgement Day.

How would Charlotte's desperate outcries fare then? Jemima remembered the aftermath of that ghastly scene, the screaming, the appearance of Dan himself, soaking wet, eyes terrible with shock—or perhaps like his daughter Nell, with hatred.

"I did it for the family," Charlotte had cried, trying vainly to get her arms round his neck like a puppy trying to embrace an Alsatian. Then: "I did it for you. That horrible drunken old man was going to die sooner or later and he was selling everything! Your heritage. Dessie's heritage. You wanted him dead. You did. You said it to me: 'I wish he would bloody well fall downstairs and break his neck.'"

So perhaps after all Lady Macbeth was not the right analogy: Charlotte had been more like one of those knights who listened to King Henry II raging against Becket—"who will rid me of this troublesome priest"—a knight who had ridden off and done the deed.

Dan Lackland himself showed no signs of ever wishing to discuss the subject with Jemima Shore once Charlotte had been arrested. When they ran into each other at the Plantaganet Club a little later, each was coolly polite: but this time there was not even a ritual kiss-on-the-cheek for Jemima, neither proffered nor desired. But that was understandable and not only because of all the terrible public pressures Dan was currently facing. The fact was that Jemima had come too close: she had come too close to the mysterious heart of Dan's relationship with Charlotte, the responsibility which was not responsibility, the irresponsibility which Charlotte's behaviour allowed him to have.

That night, that dreadful night, she had impulsively taxed him with it: "But you knew *something*, Dan! I heard you that evening at the Planty, I was in the far court. 'Get away from me,' you said, and 'It's over.' Why else did you decide to leave Charlotte for Alix?"

But Charlotte, shivering in Dan's angry grip, a man's dressing gown incongruously cast over her wet costume, had glared at Jemima now more like a tiny lioness than a puppy. They were in the Long Gallery and Nell had already been rushed away. The huge pictures of Merediths and their bejewelled and beruffed wives gazed down on the latest Meredith wife: one whose portrait would surely never in future hang in the ancestral home. Ironically enough, Charlotte was actually standing directly beneath the portrait of Olivia Lackland: another wife who had stood fast for her family. (Charlotte, if no-one else, might have directly compared their two actions.)

"He knew nothing!" Charlotte shouted. "And he would never have left me for Alix, never, I'm his wife, the mother of his *heir*." She put a dreadful breathy emphasis on the last word.

Dan, without letting go of Charlotte, swayed slightly. In the light his thick poll of wet fair hair looked white not flaxen: Jemima suddenly had a glimpse of what he would look like when he was old.

"She hinted—" he began, "the other day when I told her about Alix and the baby, I had to tell her, and she began to talk about all she had done for the Merediths and their family heritage. I had this ghastly realisation—poor little Nell—I've always known that deep down Charlotte hated Nell, she couldn't hide it from me, she hid it from the world, all that public affection, but that's why I was so careful not to spoil Nell—I didn't want to upset Charlotte. Then some of Charlotte's movements at night. They didn't quite add up. There was one time, I came back in the small hours—oh, why pretend now, I was with Alix—and she wasn't there, and her car wasn't there. That's why I was originally worried about you—you're so clever—talking to poor old Haygarth, just an uneasy instinct. Then there was the odd time when we all ended up roaming round the gardens; Charlotte hadn't been where she said she was. And I found the door to the roof staircase open. I didn't know what to do—so I just locked it. All the same, it puzzled me. But Nell! That was what finished her for me."

"But you did nothing!" Jemima knew that she sounded fierce. "Except make a promise to another woman—Alix."

"It was the Celebration," said Dan weakly. "And the Club. I had to get the Celebration over for the sake of the Club. And that was to save Lackland Court. I know it sounds terrible now, but they were both dead, nothing would bring them back . . ." His voice tailed away. Once again he looked not so much a glamorous former athlete in his late forties as an old man.

On the subject of Dan's secret foreknowledge—but it was not exactly that, more growing suspicion after the event—Jemima decided to hold her peace to everyone else. She did not think it necessary, for example, to tell the police. They were, after all, in the person of Detective Inspector Mike Spain and others, rejoicing in the very full confession which Charlotte had insisted on making, without waiting for her lawyer, duly taken down by the police.

"It's as though she wanted to be found guilty!" exclaimed Mike Spain to Jemima almost ruefully. "I can't believe it. It's too good to last. Look here, how else would we make a case like that stick? She's dishing it out to us like some bloody great soap opera. It's as though she was determined to punish him, just because the red-haired bimbo has a bun in the oven. Hasn't noticed she's doing herself in along the way."

Jemima could only agree.

It was appropriate that the fullest conversation Jemima ever had on the subject with a member of the Meredith family was not only with Zena—who had commissioned her investigation in the first place— but held once more in the cool precincts of Taynford Cathedral, where Zena had first called for that investigation. The general agreement on the identification of the Taynford Grange skeleton as that of Decimus, 1st Viscount Lackland, was followed in due course by a brief private interment ceremony in the cathedral. Gillian Gibson had wanted to attend but was prevented by a husband who had evidently not yet pardoned "those damn bones." She sent the only wreath, although Rupert Durham, who attended, along with Zena, declaimed the last "Swan" poem—beautifully—and Jemima echoed the greatest of all the love poems silently to herself. Decimus, 1st Viscount Lackland, now lay close to the plaque which in fact stated that his body was absent.

But for the time being it was not planned to alter the original tablet.

"It won't be the first false inscription in this cathedral," exclaimed Rupert cheerfully. The 18th Viscount Lackland, however, did not attend. "A horror of any more publicity" was the official reason for his absence.

"But Dan never did care much for history," added Zena bleakly. "Whereas Charlotte, it seems, cared too much. At least, that's, as it turns out, the kindest explanation."

They were sitting together in the cloisters where Jemima had once listened to Nell's tale of the phantom who was not a phantom. Rupert had bounded away to talk to the new Dean of the cathedral, a rubicund friar of a man, who promised something of interest to him to discuss, presumably concerning that great television series, *Bunk or History*. The two women sat close enough for the fresh lily-of-the-valley scent of Diorissimo—the perfume Zena and Charlotte had in common—to remind Jemima all too poignantly of that particular elusive if unhistorical detail of the Cavalier Case.

"I'm not complaining. You did as I asked. 'Whatever I find?' you said. And I agreed." Zena turned and looked at her. "But *how* did you know or rather guess? Should we have known? That's what tortures me. May God forgive me, I did think that perhaps Dan—he can be so ruthless when he goes for something, I suppose it's the games player. That's why I asked you to investigate. I couldn't bear to do it myself. And yet, I couldn't get over my awful suspicions. But Dan never knew, did he?"

"Dan never knew until the last moment." That was true—even if Jemima did not care to specify what the last moment was.

"For my part, I thought that maybe Marcus—" Jemima admitted. "You see, the costume was the clue. Charlotte's tiny child-sized costume. The costume that would only fit her. Then there were the boots, the boots with their rubber soles, they were absolutely tiny too. Nell found Charlotte's costume and boots rummaging about in the back quarters; she was always terribly inquisitive about everything going on in her home that was not quite her home. She put various things together—including the familiar smell of the ghost leaning over her at night. The costume had the same smell of course. But then she got muddled. Do you realise it was the fact you both wear Diorissimo which actually muddled her? She had a very clear sense of a person, as one does, from the characteristic smell, except it was two people! I, of course, flirted with the idea of Marcus and his terribly strong hair lotion. Or even her father's Eau Sauvage."

"How strange! Do you know why we both wear it? Dan gave it to us both for Christmas. Lazy bugger. Couldn't even think up two different brands of scent. Or maybe Alix bought it in the first place. I shall never wear it again," Zena ended firmly. "Never."

She went on: "Poor Marcus"—as usual the epithet "poor" was applied to her cousin. "I hardly think he's capable of a plan like that. And all for Dan's financial benefit too! He might do it for the good of the country or something ridiculously pompous like that. But not for the good of the family. Not enough love and too much honour, if you like." Zena seemed to be alluding to the family motto. She added: "He's terribly upright. Poor Marcus."

It was a sad epitaph on the cousin who had loved Zena so devotedly for so long, thought Jemima, to have a label of "terribly upright" placed upon him in terms of mild pity. She returned to the Cavalier Case.

"It was the motive which was missing with Marcus, however much he disapproved of your drunken old cousin, and it was the motive which finally gave me the answer. What people will do for love . . . More finally than they will ever do for themselves . . . Dan, whatever he had to gain, whatever ruthlessness he may display on the tennis court, would never finally have carried out such a plan for himself. That's where the discovery of the skeleton jolted me into a kind of vague recognition of the answer. What the beautiful pleasure-loving Lady Isabella did for love of Decimus—the midnight capture of his body; what submissive Charlotte did for love of Dan—the saving of his fortunes, as she saw it. Then, if you think of the comparison, Alix might play tennis with him. She *killed* for him." Jemima remembered her conversation with Cherry which had come back to her that night as she ran her mental "film": as Cherry happily propounded a combination of Zena and Charlotte, it was Jemima who had replied quite casually: "Oh no, Charlotte is an unreconstructed woman. She would do anything for Dan." And she had.

Jemima then related the rest of her guesses and conclusions to Zena—feeling that she must at least tell the whole story to one Meredith, a story she had already outlined (in all but that one particular about Dan) to the police. She told her for example how the interview with Babs had given her in the end one interesting bit of information, way beyond Babs' own malice concerning Charlotte, and her reiterated scorn for Charlotte's "anything-to-please attitude." How Charlotte had told Dan her baby was going to be a boy—but it turned out not to be true (that baby was Louisa). So Charlotte, in her own way, could be quite manipulative if she wanted something badly enough.

Then Nell had revealed that Charlotte had quite often visited Lackland Court in the lifetime of the old Lord even if she wasn't noticeably welcome—at least according to Nell. "No brats" had been the ukase of Cousin Tommy and Charlotte had obeyed it: so there were other times when she arrived, free and alone. It must have been Charlotte's crucial secret night visit, the entrapment of Cousin Tommy, which had somehow become known or suspected by Haygarth after his death. Had Haygarth communicated his suspicions to Charlotte herself? That would never be known for sure. What was known for sure was that Charlotte had boldy decided that he was too dangerous to live.

"And she *was* bold, unbelievably bold," concluded Jemima. "I suppose one might even admire her. Except—"

"She fooled us all. Little Charlotte the wonderful manager. She was a wonderful manager, in a sense, right up till the end. The decision to go for Nell was a desperate one. But I suppose by that time—" And Zena in the same bleak voice quoted Macbeth: "We are so deep in blood imbued—" She added: "I believe that happens to people. They don't know when to stop."

"Even then she was lucky. Nell getting concussion, not remembering. She hit her with a croquet mallet, threw the head in the river the next day. After Charlotte told this to the police, they dredged it out. But of course she couldn't count on Nell not remembering forever. Remember how Charlotte insisted on sitting by Nell's bedside when she was unconscious? That must have been fairly traumatic for her. Nell must have been living on borrowed time." They neither of them wished to pursue the prospect of Nell's fate if she had recognised Charlotte as her attacker under less public circumstances. Fortunately the return of Rupert Durham, lolloping across the green sward of the cloisters (something strictly forbidden), interrupted them. Beneath his horn-rim spectacles his eyes flashed with excitement; his wild curly hair seemed to be animated by its own similarly enthusiastic electricity.

"By God, Becky, I feel like Professor Higgins. He's got it. I think he's got it."

"Darling, got what?" Zena, Jemima noticed, like all Rupert's inamoratas, had learned to live with his purely peripheral hold of people's actual Christian names. She leapt up, murky details of the Cavalier Case temporarily forgotten.

"Come on"—Rupert looked at Zena—"Olivia." (Now that was rather a nice mistake.) "You're just the one I need. The merry old Dean has just shown me a manuscript, what he called something of local interest, which turned up with an antiquarian bookseller in London, and has been offered back to the cathedral—for a price. The idea is that since that absurdly rich Manfred woman bought the Taynford Globe and gave it back, she might buy anything for anyone in these parts. I need your expert eye. I've got a hunch about the handwriting."

Her expert eye? Jemima was astonished. Was this Rupert in the new guise of flatterer? For what could Zena, for all her admirable enthusiasm for history, contribute that Dr. Rupert Durham of Casey College, Cambridge, could not? But the answer was really very simple. The manuscript, so-called, was actually a holograph version of "Heaven's True Mourning"; and what Rupert needed to know from

Zena was whether she recognised the handwriting. Since neither Zena nor Rupert returned to find Jemima on this occasion, leaving her first to attend evensong in the cathedral—"Now lettest thou thy servant depart in peace," this time sung as it were in earnest—and then to drive back alone to London (where she had as a matter of fact a late-night date), it was two days later before a hectically excited Zena supplied her with the answer. And then the information came via a panted message on her machine.

"Olivia!" was the first word she heard: "It was Olivia all the time. Do you know, I always had a feeling . . . The style! It had to be a woman. So vivid. Quite unlike the sermons of that boring chaplain." The phrases tumbled out.

Only by degrees did Jemima understand what Zena was telling her: that the original manuscript of "Heaven's True Mourning" had not only turned up from whatever source to which it had been covertly sold off by Cousin Tommy, but had also turned out to be written by Olivia Lackland herself. Not by the (male) chaplain, as had been assumed by so many (male) scholars, but by that learned (female) scholar Olivia Viscountess Lackland, giving her own version of the family history. Including all those lavish tributes to her own modesty and virtue. Like Charlotte Lackland, there had been more to the submissive Olivia than met the eye. It was Zena who had instantly recognised the handwriting: that writing "exceeding good and fair for one who was the weaker vessel" which even Aubrey had grudgingly praised.

"No wonder she never mentioned Lady Isabella," the message ended. "So that's one more mystery solved. Not such a boring wife after all," added Olivia's direct descendant.

There was only one other message on her machine, and that was from Rupert Durham.

"Zena, my love," it began—well, perhaps that was a pardonable mistake under the circumstances. "I thought I might take back possession of my portrait. You see, Olivia—no Zena"—was he learning?—"has taken rather a fancy to sleeping underneath its baleful glance. I hope you don't mind."

Jemima, thinking it over, found that she didn't mind. And when she learnt that the obliging Lady Manfred was indeed buying back the "Heaven's True Mourning" manuscript—no questions asked of the bookseller—but presenting it to the Lackland Court library, she felt genuinely happy. One day "Heaven's True Mourning" might even be edited by Rupert Durham, with a memoir of Olivia by Zena Meredith attached. This would be her first modest venture into non-fiction, in place of that biography of Decimus which was now forever abandoned in favour of yet another Zena Meredith historical novel, *The Swan and the Cavalier*. The unexpected alliance of Rupert and Zena, the historian and the historical novelist, Jemima decided, was the one positive result to come out of the Cavalier Case. She decided to tell Cherry that she had been quite wrong about Zena: it wasn't so much a man she needed as a historian! Rupert would at last woo Zena away from her claustrophobic family and when Rupert finally went on his way—as he always did—it was to be hoped that Zena would be independent enough not to return.

Cass rang up once more and he too left a message. But that was sometime later after Charlotte's trial and prison sentence—but on a charge of manslaughter. Mike Spain had been right: the full confession of Lady Lackland had been "too good to last." The expert barrister that Dan Lackland had honourably hired for his wife—by now his ex-wife—had made short work of such a suspect document in the hands of the police. Charlotte had retracted it entirely on the grounds that she had been mad with sorrow at the time over the pregnancy of her husband's mistress and hardly known what she was saying. The impossibility of proving the death of the old Lord—for which there was no evidence except her confession—and the undoubted difficulty of proving the case regarding the butler led to some hard bargaining behind the scenes.

In all of this the evidence of Nell Meredith was of course crucial. On the one hand Nell would have to give evidence about her step-mother's attack, why she had been attacked, and also concerning those nocturnal ramblings of the "Cavalier Ghost." On the other hand, Nell was already a suspect witness with her flights of fancy concerning phantom Cavaliers—and nobody in the Meredith family, including for once her father and her mother in agreement, wanted her further mixed up in such a distressing event.

In the end Charlotte pleaded guilty to the manslaughter of Haygarth, who had, it was revealed by her defence, plunged to his death accidentally in the dark. In Dan's absence, Charlotte, hearing a noise on the roof, had gone to investigate. Each had believed the other to be an intruder. They had struggled. Somehow Haygarth had fallen. Charlotte had not previously owned up to this, fearing to inculpate herself. It was a thin enough story (why had she not called Marcus, for example?) but the police, aware of the pitfalls of withdrawn confessions, did not press their case further. And the jury, much moved by Charlotte's piteous plight, now that she was divorced and abandoned, believed her. She did after all cut a small, frail and infinitely vulnerable figure in the dock.

Cass' message concerned Charlotte's conviction. Like the jury, he seemed to feel sorry for her. But since there was one thing that Jemima had wanted to tell Cass one day, she rang him back.

"You know, Cass, in the end I saw the ghost," she said. "Isn't it strange? I don't expect you to believe me and it's not important whether you do or not. You see that last terrible night, just before the storm broke, I actually caught sight of the Decimus Ghost going down the staircase. Was it looking for the portrait which had been moved after centuries? Perhaps—but that's pure speculation. My sighting the ghost isn't speculation.

"How do I know?" she went on. "Because at first I thought it was Zena Meredith in her Decimus costume and I was rather surprised to see her, but I had, shall we say, other things on my mind. Afterwards I realised that Zena had unquestionably been on her horse outside, witnessed by the whole audience, at that point. She never went upstairs at all. And then there was the dog. That was the strangest thing of all. Kylie, the dog who had been hired to accompany Zena, bolted at the first sound of gunfire—so much for its training. But she had another dog with her—wait, I've just remembered this—she was holding its collar in her right hand, but Zena is left-handed. This was quite a different animal— much bigger for one thing—and it was actually identical to the dog in the portrait. The Lackland portrait and my portrait. My portrait as was. Rupert Durham asked for it back. He's living with Zena Meredith now, you know: a Cavalier affair. And he's got that Dave Smith working for him on his programme: a thoroughly Cavalier affair."

"What rot!" Cass sounded quite angry; it was as though his jealousy for the poet who had captured Jemima's romantic fancy was still active. "Why can't you leave the subject of that phantom fellow alone? An intelligent woman like you. At least his picture is no longer overlooking your bed. That's good news."

"No-one is overlooking my bed," replied Jemima carefully.

"I'm glad to hear it." Cass sounded relieved. He should not have done so. As a matter of fact there had been a profound and happy change in Jemima's personal life quite recently, one of those rapid transformations which can occur from time to time in the lives of persons who are young, urban and single. Oddly enough it had happened at one of Cy Fredericks' dinner parties, not normally famous for engendering romance among their participants—except of course where Cy himself was concerned.

The explanation for Miss Lewis' increasing number of interconti-nental mess-ups had proved to be not so much overwork but the hideous—to Cy, at any rate—secret of her engagement to a district surveyor in the Northern Territories of Australia. Marriage was now imminent. Cy was both distraught and uncomprehending, like a child who is told his parent is doing something called "leaving."

"But how on earth will I reach her? My Miss Lewis," he asked pathetically of more or less anyone who came into the office. No-one was cruel enough to give him an answer.

Along the way, however, Miss Lewis had become quite the Cupid. At this particular dinner party, Jemima, for example, had found herself sitting next to the loquacious and high-spirited radical lawyer Ned Silver—sometimes described as having been born with a silver tongue in his mouth—although the place card actually read: "Sir Edward Silvers." (That name, at the sight of which Jemima's heart had sunk, belonged to a heavily handsome television tycoon, whose skittish Iranian wife had just left him for a pop star.)

When Cy said to Jemima before dinner, "I've been longing to bring you two together," he did look at Ned Silver with a certain wild surmise—who on earth *was* he?—but since this was not the first time that Cy the celebrated host had been faced with this kind of probing question about one of his own guests, he knew just how to pass rapidly—and expertly—on without losing his equanimity. So Jemima Shore and Ned Silver were left talking to each other. And one way or another they had scarcely been apart, except during the hours of work, ever since. What was more there was no danger—absolutely no danger—of Ned Silver wanting to do anything like "settle down"; the very phrase was impossible to imagine in his connection. None of this did Jemima see fit to tell Cass. It was, finally, none of his business.

The only other person to whom Jemima related her "ghost story"—Cherry—was equally dismissive, if in her own much kinder fashion.

"Oh, Jem, don't you see, you projected it?" she explained. "You were in a state of terrible nervous tension—not surprisingly, about to face that little monster up on the roof—you were so tense that you *projected* Decimus."

"I damn well didn't project the dog! Now if it had been a cat. Dogs like that terrify me. And that dog was absolutely enormous. Just like the one in my picture."

Cherry looked at her pityingly. "That's the whole point. The one in your picture—the picture that hung over your bed all those weeks. You projected that as well. We don't only imagine nice agreeable things . . . Our fears too play a part . . . You see, Jem, psychologically . . ."

But Jemima always knew that she had seen the Decimus Ghost.